I0723122

Shadow Rules the Land

Samara Saward

Find your flames

Content Warning

Shadow Rules the Land contains content that may be triggering to some readers, including, but not limited to, depression, torture, asphyxiation, death, disownment, misogyny, war (including knife, sword, and axe violence), drowning, references to off-page sexual assault, suicidal ideation, PTSD, trauma, depictions of blood and gore, dismemberment and amputation, murder, and sexually explicit scenes.

Your mental health matters.

Beyond Blue (1300 224 636) provides information and support to help everyone in Australia achieve their best possible mental health, whatever their age and wherever they live.

A Guide
to Radelea

AUTUMN COURT

Kerym — *keh-RHYME* — Bria's father

Rennyn — *WREN-in* — High Lord

Gorred — *GORE-ed* — Rennyn's second

SPRING COURT

Nyana — *NIGH-ar-na* — High Lady

Imala — *EYE-marr-lah* — Nyana's consort

Argi — *ARR-gee* — Nyana's consort

Darcel — *DAR-cell* — Nyana's consort

SUMMER COURT

Ad'Starrag — *ADD-stah-rag* — Summer Court keep

Tohminic — *TOM-in-ick* — High Lord

Chlora — *CLAW-rah* — Tohminic's lover

Xaler — *ZAY-ler* — Selkie leader; Tohminic's second

Yaryn — *ya-REN (i.e. Karen)* — Tohminic's mother

WINTER COURT

Ruith — *ROO-ith* — High Lord

Tarathiel — *ta-RATH-eel* — Ruith's second

Uma — *OO-mah* — Bria's mother

Vacon — *VAH-sohn* — Ruith's guard

NIGHT COURT

Maude — *MAWD* — High Lady

Blodwyn — *BLOD-wen* — Torin's mother

DAY COURT

Warakoris — *WAR-rack-oar-iss* — Zentha's home

Zentha — *ZEN-thuh* — High Lady

Elmon — *ell-MON* — Zentha's son

Kyra — *KIE-rah* — Betrothed to Elmon

DAWN COURT

Jonik — *JOHN-ick* — High Lord

Leilani — *LAY-lah-knee* — Jonik's mate

Tasar — *t-SAR* — one of the triplets; Prince

Larrad — *Lah-RAHD* — one of the triplets; Prince

Xaria — *ZAR-rea* — Jonik's niece

DUSK COURT

Vander — *VAN-dah* — High Lord

Bria — *BREE-ah* — Our main character

Wynetta — *WIN-et-ah* — Bria's best friend

Torin — *toh-RIN* — Vander's second

Penna — *PEN-nah* — Healer

Chapter 1

WRATH.

It forces a guttural roar from my throat as I lunge for my opponent. I use that anger to strengthen my attack, as I have with every move since we entered the training field hours ago. Wrath rules my every move, it taints my every breath. It has been my companion since the Night fae first stepped foot on our land.

I cannot help but place blame. Our court would be whole, and Ulakas would still be with us if Nyree did not betray Dusk. Darkness would not weigh us down if not for Maude and Tohminic and Rennyn. Not darkness in the sense that our hearts beat with anguish and dread, but the literal darkness of night and shadow. The Mother Star did not rise after the battle. She has not graced us with her bright rays since. I fear we will never see the golden glow of noontime again.

I could have won this round, but my wrathful attack is too forceful, and I slide on the loose dirt when Vander twirls to the side. Determined to succeed for once, I spin and swipe at his thigh with a dagger wreathed in shadows. The hilt is a comforting weight in my palm, but the worn leather is slick with sweat. It slips in my grip.

A sweet breeze sends strands of my copper hair billowing behind me, the scents of lavender and orange fighting the rage with calm. Dust plumes from the ground, coating my leather boots with a fine layer of beige.

Vander's air magic is not enough to deter me — at least he is refraining from using his illusions to confuse me this time — and I pivot at the last moment, swinging my other arm around and taking him by surprise. "Don't bother, Van," I pant as I press the blade against his throat, my emerald eyes flashing with warning. "No amount of calm will soothe my haunted soul today."

"You're letting the rage rule your actions."

I pull a second dagger from my boot and press it against his chest. "So are you."

"It doesn't rule me, Princess." He brings his axe down in a wide arc, hitting my dagger away. The clash of our blades rings in my ears, almost drowning out his next words. "I let it *fuel* me. There's a difference." He twists from my grip, leaving both my daggers piercing the constant night air. He's on me again in the next heartbeat, the curve of his blade pressing against my throat and his free hand gripping my wrist.

My magic roils at losing this final round. The shadows I inherited from my birth mother snake from my palms in tongues of piercing darkness. My ice magic escapes through my ragged breaths in glittering clouds. The blades strapped to Vander's body hum when my metal bending power wraps around them. The amber threads of my animalistic magic writhe and shove against the hatch that keeps them contained.

"You have to learn how to push the anger aside." He steps back and sheaths the axe. "It's time."

I welcome the anger. It is a pleasant change from the demons, from those nightly terrors that remind me of all the red staining my hands. Of Nikolai's blood, the blood of every fae who died at Ad'Starrag, Fayeth, Ulakas, the undead who were not truly lost from this world until we disposed of them, and of everyone who died on our land. Crimson seeps into the lines of my palms and stains my ivory skin.

I am learning to move past the guilt and regret, and learning to live with the knowledge I'm not the only fae at fault; as much as I can cope with everything during the waking hours, it is during the quiet time when everyone is sleeping that my mind rebels.

"Ten days, if we can even call them that anymore, is *not* enough time to forget we're at war, let alone forget the fae we have lost."

He runs a hand over his head, his calloused palms scratching against the short ebony strands. His silver eyes darken before he runs his thumb down my cheek. "You overcame your guilt. You can climb this hill and conquer the rage, too."

The mention of climbing hills takes me back to when I first stepped foot on his land, when I was determined to earn my freedom by climbing a literal hill. I was beaten, defeated, and on the brink of death. I dragged myself to Dusk Manor, and Vander crawled with me. It was the first time in my five and seventy years I did not feel alone in my pain.

Wyn and Torin cross the training field, joining us after overseeing the rebuild in the western village. Their arrival pulls me from the horrible yet comforting memories.

A sigh flutters past my lips. "I'll be okay. It's just hard. After everything we have survived, I cannot understand why the Mother Star would abandon us."

"Because she's ruthless and cunning," says Torin. He ties his long, blonde hair back with a length of leather, making his dark eyes seem brighter. He tilts his face to the shadow that rules the land and shouts, "Did you hear that, you shiny bitch?"

"Yelling at the only being we believe in will not help matters," says Wyn.

She and Vander could be twins with their identical ebony hair, tawny skin, and silver eyes, but where Vander sparks with life, Wyn is a quiet shell of her former self. There is something different about my best friend of late. She is withdrawn since the battle that sent the Mother Star into hiding. Withdrawn and... just different. She does not speak often and keeps to her bedchamber.

Vander sighs. "No, I don't think it will. We'll hit the archives. See if we can't figure out why she refuses to shine."

"It's because of the war," I say as we gather our weapons and head towards Dusk Manor. "The first time she rose was after the ancient fae shared wine and signed the peace treaty. She won't rise again until the fighting ends." The truth of my words settles in my bones, the knowledge having come from years of studying our past and teaching it to the younglings of my home in the Autumn Court.

I wonder about Rennyn and what he thinks of this turn of events. As High Lord, his denizens expected him to choose a side. What no one expected, me least of all, was for my brother to side with my enemies. Perhaps I should have seen it coming. I disowned him, after all. I shove the image of his golden-brown eyes and hair from my mind. Thinking of his betrayal will only add to the anger swirling within me.

Wyn smooths her shining ebony hair. While it's strange for her to care about her appearance, her words distract me from the thought. "Then we focus on putting an end to the war." Rage should drip from her voice. Instead, it's flat and lacking emotion. Her air and illusion magic doesn't pulse as it once would.

I pull back from Vander and walk beside my best friend, nudging her with my elbow. "Are you okay?"

"What do you mean?" she asks in that same emotionless tone.

"You're kind of... lifeless. You've been different since the Gloom." It's a moniker we gave the battle that encompasses all the fighting brought: darkness and heartache.

Her steps are almost automated — like the technology on Earth — as we climb the hill to the manor. She does not scoff like she often would when confronted with a harsh truth. "I'm fine."

Melancholy.

She is the epitome of the word. She is not the only one.

It is the only word I can use to describe the Dusk Court. No matter where Vander and I go, whether it be the western village, the manor, or the northern village, there's an air of sadness pressing down on everyone. The fleeting happiness that followed the battle against Night, Summer, Autumn, and the Ill-fated has long since vanished. It faded when the Mother Star refused to rise, then disappeared altogether when we assessed the damage to our court.

Our efforts in rebuilding the eastern village after the undead attack and tavern fire, wasted. The bustling grid of homes and stores suffered under the cruel hands of the Night fae. The northern village is nothing more than smouldering remains, and those who live there have sought sanctuary with friends or family. Many of them claimed rooms in Dusk Manor, and the brick building has never been livelier.

I look at the manor now, where it shines like a welcoming beacon atop the hill. The winds of Dusk part around the russet bricks and envelop the manor in the scent of lavender with a hint of citrus. The onyx roof blends with the dark blanket of the sky. The only distinction between the two is the stars that glitter above.

Everything is dark now. The moon still comes and goes, as if none the wiser that its golden counterpart refuses to brighten the land. For a moment yesterday, we feared the moon had forsaken us as well, but I am glad to see the slither of silver tonight. Last night's new moon sent ripples of panic through Radelea, all assuming the worst.

I throw another worried glance at Wyn and sigh. "Vander and I are here if you need to talk. We're all enduring the same heartache. We know what you're going through."

For a heartbeat, sorrow pulls at the corners of her eyes, but it's gone within the next beat of my tortured heart. Wyn turns back to the manor, then disappears beyond the large front door. The din of chatter floats into the night from the large sitting room inside.

I let the door fall closed and turn to Torin and Vander. "She's not getting better. If anything, she's more distant."

"I kind of miss her bossing me around," says Torin. "And she hasn't joined us on the training field since before the Gloom. I'm still waiting to get my revenge for the last time she handed my arse to me."

Vander turns towards the west, where darkness veils the Night Islands. Before the Mother Star set for the last time, we could see the undulating landscape of Maude's Court, where fae with the power to control both body and mind live among the harpy population. Now, it is nothing more than an obsidian smudge in the distance.

Van's magic churns, the signature of his air and illusions pulsing around us in waves laced with the scent of cedar and apple. "She's the only family I have left." He turns his starlight eyes to Torin. "Find out what's wrong with her. I'm begging you."

It's rare for Van to show such vulnerability around anyone other than me — the twin soul bond we share leaves no room for secrecy.

Torin dips his chin, the bronze skin of his jaw hidden beneath a halo of golden hair. "I'll do whatever it takes. She's my family, too."

Though not related by blood, he has been with the Theron siblings for centuries, forsaking his Night heritage and leaving his mother, Blodwen, to her lonely life on one of the smallest islands. There is no disputing his claim: Torin is family.

"I'll help you." My body tingles with the need to help Wyn, just as she helped me when I was a captive of Ad'Starrag. I shove the memories of my time in the Summer Court to the back of my mind. "Let's meet in the northern village tomorrow and see what we can find."

"Why the northern village?" asks Torin.

Vander says, "Wyn defended the village during the Gloom. It's the last place she was before she changed."

"Well, I have a warm bed and a beautiful female waiting for me. I'll see you love birds tomorrow."

"Don't let Alizeh take too much," warns Vander. "We need you at your best. Only the Mother Star knows when Maude and her Night fae will attack again."

Alizeh, the alluring wind wraith who flits from fae to fae feeding on their air magic, is a regular in Torin's bed. He is always lacking his usual energy the next morning, and his smart remarks do not quite hit the same.

He only smirks before disappearing into the forest of she-oaks.

"She's going to suck him dry one of these days," says Vander, threading his fingers through mine as we enter the manor.

"Pun intended?"

"Bria Sutherland, you have a dirty mind."

I cringe at the use of my full name, the name given to me by my father. Perhaps I should speak with Uma about taking on the name she shares with Ruith of Winter. I still marvel at finding my birth mother after all these years, and the reminder makes me smile.

The Autumn Court was once my home, though I did not belong there. As the High Lord's daughter, there were too many expectations of me, and the earth and animal wielding denizens treated me like a pariah, purely for my title. Illegitimate Princess. What a load of horse manure.

For a long time, I believed I was born of a Spring fae, and dreamed of manipulating plants and using the psychic abilities of the Court of Blooms. I am glad my copper hair, which is a trait of Spring, is not a gift from High Lady Nyana, but from Uma, Lady of Winter.

My mother brings a rare ray of light to this shadow-ruled land.

Vander and I nod greetings to any fae we pass on the manor's ground floor, both of us relieved when we step onto the winding staircase to the third-floor apartment we share with Torin and Wyn. Somehow, we have kept it as a kind of sanctuary, a place where we can be ourselves without the weight of our responsibilities pressing down on us.

We peel apart when we enter the spacious kitchen, Vander backtracking to check on Wyn while I rummage through the kitchen for something to serve for dinner. Given how distracted we have been of late — rebuilding the villages and the extra training takes most of our time, with Vander's responsibilities as High Lord filling the rest — there's not much to choose from.

I settle on a selection of bread, cheeses, and cured meats, and have the smorgasbord laid out on the over-sized dinner table by the time Vander returns.

"How is she?" I ask as I set two pewter mugs down and fill them with plum wine.

"No different." He sags into his seat, like his body refuses to hold him upright any longer. "She was just sitting on the edge of her bed staring out the window when I entered. Her eyes were vacant, like her mind was elsewhere."

I hand him a mug and take the seat beside him. "We'll figure it out. Torin and I will spend every free moment working to bring her back."

He takes a deep drink of the wine, and his emotions flicker from concern to fear. "What if this is who she is now?"

I grip his hand and repeat, "We'll figure it out."

The lone fae light overhead casts an amber glow on the spread of food, and I focus on the colours while picking at a slice of dense bread. So much has changed in recent times. I have evolved from a magicless, rebellious bastard seeking adventure to a courageous fighter with a quartet of powers. I have overcome hill after hill. Guilt, regret, the red coating my hands, all hills I have climbed. But they just keep coming.

We pick at the platter in silence, each of us lost in our own thoughts. Mine revolve around researching the Mother Star and when she rose for the first time eons ago. Vander's emotions change from anger to sadness to fear to frustration faster than my heart beats.

The food is almost gone when Torin races into the room, his dark eyes wide with both fear and excitement. "Come quick." His words slip between his ragged breaths. "There's something you need to see."

"What is it?" Van asks, using the table to help him stand, wincing when the scar on his thigh pulls.

"It's good. It's so good." His eyes flick from me to Vander. "Ruith has declared war on Summer in the most spectacular way possible."

"How?" I ask, taking a single step towards him.

Torin smirks. "He's captured their High Lord."

Chapter 2

M Y MAGIC CHURNS. THE shadows and ice meld together and whip from my hands in tongues of frozen darkness. The fae light hovering overhead flickers out, throwing us into an impenetrable darkness the return of the Mother Star could not hope to lift. My fingers caress the invisible pelt of an animal when my Autumn-born power rushes to the surface. The pewter mugs shatter, the cracking of metal deafening in the now silent manor.

"Breathe, Princess." Vander is beside me in a heartbeat, his warm hands cradling my heated cheeks. That he made his way around the table to comfort me in this darkness is nothing short of a miracle. "Ruith captured Tohminic. *Captured*. He will not harm you."

I startle at his proximity, flinching back as if scorched by the words he speaks. I curl my hands into fists, fighting to ease the shaking while gasping to control my harsh pants. Even through the darkness, I am aware of my vision tunnelling, aware of stars flashing across my eyes and trying to obscure the haunting image of Tohminic's sneering face.

Mouse-brown hair and yellow eyes that belong to some kind of feral animal taunt me while the echo of the Summer Lord's fire magic scorches my skin. Carrion invades my nose with so much strength, I choke on the arid odour.

"Bria."

I trail my trembling fingers over the grid-like scars pressing against my black leathers, and every raised line of clammy skin takes me back to those days. A cage of iron. An undead guard. Taunt after taunt after taunt. My knees give way, and I only remain upright when Vander catches me in his muscular arms.

He cannot be here.

This is my sanctuary.

I grip Vander's arm for dear life. "I can't go through it again."

"You won't." Though his tone is calm, rage and vengeance ripple along our bond. "You're not alone, Princess. Tohminic —"

"Is trapped," finishes Torin, "in the very cage he held you in. Broken wheel and all. He can't touch you. Even if he could, do you think Vander and I would allow him to get near enough to so much as *breathe* on you?"

My shadows begin to retreat, clearing enough that Vander's face swims into view.

He crooks a finger under my chin and forces me to look into his mesmerising eyes. Silver. Not red. Not yellow, like Tohminic's. "You're safe. I vow it."

The image of crimson-stained fish and rice flashes in my mind, melding with the memory of Nikolai in his last moments. He was brave beyond measure, stoic, as that awful sword careened for his throat. That same expression remained on his lifeless face while the Summer Lord used his necromancy magic to torture me with the knowledge that Nik's death was my fault.

The room shimmers. The darkness contorts until I am looking at a hazy image of me as I fight free of Tohminic's hold on the battlements of Ad'Starrag, then run for the corner tower. My memory snags on the details, like the weight of the blade in my hand as I fought for freedom beside Wyn, the kiss of cool water when she dragged me into the churning ocean, and the feel of solid ground when we folded to Vander on the curling land bridge outside the Summer keep.

I got out. *I. Got. Out.*

Vander soothes the panic away with firm strokes along my spine, whispering encouraging words while I regain control. "That's it," he says, his thumb making a small circle over my shoulder blade. "You've got this, Princess."

Though my lungs burn in protest, I force them to cooperate, dragging thankful breaths in through my nose to ease the pants. Slowly, they turn from ragged to shaking, then at last, even and deep. My shadows and ice recede completely, the fur skating across my palms fades, and the rusty tang of metal disappears from my tongue as my magic retreats into my mind.

"Okay." I straighten, standing on my own two legs and no longer relying on Vander to keep me upright. "Okay. I've got this. I can do this." In a whisper, I add, "Help me do this."

He releases his hold on the illusion, and the image of me fleeing the battlements fades. Moonlight filters into the dining room, illuminating the lines of his face. "I will always have your back."

"I don't mean to be insensitive," says Torin in a voice that says otherwise, "but can we go now? Ruith refused to let me so much as look at the flame-wielding arsehole without Bria there."

Ruith, the High Lord of Winter and my stepfather, was once an ally of the Summer Court. He's our ally now, claiming he has no choice if he wishes for his mate to live in happiness. Which is why I wonder... *What in the Blessed Mother Star has he done?*

"Yes. Let's go." I'm pleased my voice doesn't show the raging emotions coursing through me.

Vander offers me his hand to keep me steady, and together, with Torin all but bounding in front of us, we make our way down to the safe room.

I have not stepped foot in the terrace-level chamber, though I have entered the training room to its east and the infirmary opposite. Our healer, Penna, would have had my head if I tried to sneak away instead of healing, so exploring the lowest level of Dusk Manor was never an option. Not to mention I have not had use of the room, let alone felt a desire to enter it. The only thing I know about it is the walls are made of iron and rendered with some kind of clay to prevent the deadly metal from injuring anyone.

A prickle of magic washes over my skin when I cross the threshold, freezing me in place when the stronger wards warn against entry and probe my mind for intention. As if realising I am friend, not foe, the magic slithers away and grants me access.

The wall along the far end — so far away that my enhanced eyesight can only just make out the details — holds timber shelves laden with scrolls, jars, weapons, and small wooden chests. To the left, weapons gleam under the bluish fae lights clinging to the ceiling. On the right, arched doors are open to bedchambers. My eyes skim over the assortment of animal pelts covering the iron floor, the wooden furniture placed without rhyme or reason, and the many barrels and crates in clusters.

I disregard all the details, my eyes going straight to the dense shadows in the middle of the room and the brown-skinned male beside them.

"Well met, Stepfather." I dip my chin in respect for his title. "Torin said you captured Tohminic. Is it true?"

His eyes, such a dark brown they are black in the low light, hold an edge of anger. It recedes when he sees how calm I am. "Well met, my daughter. The Wind Whisperer speaks the truth. I have veiled Lord Tohminic with my shadows, and I will only reveal him to you when I am sure you can handle it."

"She can handle it," says Vander. As if in afterthought, he adds, "Well met, Ruith."

"How's Uma?" I ask Ruith, choosing the only topic that will distract us both — Ruith from my reaction to Tohminic, and me from facing my captor for the first time since escaping his cruel hands.

He sighs and the temperature in the room plummets when his ice magic seeps from his palms. "As much as I wished to keep her in the dark about the war, when the Mother Star did not rise after the Gloom, I had no choice." He eyes the shadowed cage. "Hence the retribution."

"She didn't take it well?" Having spent the past five and seventy years hiding in her chambers, the last thing Uma needs is the fear of war. "Shall I visit?"

"She was more courageous than I could have imagined. In fact, she did not so much as balk." A proud smile pulls at his full lips. "I am in awe of her. Yes, I would be very grateful if you would visit. I think Uma would appreciate the sentiment, too. She worries about you."

"And I her." I offer Ruith a smile of my own. "I will come tomorrow evening. Perhaps we can dine together?"

His sable hair catches the light when he dips his chin. "And your mate?"

"I will come too." Vander's tone leaves no room for disagreement. "Enough of this. Let's see the Summer Lord and delight in how far he has fallen."

Torin rubs his hands together and approaches the dense shadows, their form encompassing a shape I know all too well. "Unveil him." He cracks his knuckles with menacing intent.

"There is something you must know before I lift the shadows." Ruith's tone is so sincere that I whip my eyes to the cage. "He is not what he once was. He is… I suppose you will see." He drags his shadows back, gathering them in his palms before they retreat beneath his dark brown skin. They are a stark contrast to the white tunic he wears.

As his shadows disperse, an icy shiver that has nothing to do with Ruith's magic crackles down my spine. Gooseflesh prickles along my arms and over my nape in a warning to flee the male within the cage.

But I make myself look. I force my eyes to watch as the shadows fade and reveal a cowering male. I force myself to acknowledge his ostentatious gambeson — the red leather and lace detracts from the armour. He is lucky to be fully clothed, the only skin to endure the scorching iron is his bronze hands and face. I frown at his unkempt and unexceptional hair, then move to his animalistic eyes. This is where I pause.

His eyes, eyes I know can hold sparks of fury and the promise of punishment, now drip with remorse and heartache.

I tilt my head to the side, seeking answers I cannot gain from observation alone. With his knees bent to his chest and his arms wrapped around his legs, he looks weak. He looks vulnerable. The red lining his swollen eyes suggests my tormentor does, in fact, suffer the same emotions as the rest of us.

The male before me is a far cry from the abuser who taunted me with his words. *War is not kind. You will learn how cruel it can be soon enough.* Since my escape, I have dreamed of throwing those words back at the High Lord, but seeing him now, so broken and on the brink of giving up, the words turn to ash on my tongue.

He is slow to lift his head, as if each of his tears weighs heavily on his soul. "Help me. Please, help me. It will not stop. She will not stop. Help me." He repeats the same words over and over, each syllable growing quieter until his words morph into a whispered chant.

The only 'she' he could be speaking of is Chlora, his lover and the daughter of his Commander General. Now I think of it, Xaler is Tohminic's second, which leaves no room for another commander of his armies. Something does not add up with the female.

"It is all he has said since I detained him," says Ruith.

Torin inclines his head, closing his eyes against the vision before him while he listens for whispers. He places a tanned hand against the remaining wheel of the cage. "He's right. The

Summer Lord has said nothing but what you hear now." He turns to Ruith. "How *did* you detain him?" The menace in his tone has dimmed upon seeing Tohminic.

"I requested a meeting during the Gloom. While his denizens were distracted by what was occurring here in Dusk, I met with Tohminic under the guise of discussing reestablishing our alliance. He was more than happy to indulge me." His tone changes to once of disgust. "This thing was in his war chamber, where he foolishly met me alone."

"How did you force him into it?" I do not take my eyes from Tohminic.

"My ice magic is a marvellous thing, dear daughter. All it took was one well-timed attack, some questionable skills in getting him through the cage door, and a lot of shadow work on our exit of Ad'Starrag. Thank the Mother Star his denizens were otherwise engaged."

"Otherwise engaged?" asks Torin, with a hint of curiosity.

I spit out, "They host sex parties quite regularly. They gather in the rotunda and everyone... partakes."

"Sounds like my kind of scene." He does not hide his amusement.

The image Ruith paints with his words is easy for me to conjure in my mind. The Winter High Lord, seemingly innocent, freezes the Summer Lord and shoves him into the same torturous cage I endured, wreathes the entire thing in shadow, and heaves it through the sandstone keep at the realm's eastern border. Some details are lacking — like how Ruith dragged that cage all the way to the wards without detection, when it took two guards to push me to my chambers at Ad'Starrag, and they still struggled — but I let the curiosity die. I don't care to know *how* he managed it, just *why*.

"You said you did this out of revenge." I face my stepfather, my brows rising. "Please explain."

He clasps his hands behind his back, his upper lip twitching into a snarl. "No one, not even a fellow High Lord, causes my family such pain. I considered his demise when you first came to me, requesting to meet your mother after all these years. My plans were in place not long after. When circumstances forced me to reveal everything to Uma, and she broke down upon hearing of all you endured, I acted on those plans. No one hurts my family, Bria."

I stare at him for a moment, thoughts spinning while I come to terms with what he is saying. My true father would never seek vengeance on my behalf. Blessed Mother Star, he would not send an army to rescue me from the Summer keep. Rennyn cares only for his new role of High Lord and will do nothing that may threaten his life of opulence.

For five and seventy years, not a single fae has had my back. Now, after forsaking my home court and living life how *I* want to live it, I have a handful of fae I consider family. Vander, Torin, Wyn, Ruith, and Uma. Little by little, I am opening my heart to these fae and letting them see the real me. And what I am receiving in return is beyond anything I could have hoped for.

The war threatens all of that. Suddenly, those words that turned to ash on my tongue fight for freedom.

I turn to Tohminic and say, "War is not kind, Tohminic. You will see just how cruel it can be soon enough."

He is a broken male as his tear-filled eyes clash with mine. "Help me. She will not stop. She will not free me. Please, help me." He slams his fists against each side of his head and, through gritted teeth, continues to chant, "Please. Bring the shadows back. Help me." It's as if he did not hear a single word I said, as if he has no control of his body and mind.

Ruith obliges and blankets the iron in swirling onyx. "He is quiet in the shadows. Calm. Whatever haunts him does not pierce the darkness."

"I have an idea." Torin sounds as though he would rather not voice his plan.

"Go on," says Vander.

Torin runs his fingers through his long hair, toying with a loose strand before letting his hands fall to his sides. "To find out what torments him, we need a Night fae. We need my mother."

Chapter 3

"WHAT DO YOU THINK about asking Blodwen for help?" I ask Vander when we are alone in his bed-chamber. "Is it worth contacting her?"

There's no point stating my point. He knows I am talking about the sacrifice Torin's mother will demand if we ask for her help again. Last time, when she accessed my memories so we could discover how to create a stronger ward stone for our court, we offered her five undead fae. *Five.* We later learned those fae were not dead. The knowledge is haunting.

Her desire for tormented souls to feast on knows no bounds, and the prospect of seeing the Night female again causes nausea to churn in my stomach.

"Something isn't right with Tohminic. When we last saw him on the battlements of Ad'Starrag, he was cocksure and taunting. I wonder what makes a powerful male go from that to a mere husk of themselves," says Vander.

I move to the lone window and look out over the eastern horizon. The slither of the moon hanging low in the sky does little to illuminate the land, though I know the Autumn and Summer Courts to be in the distance. If the Mother Star rose,

I would see the rolling hills of the former and arid desert of the latter.

"It reminds me of Wyn," I say with caution.

"In what way?" Sheets rustle when he sits, and the tell-tale thud of leather boots hitting the floorboards reverberates through the room.

I give my back to the view of everlasting night and face him. "How he doesn't seem like himself. He kept mentioning a female, saying she won't stop. At the time, I thought he was talking about Chlora. Now, I'm not sure. The more I think about it, the more I realise something doesn't add up."

He runs a hand over his shaved head and sighs. "Wyn's just overwhelmed with everything that happened. Father died, which caused the illusions over our court to fall and reveal us to the rest of Radelea. Being held captive with you affected her more than she lets on. Now we're at war. She fought valiantly to protect the northern village, and I think it was her breaking point."

I move to stand between his legs and cup his face. "You're worried about her." I do not voice it as a question; his emotions buzz in the back of my mind, mingling with my own and sometimes taking control.

"I can't help but wonder if there's anything I could have done differently to make this easier on her. It's clear she's not coping. I just don't know how to help her."

The notion that whatever is haunting Wyn and tormenting Tohminic is the same thing burns hotter through my body, and I believe in that idea with every fibre of my being.

As true mates, blessed by the Mother Star, Vander and I will often have differing opinions. It is why we're so good together. We complete one another. Where one believes in inner demons, the other acknowledges outside forces may be at play. Where one is suffering and cannot see through the darkness in their soul, the other is a voice of reason enticing them into the light.

Yes, we will have differing opinions. Yes, there will be times when I dispute his words with my own, when I disagree to the point of arguing. But now is not the time. Vander doesn't need verbal sparring; it will not do him well to think he allowed something to happen to Wyn — he's struggling enough thinking her emotions are ruling her — and he does not need to be reminded of her torment.

No. What he needs is a distraction.

And if I'm being honest with myself, so do I. I need a distraction from the iron cage in the safe room, from the war that is sure to change Radelea, and from the weight that pushes me down more and more each day. More and more every time the Mother Star doesn't rise, and more every time I visit either village in Dusk.

I stroke my thumb over his full bottom lip and move closer, pressing against his thighs. My heart beats hard in my chest when I slide my hand from his cheek to his black leather jacket and pull on the strange zipper contraption to reveal his defined chest.

"I know what you're doing, Princess, and I have one thing to say," he starts, then grips my hips and pulls me impossibly closer. "It's going to work."

He trails a hand up my spine with a pace so slow it sends tingles through my body, his silver eyes boring into mine. That intense gaze does not falter when his fingers slide over my shoulders and down my arms. If anything, the burning desire increases when his hands skim over my breasts before moving to the buckles of my leathers.

One by one, Vander releases the clasps that hold the top half of my fighting gear together, and each time, I'm rewarded with a graze of his calloused skin against the soft ivory flesh of my torso. When he releases the last buckle, he sets his warm hands on either side of my waist, then drags them to my shoulders, marking me with a trail of scorching heat that leaves me wanting.

I graze my teeth along my bottom lip, fighting the urge to rip his pants from his body and take what we both need. He doesn't need this to be fast and fuelled by lust. He needs to be loved. Adored.

The cool air nips at my skin once my top half is free, and my nipples harden from both the temperature and the look on Vander's face when he drags his eyes from mine to drink in the view of my breasts. A whisper of air sighs through the chamber, as if it, too, has been waiting for this moment.

Mirroring his actions, I drag his jacket from his shoulders and plant a soft kiss on the curve of his neck, inhaling that addictive scent. It envelops me with the freshest of breezes, the ripest of apples, and the rain on a summer's eve. It is the forest cedars and the salt of the beach. His scent is many things melding together to create that one perfect aroma. Home. He smells and tastes and feels like home.

I discard his jacket on the floor without looking where it lands, then move to the laces of his pants, pulling the string free and loosening the waistband with deliberate slowness. Every nerve in my body tingles with expectation and exhilaration, and my mouth runs dry at the sight of the magnificent male before me.

Vander helps me dispose of his pants by lifting his hips from the bed, and throughout the tugging and pulling of leather, his hands never leave my shoulders. His thumb moves in circles over my scarred flesh while he watches me peel off my leathers, then add them to the pile of onyx in the corner.

Standing naked before him, I moisten my lips and whisper, "I need you."

"Then come get me." The corners of his lips curl up in challenge.

Before I can so much as lift a leg to climb onto his lap, he peels himself from the bed and moves to stand behind me. He keeps one hand on my hip, his fingers taunting as they skim close to just where I want them, while he drags the other across my front to cup my breast.

He plants a gentle kiss to the curve of my shoulder, where I know a scar to run across the bone. "A loving kiss to replace the sting of betrayal by your father." His tongue slides across my skin to another scar, his tongue darting out to run the length of the angry red line. "A caress, for all you endured in that cage."

A whimper escapes through my parted lips. I am supposed to be loving *him*, not the other way around. But I cannot force myself to move, to return the favour, not when he is moving from scar to scar and replacing every horrible memory with the feel of his lips and tongue.

"For the life of taunts. For Fayeth's hatred. The ogre attack. Almost drowning off the coast of Dusk. What you witnessed in the rotunda. For Rennyn, Chlora, the Autumn fae." A delicate kiss for every terrible thing that has happened to me. His finger flicks my nipple when he kisses the last scar. "These are not scars of what has happened to you, Princess, but scars of what you have overcome."

I can take it no longer. I twist in his arms and crush my mouth to his, tasting the remnants of mead on his lips. He is all I know as my tongue slips into his mouth, all I am aware of when his tongue meets mine in a dance of desire and need. The entire realm fades away until Vander and I are all that remains. Just us, his growing need for me pressing against my stomach, and the increasing wetness between my legs.

I skim my fingers over his jaw and cup the back of his head to hold him close, then nip at his bottom lip while trailing my other hand over the grooves of his abdominal muscles.

Vander tuts and pulls away, turning me back around in one swift move. "You must learn restraint. Now, where was I?" He hums, then adds, "That's right."

I moan when his fingers return to my breast, kneading and caressing, before he pinches my nipple between his thumb and forefinger. My head falls back against his shoulder and I watch how his face changes with every flick of his finger against the hardened bud.

He trails his tongue up the curve of my throat, his free hand travelling down my body at the same pace. They both leave gooseflesh in their wake; they both leave me panting for more, yet I hold my breath when he runs a finger along the length of my centre then pushes it inside me, curling it until he hits that incredible wall of bliss.

A keening moan rushes free, and I snake an arm behind me to hold his hip. It serves as an anchor, so I do not lose myself entirely to the sensations. I have not forgotten my vow to shower him with adoration.

He presses his thumb against my clitoris, the pressure firm and tantalising while he glides his finger in and out. Light tremors spread from my core to my limbs, tightening and releasing with every thrust of Van's finger. He has me aching for more every time he flicks his thumb, and I cling to him harder.

"That's it, Princess." His breath is a gentle whisper against my ear. "Let it all go. Give yourself to me."

The tremors grow wilder, increasing to rumbles of searing bliss. My shadows snake from my palms and writhe through the room with Vander's wind, their sighs muted compared to the gasping moans pulling at my throat.

"Vander." His name is a prayer, a reverence.

A second finger joins the first, and I buck against his naked body. The feel of his erection against my lower back is exquisite. His thumb moves in a feather-light circle, and he nibbles at my neck while angling his fingers once more.

The rumbling euphoria quickens before erupting into a thundering earthquake that shatters my body and mind. I shudder and buck as an orgasm rips through me, and I scream his name so loud the Mother Star is sure to hear. I grip his wrist and hold him to me, clenching around his fingers and riding out the last trembles of ecstasy until they fade to a dull ache.

He removes his fingers and subtly rubs his wrist. "You're magnificent, Bria. So beautiful," he says when I spin in his arms and rub my hands over his chiselled chest.

I urge him closer to the bed, our bodies pressing against one another and fitting with heart-warming perfection. "As are you." I lick my lips, and my eyes dip to his lower half.

He shakes his head. "I need you. All of you, not just your mouth." The backs of his knees hit the mattress, and he sinks down, pulling me with him. His eyes glow like beacons in the night, shining through the tongues of wind and shadow as I climb on top of him, angling my hips until I'm settled over the tip of his cock.

Van grasps my hips, his fingers splayed wide, and pulls me down. His breath hisses from between his teeth while I release a ragged whimper. There is nothing more perfect than the way he fills me, nothing as euphoric as stretching around him and taking him as deep as I can. We are joined in the most intimate way possible, our minds linked and our bodies melding.

I cup his face and rest my forehead against his. "I thank the Mother Star every day for bringing us together." My lips slide against his, soft and tender. Through our mind link, I say, *"I love you, Vander."*

He trails his fingers along my spine and tucks a stray strand of copper behind my ear, grazing over the shorn strands on the left. *"I love you, too."*

I savour the moment for a heartbeat longer, delighting in the utter completeness coursing through my veins. Unable to remain still any longer, I roll my hips. His groan is animalistic. It is sexy as sin. I pepper soft kisses along the curve of his neck and grind my hips again. A coil tightens inside me, a tornado of simmering divinity.

Vander worships every line of my body he can reach with tender caresses and gentle kisses. His rough hands stroke and explore, his tongue lathes, and his lips stir a raging need inside me.

Desperate for more, I slide up his throbbing length, then sink down once more, crying out when he hits that magical place deep inside. I force my legs to work harder, rising and falling onto his cock faster and faster as my fingers trace the lines of his face and my eyes lock on my mate's.

An aching well of emotion bursts inside me, and I know I will never recover if I lose him. The thought has me wrapping my arms around his neck and pulling him close. Love is not a strong enough word for what I feel. It is soaring to a height I never knew was possible, and it is the grey between the black and the white. It is all-consuming. Indescribable.

The coil within me tightens further, thawing every wall around my heart and pulsing with a thrilling rapture. With each smack of skin against skin and each roll of my hips, with each groan from Vander and each thrust inside, I slowly come undone.

Sweat clings to my body, my breaths are harsh and ragged, and my legs protest at the repetition, but I don't dare stop. My movements become jerky as I give myself to the feeling. My breaths are harsh against Vander's shoulder when I allow the love and adoration to consume everything I am. I pull back and claim his mouth with my own, slipping my tongue between those glorious lips and tasting him. It's a move that sends us both reeling.

He tightens his hold on my hips and slams me down with a delectable force that has me quivering. It shatters what remains of my control. I throw my head back and cry out his name as a second orgasm tears through my body like a ravaging wind.

He stills beneath me, and the throbbing of his cock as he spills inside me only strengthens the waves of ecstasy pulling at my everything. Our magic tears through the room, curling around us and creating the sweetest destruction. It's the destruction of true mates who would do anything it takes to protect one another, a chaotic symphony of love and respect and protection. It is a bubble of safety I will do everything in my power to keep, no matter the cost.

Chapter 4

T HE MOMENT VANDER AND I fold the Winter Court towards us and step through the void of time and space, leaving the stillness of Dusk behind, I regret my decision to wear a traditional fae gown. The bronze skirt, though woven from a thick cotton, does little to protect my legs from the bitter cold, and the eggshell white frills beneath the amber corset itch my skin. I much prefer my leathers. It's a wonder I managed so many years wearing something as uncomfortable as a gown.

My nose is numb within two heartbeats, with flecks of snow settling on the pinked tip and clinging to my eyelashes. I draw my travelling cloak tighter around me, though it does not help much.

Vander takes my hand to help me along the precarious slope in the Bolbala Ranges, a frozen wasteland of mountains in Radelea's north-west. "Let's get moving," he says, crystals of breath pluming, "before we freeze to death."

"Being born of Winter should mean I don't feel the cold," I whine as we begin the short walk to Kol, the tallest mountain in the ranges and Ruith's home.

"It doesn't work that way, unfortunately." He helps me over an iron-coloured boulder that pierces through the thick snow. "How did your meeting with Torin go this morning?"

A harsh wind tears at my hair and gown, threatening to freeze me where I stand. "I tried talking him out of bringing his mother here, but he wouldn't listen. He left for the Night Islands at noontime."

He hums. "Whatever changed Tohminic is something to fear. I'm okay with Blodwen coming to the manor to help."

"What of her payment?"

A cloud shifts, revealing a streak of glittering stars. It's a small detail everyone in Radelea relies on to determine time. The stars, and the moon. Kol is a dark mass before us, piercing the dark sky with its crooked apex. Last time I came here, I was alone, and folded onto the peak of Kol. This time, Vander and I are searching for a lower entrance, the mouth of a cave somewhere nearby. It leads straight to Ruith's private wing.

"We'll consider anything," he says. "Though I'm hesitant to provide her with more souls to torture. Did the two of you talk about Wyn? It was the reason for your meeting, wasn't it?"

The first of the obsidian statues appears when we crest a small hill, then the entire snaking line of Winter's previous leaders, followed by a mere slither of darkness. I increase my pace, all but dragging Vander with me, the call of the warmth within the castle beckoning.

I flick a glance at him. "He wants to figure out what's wrong with Tohminic first."

"His reasons?"

"If whatever haunts Tohminic also haunts Wyn, and Blodwen can determine what that is, we're best to use the Summer Lord as a trial run. His words, not mine."

He's quiet for a moment, contemplative while we pass the dark statues. It isn't until we are slipping inside the cave that he says, "It's smart thinking. If Blodwen's mind magic causes pain or damage... We can't risk that with Wyn." But we can with Tohminic. He does not say the words out loud, but we both know it is the truth.

The cave's antechamber reveals nothing about what lies beyond the heavy-set door to the right. Icicles as long as my legs drip gelid water from above, and patches of ice obscure the uneven ground. We move around them and pause before the onyx door.

"Are you ready to meet my mother?" I ask, a smile pulling at my lips.

He brushes the sleet from my cheek. "Anything for you, Princess." He knocks twice, the boom echoing through the antechamber and threatening a cave-in.

I glance at the icicles when a concerning crack follows Vander's knock.

The door creaks as it opens, and a burst of heat flutters over my frozen skin. "Well met," says Ruith with a welcoming smile. "Step into the warmth."

"Well met." I curtsey, then drag Vander into the opulent foyer.

A gold and obsidian double staircase parts around a statue of Uma and Ruith, both looking lovingly into the other's eyes. The twisting banister glimmers under the bright fae lights overhead, but the shine has nothing on the tinkering chandelier in the centre of the space. It has to be larger than I am, and twice as wide. The sparkling gems dangling from the golden whorls and hooks create a rainbow of colour on the black marble floor. It is a breathtaking sight.

"Come," says Ruith. "Uma waits for us in the dining hall. I trust your journey was acceptable?"

"It was cold," I say, releasing Vander's hand and following my stepfather through his home.

The walls are a creamy white, and the wainscoting a delightful touch. The dark floors make the space feel smaller but bring a certain richness to the winding hallway.

"I will amend the wards so you may fold into the antechamber," says Ruith, pausing at an open door.

"That would be wonderful."

A male appears from within the dining room and holds his hand out for my cloak. I unclasp it and hand it to him with a smile, but he turns and disappears without a word.

I arch an eyebrow at Ruith, who only shrugs. "We protected your vulnerable for mere hours, yet my denizens miss the younglings and babes of Dusk."

"The younglings still talk about their adventure to the Bolbala Ranges," says Vander. "Some of them wish to return soon, with your permission."

"Of course, of course. They are more than welcome," says Ruith.

He leads us into a small dining hall, the same wainscoting and dark floors flowing into the rectangular space. Velvet curtains in a pale blue hang limp at the windows, and I wonder if it is ever warm enough in the Winter Court to open them and bask in the view of the ranges beyond. In the middle of the hall, a gleaming table groans under the weight of too many carafes and pots for four fae. The aromas wafting from the array of food and drink is mouth-watering.

Vases filled with small flowers line the centre of the table. Their dainty petals are lilac at the edges but in the middle they darken to a violet so deep it is almost black. They remind me of the jade flowers in Autumn, found in abundance in the gardens to the east, and the pink and red flowers dotted throughout the fields of Summer.

"Dame's violet," says a musical voice that stars in my dreams.

I turn to Uma with a wide smile. "Well met, Mother. Let me introduce my unofficial mate, High Lord Vander Theron of the Dusk Court."

She hides her shock well, smoothing the skirt of her lapis lazuli gown as she stands. The white corset makes her pale skin seem tanned, a real feat for someone who lives inside a mountain. Her copper curls fall over her shoulders when she lowers into a curtsey and dips her chin. Her ice-blue eyes crease at the sides, so filled with life and excitement it makes my heart lighter. "Well met, Lord Vander. Ruith speaks highly of you. I am pleased to see he speaks the truth."

"It's an honour." Vander takes Mother's hand and presses a chaste kiss to her knuckles. "I can see where Bria gets her looks."

She blushes the same blush that creeps along my cheeks when I'm embarrassed. I enjoy finding the small similarities between us, having spent my entire life with only Father to compare myself to. I share his emerald eyes and quick temper, but everything else, everything good, I get from Uma.

Ruith chuckles. "Enough of that, now." There's enough warning in his tone that Vander takes his seat without another word.

"I was ever so surprised when Ruith told me of the war." Mother scoops yellow rice onto her plate before she continues. "How goes the rebuild of your northern village?"

Accepting the serving spoon, I say, "It's slow. The Night fae destroyed it beyond recognition. We had to start from scratch. The homes, stores, market. Everything is gone. It's heartbreaking to see."

"Such a shame."

"The western village is nearing completion," says Vander, helping himself to a stew. The chunks of carrot, turkey, and sausage glisten with an aromatic sauce.

Ruith says, "I am very glad to hear it. My denizens whisper of the destruction to your court. They will be relieved to know things are not as bad as they feared. Autumn, however, we cannot say the same for."

Ice crackles down my spine, and I freeze, the serving spoon dripping grains of rice onto the table. "What do you mean?"

"Lord Rennyn is eager to please the nobles of his court. In his quest for respect, he allows Lord Gorred more say than is wise. I have heard the court is on lockdown. No fae may enter or leave."

Fear trickles down my throat and settles in my stomach with the weight of an anvil. Lord Gorred, Father's second and the commander of the Autumn army, is a despicable male. The number of times I was forced to wear a smile while enduring his wandering eyes and straying hand...

"Are you okay?" Vander asks through our bond.

"Gorred cannot be allowed control of any kind. We have to intervene. The females don't deserve such a fate."

He stills beside me. *"Meaning?"*

"Meaning Gorred will see to it that his way of thinking becomes the norm. He's an abuser, Van." Before we get carried away with our mind-to-mind conversation, I ask Ruith, "How accurate are these rumours? Where did you hear them?"

"Explain."

"Later. I promise. Let's just enjoy tonight, please."

"My shadows pierce even the brightest of corners, Bria," says Ruith. "It would be foolish of you to think I do not have spies in every court. Even yours."

"I would take offence," says Vander, "if I didn't have spies here, too."

The Winter Lord throws his head back and laughs. "Oh, I do like you, Vander of Dusk. An honest male who does not back down. I had my reservations about you back when you appeared at Rennyn's born day ball, but you have proven yourself worthy."

"Worthy of what?" Vander spears a chicken thigh with his fork and dumps it on his plate with more force than is necessary. It's a show, for Ruith's sake, that warms my heart.

"Of my daughter, of course."

Uma and I watch them, each of us wearing a bemused smile. I offer her a shrug when our eyes meet, and we both shake our heads and start on our food while the males continue to jest and bond.

Bursts of herb and spice coat my tongue as I eat, and paired with the tender meat and sweet sauce, a warmth settles in my stomach, though I am not sure it has much to do with the stew.

An image of the life I could have if war did not exist flashes in my mind. A life of dinners in Winter, strengthening the bond I share with my long-lost birth mother and her mate while Ruith and Vander argue about politics and purposely aggravate one another. A life of breakfasts in Dusk, with Torin and Wyn and whoever they choose to spend their lives with. Life unguarded and free.

Despite the darkness and the war, life is good right now. I have a male who I love, and who loves me in return, and a group of close friends I am happy to call family. I have a home, a roof over my head when many do not. Food is not an issue — though I remember the pain of hunger from my time in Ad'Starrag — and I will never be without clothing or a bed to sleep in. My life, even with the downfalls, is *good*.

It is a far cry from what I thought mere months ago, when I was so reckless that I would sneak from the Autumn castle to meet Nikolai on his ship and spend the night lost in bliss. The reminder of Nikolai brings a dampener to my elated thoughts, and I return my focus to the conversation at the table as a distraction from the red creeping into my mind.

I'm getting better at shoving the demons away.

"I just want to make sure Tohminic hasn't been planted by our enemies," says Vander. "I am certain capturing him was difficult for you, especially after you were allied to the court of flame and necromancy for eons, but it all seems too easy. You must understand my hesitance after everything that happened with Nyree."

The betrayal from the leader of the Ill-fated — fae who were unfortunate enough to be stuck on Dusk Island when the original Night Court broke apart — will haunt Vander for a long time. And even now, days later, I cannot find it within my heart to feel guilt for Nyree's unexceptional death.

"Of course I understand. I thought the same. With the behaviour of the Summer fae, I would be surprised if they knew the month we are in, let alone hear a cage being dragged through their keep. They acted different from the last time I visited," says Ruith. "Hollow. Mindless."

"Like their leader?" I ask, and an idea rushes in, though I shove it to the far reaches of my mind to assess later, when I'm sure everything we know to be true will not come crashing down around us.

I need to speak with Tohminic again. As much as I detest being in the same room as the High Lord of Summer, it is necessary so I can begin placing the pieces of this puzzle together. I have to be certain if I am to broach this subject with the other High fae.

"Precisely," says Ruith, soaking up the last of his gravy with a chunk of rye.

Uma leans forward, her pale arms a stark contrast to the dark wood of the table. The way her copper brows are arched high, and the slight downturn to her lips — the same frown I wear when I'm not pleased by a realisation — are sign enough she has also put the pieces together.

"Mother, would you pass the wine, please?" I ask, giving an almost undetectable shake of my head when she looks at me.

Though she frowns, she says, "Of course." Her hand clenches around the handle of the carafe when she pours a dark red wine into my goblet.

I'm saved from reacting by three females who flit into the room and replace the pots of stew with a single platter of bread and butter pudding sprinkled with slithers of almonds, juicy sultanas, and crushed pistachios. The scent of nutmeg begs me to take the entire platter for myself.

The conversation steers away from betrayal, war, and allies, and back to how Vander intends to rebuild our northern village, and to what style. I let the males talk once more, enjoying the fruity tang of the sultanas every time I take a bite of the pudding.

We stay well into the night, the conversation between everyone flowing with ease and comfort while we relax in the sitting room. The black leather seats are so comfortable, I think I could live in them and be happy with my hand in life.

Being curled into Vander's side, with my mother and stepfather sitting opposite, even with the corset digging into my ribs, is just what I needed to reset, to let the anger I have been holding onto drift into the void, never to return.

Perhaps it is a dream. Perhaps I will never let go of the rage I feel every time I think about the Gloom and the lives lost that I am responsible for. But in this moment of peace and family, with the wine likely tricking me into a false security, I cannot imagine feeling such an emotion.

When I drift to sleep in Vander's arms, and he declares it time to fold home, I am unwilling to leave the peace of Winter. But

I relent, allowing Vander to fold us to Dusk. The moment we step onto the sandy shore, I wish I had been more stubborn. To think of Winter as a false sense of security was right.

Chapter 5

V ANDER LOWERS ME TO the sand, but keeps his hand on my elbow while he listens to the shouts, trying to determine where they're coming from. His free hand lifts to chest height, his fingers splayed and a tongue of wind rushing from his palm.

The wind ravages the she-oaks lining the beach; it rustles the leaves of the pines and oaks, and it whistles through the buildings in the distant western village. The sounds repeat when the gust returns, bringing with it the sound of chaos. "But what is it? There is too much blood. Someone get Penna! It was so loud. I have never heard anything of the like. Drag her outside." The words are a rush of panic, all merging into a single breath of air.

"The village," I whisper. "Not again."

"It doesn't sound like the undead," he says as we take off at a rapid pace. "They sound confused, like they don't understand what they're seeing."

My gown rustles with every step, trying to weave between my legs and get tangled around my ankles. I yank it free and hoist it up to my knees with a growl — I should have worn my leathers.

I graze my fingers across the spindly leaves of a she-oak encroaching on the dirt path that winds through the southern forest, taking a breath of calm when the needle-like branches caress my skin. It is all I need to hold the panic at bay; the branches have been my constant since I first came to Dusk. They are my lifeline, an anchor to keep me grounded and prevent the demons and red from dragging me into the depths of despair.

Dark clouds move over the stars, their menacing energy a mirror of Vander's emotions. As High Lord, he needs to have control of himself, or the weather will reflect his mood. A crack of thunder rolls across the sky, a trio of flashes illuminating the path for a heartbeat.

We veer west, towards the village, and I cannot help but think the rebuild we have put so much time and energy into was for nothing. Every time we take a step towards recovery and returning to the life we once led on this island, something sends us careening backwards and fighting for traction.

Delicate scents of zesty orange and calming lavender do little to soothe my frayed nerves as we break through the last of the trees and all but slide down the slope to the first row of brick buildings. The sight of the village's grid often sends waves of peace coursing through me, but tonight, all I feel is a burning rage. The wrath has returned, sizzling through me and tensing my muscles.

Thunder rumbles once more, followed by a fork of lightning that hits too close to the village.

My hands curl into fists, my pace increases, and my breaths hiss through my teeth in harsh pants. I beg the Mother Star for mercy, for a reprieve from the torment of war. I beg her to return to us, to shine her golden rays on our melancholic island and bring light to Radelea once more. Perhaps then, with her renewed blessing, the war will stop. I beg her and beg her, harder with every step I take towards the village square, knowing I cannot take much more of this. The fear, the anxiety, and the regret, they churn in my stomach and feed the rage.

"High Lord Vander," a male calls from outside the rebuilt tavern. Not a trace of the fire that scorched the walls remains. His voice is a rush, the words all blending into one as he says, "I don't know what happened. There was a crack through the night, then she screamed, and —"

"Take a breath," says Vander, stopping before the brown-skinned fae, "and tell me what happened."

Raised voices drift from the tavern, the silhouettes of fae moving about and casting lines of shadow on the ground outside. The amber glow of the fae lights streaks across the tavern's façade, creating dense shadows where the uneven bricks jut out.

"My brother and I were enjoying an ale when we heard a booming crack from the kitchens. Of course, we were stunned for a moment, having never heard such a sound before. When our senses returned, and the tang of blood filled our noses, we rushed behind the bar to see her —" He closes his eyes and shakes his head. "The cook is dead. I'm to find our healer and bring her here."

"Where?"

"In the back alley." He forces his golden eyes open once more. "My Lord, I have never seen a wound such as this. It looks like a spear pierced her heart, but the hole is smaller. Smaller and too neat. There was nothing we could do. She was dead when we reached her."

I step forward and rest a hand on his shoulder. "I'm sure you and your brother did everything you could. Go. Find Penna and bring her here. We'll go see what we can do."

"Thank you," he says, flicking a worried glance over his shoulder. "I... I'll be back as soon as I find her."

The thunder growls again, farther away this time, but no less fearsome.

"She'll be in the manor infirmary," says Vander. His worry pierces through our bond and settles in my mind, tempering the rage.

Instead of going through the tavern, we take the long way around, finding the narrow alley that snakes behind the irregularly shaped stores. The dirt path is too small for the delivery wagons, with crates and barrels stacked against the brick walls on either side. It is a maze, with twists and turns and the occasional rat darting from barrel to barrel, that delays our arrival, but if the attacker left any clues, this is where we will find them.

Unfortunately, we find nothing out of the ordinary, other than a small keg of mead that someone has helped themselves to. No doubt Alizeh, the wind wraith.

The closer we get to the rear entrance, the stronger the scent of rust and salt becomes, so strong that the back of my hand, which is pressed against my nose, does nothing to block out the odour of blood. I detest this alley all of a sudden.

The last time I raced along the narrow path, I was running to free the cook from a raging fire Nyree had set. Her plan worked; Vander, Wyn, and Torin thought the Summer fae were behind the attack. I was the only one who saw the flash of pearlescent hair, the only one to realise Nyree was betraying the court.

"What are you thinking about?" Vander asks through the bond. He pauses at a crate and rummages through it, no doubt searching for more clues we will not find.

"Last time I was in this alley, when we saved the cook from the fire. I don't understand why the Mother Star would show her mercy then, only to end her life now. It's cruel."

He sighs when he finds nothing of interest in the crate. *"I'm starting to wonder if we place too much trust in the sun. She's a manipulative bitch."*

I fight to keep the smirk from my face. If the Mother Star ever heard him talking about her in such a derogatory way, she would rise out of spite and burn him where he stands. Me, too, if she discovers my amusement.

Another brown-skinned male heaves a limp body into the alley two doors ahead, and we cut our conversation short to help him with the cook.

A smear of crimson mars the ground, disappearing beyond the door and into the tavern's kitchen. It's more blood than I have ever seen from a single wound. The stench is overpowering. My stomach clenches as bile burns the back of my throat. My mind deserts me, and replacing the rage and jumble of thoughts, an incessant buzzing.

"My Lord." The male steps back and sags against the brick-work. My heart clenches at the pain crossing his features. "There was nothing I could do. Nothing..." His words end in a choked gasp, his shoulders heaving.

Vander kneels beside the cook after thanking the male, and presses his fingers to her blood-stained throat. The moment he realises her soul has moved on from the world, his entire face crumbles. The thunder cracks one last time, fading to a muted rumble before the clouds converge, and a torrential rain cascades from above.

He is gentle when he unties her apron and pulls it from her body. He shows the cook utmost respect when he pulls the collar of her tunic aside to inspect the wound. The rain is a constant downpour, drenching us in an instant, but he ignores the cool drips clinging to the tip of his nose, the trembling drops hanging from his eyelashes.

Rain and blood washes over my boots, scaring the alley's rodents into hiding as it races along a shallow rut in the dirt towards the exit. Splashes of pink stain the barrels and crates and brick.

I wrap my arms around my torso and force myself to take in the cook's features. A slightly hooked nose, thin lips, and wide eyes of such a captivating hazel that I am lost in their depths for a moment. Even after saving her from the fire, I did not bother to learn her name. I did not return to the tavern to see how she was afterwards.

My lungs grow tight, and I struggle to draw breath as my gaze trails over her chin and to her chest, where a small hole trickles blood. The size of my fingernail, the wound is clean, with mottled purple blooming around the edges.

"What is it?" I wheeze, my lungs still refusing to cooperate.

"I'm not sure," Vander murmurs. He spares me a glance. "Are you okay?"

Vander should not be worrying about me; the cook deserves his attention. My nod is frantic. "I'm fine. What has the power to kill a fae like this? Why didn't her enhanced healing save her?" They are questions that have been bothering me since we arrived.

"I don't know," he mutters. "I just don't know. But I think…" He shifts his sight to over my shoulder.

Hurried footsteps bounce off the walls, growing closer and carrying Penna's voice as she says, "I have never heard of such a wound. Not here, not in my home in Dawn. Describe it again."

"See for yourself," the male says before darting to his brother. "Let's go home. We will only get in everyone's way here."

His brother nods.

Vander moves aside for Penna, then faces the brothers. "Where can we find you if we have questions?"

The males direct him to a two-bedroom hut on the outskirts of the village they've been sharing with their mother since the Gloom, then disappear into the sheets of rain with their arms wrapped around one another for support.

Penna's silvery-blue hair clings to her forehead, the usual spikes limp and dripping water into her cobalt eyes, which narrow at the wound. She tuts. "He was right. I have not seen something this neat and small in all my years as a healer. Do they have any idea what caused such a wound?"

"They heard a loud crack and a scream. That's all they told us," says Vander, leaning back on his heels. He runs a soaked hand over his head. "We need Torin."

"He's in the Night Court still," I say through our bond, not trusting my voice to remain steady if I speak out loud.

The wrath I felt running through the she-oak forest has long since disappeared. All I feel now is regret and guilt and confusion. War demands sacrifice, I know that. I just did not think it would come in the form of an unknown wound on a female who deserved so much better.

"Does she have any family?" I ask Vander.

"No. Erthana lived alone."

Erthana. I commit her name to memory, refusing to let it slip through the cracks like I did after the tavern fire, because I am certain someone would have mentioned her name then. Although I fought hard to save her from the flames — and lost the hair on the left side of my head in the process — I didn't care enough about her to learn her story. I care now. I am *forcing* myself to care now. How can I dwell on regret and guilt if I do not have the decency to learn something as simple as a name?

Penna says, "Help me roll her over, My Lord."

"Why?" asks Vander, though he gently grips Erthana's shoulders and pulls her body towards him.

Penna unsheathes a dagger from her thigh and slices through the cook's tunic, revealing the freckled skin of her back. A deep purple bruise is setting in between her shoulder blades, splotches of deep red intertwining with the violet.

"No exit wound," she murmurs. "Set her back down, Vander."

He does as instructed, then pushes himself up and moves to stand beside me, his elbow brushing mine.

Penna hovers her hands over Erthana's chest, tendrils of white light snaking from her palms and probing the still bleeding wound, only to retreat. They do not heal the wound. They cannot.

"I wonder. Yes. It is possible." Penna turns to me, her brows furrowed. "Bria, would you mind investigating the wound? I am curious to know if any remnants of the weapon remain."

"How... How can *I* help?"

She arches an eyebrow. "With your metal bending powers."

In response to her words, the silver threads of my metallurgy magic writhe within the chamber in my mind, rattling the hatch I use to keep them contained.

I kneel beside Penna, my hands shaking as I hold them over Erthana's chest. Closing my eyes against the sight of the wound, I tease a ribbon of power free and bring it to my palms, where it awaits the command to investigate. A single thought, and my magic slips from my grasp and seeps into her body, seeking any hints of metal.

Steel, bright and silver against the veins and muscle in her hands, remains from many cuts. The life of a cook is a dangerous one, if the many traces of the alloy are anything to go by. There are slithers of silver in her leg, taking the shape of a small hook. I can only guess at the injury and cause, figuring it is some kind of angling mishap. Gold, warm and beautiful, shines from her ears.

But it is the dull and dark metal in her chest that catches my attention. Burning, scorching. Tormenting. Memories flood in, and I recoil, my eyes springing open. I leap to my feet and stagger back.

Vander wraps his arms around my waist, preventing my escape. "What is it, Princess? What did you see?"

Burning. Red. Bars.

My breaths turn ragged, and I shake my head. "Iron. I saw iron."

"Iron?" repeats Penna, her silver brows dipping as she turns back to Erthana. "Traces?"

"No. A chunk, still burning her flesh."

Vander's grip tightens. He whispers into my mind, *"Breathe, Princess. Breathe through it. You are the master of your fear."*

A sharp inhale through my nose, and a long release through parted lips, and I am calm enough to say, "We have to take it out. I don't know what it is, but it's still hurting her." My voice breaks as I repeat, "We have to take it out."

Vander rubs a hand over my back, his warmth fighting the rain's cold. "Can it be done?"

Penna twists her mouth. "Perhaps, if Bria can draw the metal out with her magic. We will need help, though. If she loses focus and the iron slips back inside, we may never retrieve it."

"We'll get you anything you need." Vander's tone is fierce. Determined.

"A stable surface to work on," Penna says, standing and looking to the sky before narrowing those deep blue eyes at Vander, "where the rain cannot interfere. Leather gloves, so we may handle the iron upon its release, a container to hold it in, and help."

"Help?" I ask, determined to do as much as I can. "I'll do whatever it takes."

"Then you will escort me to the Dawn Court. I trust no one but High Lord Jonik with this."

Ulakas.

My heart clenches as the memory of his death floods my mind. How he smothered me with his body to free me from the bone and blood magic of the Night fae. How my hands glistened with crimson as I tried to stem the flow of blood. The sorrow on Larrad's face, the heartbreak in Tasar's... The memories have haunted my nights since the Gloom.

I struggle to swallow around the lump in my throat, and my chest constricts to the point of pain as I sag in Vander's arms. Ten and one moons of darkness. Ten and one moons of avoiding the Dawn Court and the males I know are grieving the loss of a loved one. Because it is *my* fault he's dead. If I had not been so weak, so vulnerable that night on the beach, he would not have fought to save me, costing him his life.

"You are brave enough to face this, Princess," Vander says into my mind.

I can only hope.

Chapter 6

A HARSH WIND TEARS at my face, the bitter cold pinking my cheeks and numbing my nose. My leathers are soaked, the torrential downpour having refused to let up during the time it took to find a canvas stretcher and for Vander to return to the manor to ask Wyn if she would like to join us in Dawn.

She refused.

The crisp white blanket draped over Erthana's lifeless body feels wrong. It's too bright, too clean as we come to a stop at the water's edge.

"Are we ready, then?" Penna asks, using the back of her hand to brush water from her brow.

"Are you certain you can't do this on your own?" Vander asks for the third time. "You know I would much prefer to stay here, especially with Torin in Night and Wyn —" He swallows his words, perhaps not knowing how to describe the torment his sister endures.

I squeeze his fingers, which are tightly wrapped around the wooden posts supporting a canvas bed, and place a soft hand on Erthana's foot to guide her through the void, then turn to Penna. "We're ready."

"Very well." A faint shimmer surrounds Penna when she gathers the magic of the realm and steps through the fold.

Vander and I entwine our magic with the remnants of Penna's, his illusions and wind caressing my quartet of powers as we step from the firm sand and onto soft grass.

The shining lake before us glitters in the starlight, and a trio of merfolk drift with the slow-moving current. The palace backdrop is just as I remember it, with azure walls and golden balconies jutting from every side to mark the five levels of Jonik's home. But unlike the last time I was here, there is no joyous atmosphere. There is not a breath of wind, not a sigh of the weeping cherry blossoms dotting the landscape. In fact, if I could refer to today's Dawn Court as anything, it would be lifeless.

The temperature is neither hot nor cold, not humid and not fresh. It just is. While the merfolk have surfaced, which is a normal occurrence in the court of light and healing, their expressionless faces might as well scream with pain.

This is a court in mourning.

I squeeze Vander's hand when the memory of our last trip here resurfaces. After stealing a finger bone from Baba Yaga's hut, we had come to Dawn to create a stronger ward for the Dusk Court — if only the humans appreciated our efforts in protecting Earth. Vander's blood stains the grass we now stand on. The gaping hole in his thigh is one of the more gruesome wounds I have seen, including anything I saw during the gloomy battle that enraged the Mother Star.

Tendrils of white smoke flow from the windows of the palace, fading to a wispy haze as they drift closer to the ground. The scent of incense is so strong, I am certain my leathers will smell of it for days.

I release Vander's fingers and Erthana's booted foot and take the first step onto the curved bridge that stretches across the lake and towards the palace. My footsteps are harsh in the quiet night, the thuds as booming as the beats of my heart. The lanterns on either side cast an amber glow over the dark water, specks of golden light reflecting in the depths.

Any other night, I would think it a beautiful, calming view. Tonight, I am only reminded of my shortcomings. Like learning Erthana's name and realising I am not as noble as I believed, stepping foot in this court tears open a gaping hole inside me. I should not have avoided coming here.

Water ripples and splashes to my right when the trio of merfolk disappear below the surface of the water, their blue, gold, and teal tails glittering as they dive deeper, disappearing in the darkness when they're too far from the glow of the lanterns and fae lights.

"It is strange to be here when it is so quiet." Penna's voice is low, as if she does not wish anyone to overhear. "Even the splash of the merfolk is veiled in grief."

"How long will they be in mourning for? Is it considered discourteous of us to interrupt in a time of grieving?" I step from the low bridge and turn to watch Vander and Penna carry Erthana across. "I don't want to upset Jonik and Leilani."

Penna's face tightens. "There is no timeframe for such a thing. Grief is like the light we wield; it comes and goes, flickering in our minds and reminding us of what we have lost. Sometimes the light is dull and easy to manage. Other times, it is a blazing brightness that threatens to blind. All we can do is learn how to live with the light, to remember the golden rays and let them guide us like a beacon until it calls us to the beyond."

I blink away tears. "Such beautiful words."

Her smile is sombre. "Beautiful words for a horrible emotion. Sorrow," she sighs. "If the Mother Star offered us a chance to live without it, every fae in Radelea would beg for that chance."

"I think you're wrong. A life without sorrow is a life without joy. It is a cycle. We experience grief because we lived with joy. And how can we have joy again without having the strength to overcome sorrow?" I ask.

Though my question is rhetorical, Penna says, "Perhaps you are right. There must be a balance in life. I often wonder if that is why we are at war."

Vander steps onto the pebbled path that leads to the entrance of Jonik's palace, and readjusts his grip on the stretcher. "What do you mean?"

She somehow shrugs while holding the wooden posts on the other end. "Just that there has been much darkness of late. War, broken alliances, and bloodshed. It is no wonder the Mother Star abandoned us. She requires balance. There has been too much negativity."

We pass under a golden arch, the angular structure catching the starlight. When the moon is full, the Iassujin Arch glows brighter than the sun. Iassujin. It means *Welcome, friend* in the ancient language of the fae. Tonight, I do not feel welcome at all. Rather, I feel as though I am imposing on something deeply intimate. Something I have no right to witness.

The strain of carrying Erthana's body pulses through my bond with Vander, his efforts filtering into my hands. A dull ache throbs in my palm, and I rub my thumb along the lines to ease the discomfort before rapping my knuckles against the bifold doors at the palace's entrance.

The scents of straw and carved wood blends with the aromatic incense when a gold-clad guard opens the door on the right. "Welcome to the Court of Light. State your business."

I bow my head. "You have my thanks. We are here to beg Lord Jonik's help in a matter that concerns the realm."

"Names?"

"High Lord Vander of Dusk, healer Penna of Dawn, and Bria of Dusk." It's the first time I have voiced the title out loud. It rolls off my tongue like I was born to repeat the name. Of course, I am not a true Dusk fae, but the island court is my home. Moreso than the court I was born into.

"Come."

We remain silent while the guard leads us through the palace. We climb a curling staircase, passing circular windows that offer a northern, mountainous view. When we curl to the west, the view changes from the Dawn mountains to the flat plains of Spring, changing to the rolling hills of Summer and Autumn when we continue to spiral.

We exit on the fifth floor, entering a hallway lined with paintings of cherry trees and merfolk, the golden lanterns casting lines of shadow over the panelled floor and walls. The scent of incense is stronger up here, wafting from an open doorway on the left, where the herbaceous and flowery aroma pairs with the lilting notes of a harp.

I peer into the chamber as we pass, and slide to a stop at the sight of Tasar and Larrad lounging on hammocks with a lone harpist plucking strings in the corner. Acrid smoke hangs in a haze just below the ceiling, the stench unmistakable this close.

The males might indulge in Radelea's vinlaf — a mind-altering substance that makes you too friendly and relaxed — but that is too much smoke. If they take any more, the hallucinations will encroach on their minds. Not something I recommend five floors above the ground.

I step into the room, ignoring the protest from the guard, and curtsey. "Well met, my princes."

Tasar startles and tumbles from the low-hanging cocoon of canvas.

Larrad peers over the edge of the midnight blue fabric, his long dark hair falling over his face. "Ah, Bria." He sags back into the hammock and places a dried vine in his mouth, one end glowing red. "What brings you to Dawn?"

Tasar pushes himself up, but remains sitting on the gleaming floor. "And why is Vander carrying a dead fae?"

"Please excuse us," says the guard, slipping past Vander and Penna to drag me back. "My apologies for the interruption."

"Leave us," says Larrad, smoke wafting from between his lips.

The guard frowns but does not dare disobey an order from a Dawn prince. He seethes as he disappears into the hallway.

"My friends..." I begin. The words die before they can form.

"Do not," says Tasar, standing. "Do not apologise. We do not need to hear it. We told you during the Gloom, and I will tell you again now: You have nothing to be sorry for."

I cast my gaze to my feet. "I should have visited, should have sent flowers or... or something. Anything."

Tasar's feet slide against the floor as he approaches. "You owe us no dues." I peek up at him to see his dark eyes, the same eyes he shares with Jonik and his remaining brother, shining with truth. He adds, "Explain the body."

Larrad peels himself from the fabric, extinguishes the glowing end of the vinlaf, and joins his brother. The males are a mirror image of one another. They are but two of a trio, their usual air of jesting nowhere to be seen without Ulakas to encourage their antics.

"We came to ask your father for help. The cook from the village tavern, Erthana, has died from an injury we have not seen before," I say, gesturing towards the canvas carrier.

"Say no more." The shadow of a smile curls Larrad's lips. "That is a respectable trait you are revealing, Lord Vander."

Vander lowers his brows, though a glint of amusement shines in his eyes. He, like everyone who has encountered the Dawn Princes, knows they cannot hold conversation for long without insulting somebody.

"To understand when the skills of others outrank your own," clarifies Tasar, his smile matching Larrad's. I am pleased the males can still jest, even while mourning. It seems not even the death of their brother can take their joking nature away from them.

Vander shakes his head. "Joke all you want, Light Wielders. You'll be just as confounded as us when you see it."

Larrad snorts and beckons us to the door. "Come on. We will take you to Father."

The chambers Jonik shares with his mate, Leilani, are at the far end of the highest level. Paper screens separate the five areas, each of them decorated with precise brush strokes that depict their love story.

I pace the length of a screen that depicts Jonik on one knee, wringing my hands together and flicking glances at Jonik's back while he inspects Erthana's wound.

"The metal remains inside?" he asks, looking at me over his shoulder.

I nod. "I'm certain I can draw it out, but Penna doesn't want to risk the iron retreating if I lose concentration. If it causes more damage, we may never determine the weapon used."

His eyes crease at the sides and a hint of pride shines within the deep brown when he looks at Penna. "You were always my favourite student."

"And you were always my favourite mentor," she replies, tearing her eyes from Xaria to smile at Jonik.

Larrad laughs. "You are not brave enough to say otherwise. I always detested my High Lord and mentor being one and the same."

"It is undeniable that it limited the fun we could have had," agrees Tasar.

While it is strange for someone in Jonik's position to educate his denizens on the use of their gift, it speaks highly of his character. I have always liked the High Lord of Dawn, and this only strengthens that claim. He is one of the rare fae. Those with so much kindness in their hearts that it hurts to think about.

Xaria chuckles from the low stool she sits on and pulls her eyes away from Penna — I have caught both females admiring one another a handful of times, and hope blossoms in my chest that they might find love with one another. She says, "I have always admired him. Though your sons are right, Uncle. You left no room for fun in our lessons."

Jonik pins her with a knowing look. "It did not prevent you from sneaking into the lake and bedding the merprince instead of practicing your healing, dear niece."

She blushes, but shrugs and sips at her green tea. "It was worth it."

"Tell me, cousin," says Tasar. "Where do the mermales hide their cocks?"

Xaria spits the tea over her gown, glaring at her cousin. "It is a secret I will take to the stars when I die, as I have told you countless times. Besides, the females are better lovers." Her eyes find Penna once more.

"Bria, if you will," says Jonik, gesturing to the floor beside him and ignoring the antics of his sons and niece. Perhaps he is used to it by now, and no longer finds their jesting amusing. Unlike Vander and me, with both of us fighting to hide our smiles.

I am thankful for the light-hearted banter, thankful for the distraction it has caused. Arriving in Dawn, I assumed the palace to be as melancholy as the Dusk Court. It pleases me to see the fae here so... lively.

"Work on bringing the metal to the surface," says Jonik, "and I will heal the path it leaves." White tendrils of smoky light emanate from his palms.

I close my eyes, and as I did behind the tavern, I free a ribbon of metal bending power from its confines. Wrapping it around the pulsing metal within Erthana's chest, I command my magic to drag the iron to the surface. It writhes against my order to move slower, the harsh nature of the power yearning for destruction.

As carefully as I can, I pull the piece of metal free. My breaths turn ragged, sweat dots my brow, and my limbs grow weak, but I persevere, determined to uncover the secret behind Erthana's untimely death.

There is something about the metal, something menacing my mind and soul rebel against. Even removing the metal from the wound it caused has me screaming in silence. It's the flashes of memory, of iron bars and flame-stitched lace.

By the time the iron is resting within the container in Penna's hands, and Vander is pulling leather gloves from his hands, I am shaking and sagging into Vander's warmth.

"But what is it?" Xaria sets her teacup down, her hand shaking.

I frown at the unassuming piece of metal, rounded on one end, flat on the other, and a little twisted, as if the impact deformed its shape. There is nothing in my memories about such a weapon. A weapon so small, yet so destructive that it took the life of a fae with enhanced speed and healing.

Vander's arms tighten around my waist when he tenses. "I feared as much when we first saw the wound. It's a bullet."

Everyone turns to him, brows lowered.

Larrad asks, "What is a bullet?"

"It's a human-made weapon. They insert them into something they call guns, which fire the chunks of metal at incredible, deadly speeds." Vander releases a hand from my waist to run it over the stubble lining his jaw. "But what's a human weapon doing in Radelea?"

Chapter 7

"Guns and bullets," says Tasar. "You might as well be speaking in riddles."

"I suppose the humans rely on such forms of defence. They are fragile beings, after all." Jonik uncurls from the floor, freeing his ebony hair from the worn leather strap before pouring a round of brandy and handing a chalice to each of us.

"They wound one another with these?" asks Xaria. She has not touched the teacup since she placed it on the low wooden table, but she drinks deeply from the brandy, finishing it in one. Her tawny skin pales, her mind likely conjuring images of a world so broken *bullets* are used as weapons. But perhaps we are no better than the humans, with our lethal physical magic and fierce intangible powers. I'm certain the humans would find abilities such as necromancy and mind control as loathsome as we find their guns.

Vander's chin brushes my hair when he nods. "They do. Although, these are tame compared so some of their more destructive weapons. Bombs, for instance —"

"I think we have heard more than we can handle already," says Jonik. He crosses the room to sit beside Leilani, the fae lights throwing shadows over his light brown skin. "Where was Erthana when she was wounded?"

"She was shot in the tavern kitchens. We're waiting on Torin's return before investigating further. His ability to read the memories of inanimate objects will provide us with answers," says Vander.

The throbbing in my skull subsides enough that I can sit upright without his help, and I heave a sigh when I straighten. I bring the brandy to my lips, the nutty and woodsy aroma tantalising. "He's due back at the moon's lowest." The brandy is smooth on my tongue, bursting with flavour and warmth. It soothes me like a calming blanket, bringing feeling back to my fingers and toes.

Tasar snorts. "Such a sweet way to say, 'at the sun's rise', Bria."

"Refusing to acknowledge the Mother Star's absence will only anger her," says Leilani. "We must go on as if she still rises every morning."

"It's not that I don't acknowledge it." I stand on shaking legs. My leathers squelch with the movement, still soaked from Vander's downpour. "I just don't know what to call things now. Is it called the sun's rise if the Mother Star will not grace us with her golden rays?"

Larrad chuckles and tilts his chalice towards me. "You overthink."

"I wish I over-thought when I allowed you to enter that ridiculous mating tournament Father forced me into." I arch an eyebrow in challenge, struggling to keep my lips straight. The back-and-forth banter with the Dawn males has always made me smile.

Larrad and Tasar throw their heads back and laugh, the latter elbowing his brother in the ribs and saying, "She has you there, brother."

"It is late," says Jonik. "The three of you are welcome to rest here before your journey home."

It's a dismissal if I have ever heard one. "You have our thanks, Lord Jonik. Although, we would prefer to sleep in our own chambers. There is something soothing about the familiar scent and feel of home, and I think we can all agree tonight has been difficult. Besides, we should be there when Torin returns."

"Where is he?" Tasar crosses an ankle over a knee and reclines into the padded seat. "Bedding another wind wraith?"

Vander chuckles, but says, "No. He's collecting his mother from the Night Islands." He goes on to explain Lord Ruith capturing Tohminic, and how different the Summer High Lord is, how we suspect his mind is not his own, and we how need Blodwen's magic to make sure.

"But who is the 'she' he speaks of?" asks Xaria. "Chlora?" Her dark eyes meet mine, and we share a frown. Neither of us like Tohminic's lover, Xaria having overheard her scathing words all those moons ago.

Before the duels of weapons and magic, Chlora warned me to stay away from Tohminic. I suppose her words were not as scathing as I remember them, but they were a threat all the same. It is no secret she despises me, yet I cannot help but wonder why. It cannot be because I considered Tohminic as a mate. Not when she allowed others to join their nightly love making.

"We don't know," says Vander, dragging me from my thoughts and back to the conversation. "We intend to find out."

"Let us know what you discover," says Jonik.

I dip my chin. "We thank you for your help and bid you goodnight."

"Leave the body, if you wish. We will dispose of it," says Larrad.

"Actually, we would prefer to do that ourselves. Her clothes may hold memories for Torin to read. And our denizens will wish to bid her farewell," I say.

Gratitude flows along the twin soul bond, thrumming and caressing. Vander says, "I apologise for bringing this to your home. As our allies, I suspect you may be targeted, too. Be on alert. I will send a messenger to Day telling Zentha the same." He wraps his hands around the rungs of the stretcher, then motions for Penna to lift the other end.

Another farewell, and another insistence from Larrad and Tasar we update them on any findings, then we are moving through the palace towards the exit, all of us silent.

Coming here was not as difficult as I thought it would be, and I berate myself yet again. How could I be so unkind? I should have known none from Dawn would see me as an enemy. No one places the blame for Ulakas on my shoulders.

It's humbling to know I have friends here, as well as in Dusk.

The flames of the pyre crack and hiss, the roar deafening in the otherwise silent village square. Thuds boom from within the amber and ruby as branches take their last breaths before succumbing to the scorching heat and joining the ashes at the base. My eyes do not stray from the hues of orange that obscure the too-white sheet covering Erthana's body.

This is all she is now, tongues of flame and churning white smoke and thunderous cracks ringing through the heart of Dusk. A vibrant female, they called her; her patrons spoke of her kind nature and booming laugh before setting the pyre alight. They told a short tale of warm bread and cold ale, of welcoming arms and an open heart.

Erthana did not deserve this fate. If all I can give her now is to remain here until the last embers flicker to onyx coal, then that is what I will do.

The stars twinkle above, some of them hazy from the smoke, as if the night sky is watching with me. Ashes spiral in the smoke, arcing through the sky and catching on a breeze of fresh ocean air that will take them far out to sea, where Erthana will rest at last. All that will remain of the beloved cook will be her charred bones, which we will bury in the she-oak forest with an etched stone marking her grave.

Wyn is rigid beside me, with one hand clamped around the wrist of the other, hiding the tarnished snake bangle she never removes. It is the last reminder she has of her mother, and she often twists it around her wrist when she's nervous or angry. She hasn't touched it since the Gloom.

She didn't say anything when we told her of Erthana's fate, did not so much as blink when she joined us in the village square moments later. Silence has been her constant while the flames flicker and dance.

More ashes join the spiralling first ones, and fae peel away from the watching crowd. The flames shrink, and the group surrounding the pyre thins. By the time there is nothing but glowing embers, Vander and I are the only two who remain.

The stars flicker from existence, leaving a cloud-streaked obsidian sky behind. Vander wraps an arm around my shoulders, pulling me into his warmth, and we patiently wait while each ember stutters out. My limbs are heavy with exhaustion, my eyes gritty. Still, I wait with Vander. The ache in my feet is enough that the desire to move almost overwhelms me. Despite that, we remain.

The morning is silent. Gone is the sweet melody of birdsong, the buzz of waking insects, and the whispers of wind caressing the tired faces of the Dusk fae. The only sound is my slow breaths, in time with Vander's, pluming small clouds of glittering white before my face.

"It's time," he says, squeezing my shoulder before releasing me.

I miss his warmth straight away. The brisk morning warns of the approaching winter season, hinting at an especially cold one.

Vander's feet crunch over coal and ash as he gathers Erthana's remains in a hessian sack and hoists it over his shoulder, the thud against his leather jacket bringing bile to my mouth. He wordlessly takes my hand, and we turn as one towards the southern side of the village, where the forest path waits, shrouded in darkness.

A confused owl calls through the silence; though its body is weary, the darkness smothering Radelea fools the night bird into thinking it needs to hunt. It is but one impact the desertion of the Mother Star will have on the realm. I can only hope the wildlife adapts without too much issue.

Vander and I do not speak until we are among the pines and she-oaks, the leaf litter cushioning our steps as we wind through the trees and to the centre of the forest.

My fingers dance across the needle-like leaves of a she-oak encroaching on the path. "Something has been bothering me."

"What is it?" he asks, running the pad of his thumb over my knuckles.

I graze my teeth over my icy bottom lip. When I voiced my thoughts about Nyree to Vander, Torin, and Wyn, they ignored my concerns and told me to move past my dislike of her. They did not want to hear my reasons for thinking she was betraying them. Even Wyn, my best friend in the realm, walked away from me when I broached the subject.

I don't see how this will be any different from those days when I felt so alone, even surrounded by fae. Telling Vander everything he has ever known to be the truth is in fact a lie, will not go down well.

Vander sighs. "I can feel your emotions, Princess. Why are you so anxious?"

I free my hand from his and wrap my arms around my middle. "It's about what you said back in Dawn, about how the bullet is from Earth." I take a deep, shuddering breath. "The leader of the government in the human realm, the male with the lined face... he said Nyree tried stealing their weapons. Do you think she succeeded?"

He's quiet for a moment as he takes care to pick a route off the main path. We are deep within the trees when he speaks at last. "If she did, I'm sure we would have known. She was trying to get to the portal during the Gloom."

Right before she died. I remember our combat outside the infirmary.

"So, she can't have made it back to Earth to steal their weapons?"

"I don't think so, no." He moves the sack of bones to his other shoulder and adjusts his grip on the spade he collected from the edge of the village. "Why?"

I snap the branch of a she-oak from the nearest tree and thread my fingers through the leaves. "Then someone has. I always thought Nyree was working against us. Now I wonder if Maude is finishing Nyree's work."

"What makes you say that?"

My lips turn down. "I think Nyree stayed in Dusk to spy on us on Maude's behalf. I also think she managed to sneak weapons from Earth and hide them here for her Ill-fated followers to find when the time was right."

"And now is that time?" he asks, setting the sack down and piercing the ground with his spade.

I lean against the wide trunk of a pine, the scented leaves brushing the top of my head. "Yes. Just when we think everything is returning to normal. Something is brewing. I can feel it."

He grunts when he slams the point of the spade back into the hard ground. "Then why didn't the humans notice? They warned us against returning to Earth."

I shrug, even though his back is to me. "I don't have an answer for that."

Considering everything while he digs, I wonder if Nyree *did* manage to sneak into Earth and steal guns. If she did, there's a weakness in our wards we need to know about. But Vander is right. Nyree was fighting her way towards the war room during the Gloom, aiming for the hatch beneath the table that leads to a tunnel, then onto the portal to the human realm. Why would she need to enter Earth if she already had the weapons she needed?

By the time Vander finishes digging, my head is throbbing from trying to figure everything out. There's information we're missing, something vital that will help us know for sure what we are dealing with — fae with a vendetta, or humans who know no better.

I decide there is little to nothing I can do about the human weapon in Radelea without more to go on. Leaving the investigation to Torin and Vander will not only save me a lot of headaches, but free up time to research something I have been putting off: the first rising of the Mother Star.

Vander gently empties the scorched bones into the miniature grave, and I help him cover them with loose dirt. Grime gathers in the curves of my fingernails, and black imbeds in the lines of my hands, but it is worth it to give Erthana this last slice of respect.

Van wraps a dense pocket of air around a large boulder and settles it over the compacted dirt. We both free our daggers from their sheathes and engrave her name into the rock. We etch the letters together, our emotions wrapping around one another and our shoulders brushing.

In this moment, we are the very definition of true mates. Working together to bring peace to a lost soul, with sweat beading our foreheads, our breaths harmonised, and our hands aching from gripping the hilts of our daggers so tightly... we are one.

Chapter 8

VANDER'S CALLUSED HAND BRUSHES over my exposed hip, sending waves of warmth and lust through my body. A small smile plays on my lips as I imagine how we can spend the morning. Then my thoughts catch up to reality, and I remember the Mother Star no longer rises. Waking to darkness is a subtle torture; there are those quiet moments when I am oblivious to the realm around me, the remnants of sleep clinging to my eyes, and then reality slams into me with the force of the quaking earth.

I groan and roll over, glaring at him. "I'm certain I have only been sleeping for an hour. Why are you up?"

"Torin has returned."

I raise my eyebrows. The flick of the dark arches is a question in itself. *Is Blodwen with him?*

He runs a hand over his head, the scratching of the short hairs against his palms loud in the quiet chamber. "You'll never guess what his mother demands as payment this time."

Considering we offered her five tortured souls when she accessed my memories, I hate to think what she demands today.

I shake my head. "Just tell me." I purse my lips when he hesitates. "Vander."

He slides his arms into his leather jacket, the supple fabric clinging to the curves of his biceps. "She wants to live here, in the manor."

Every muscle in my body tenses, but my eyes narrow. "Why?" I rub the heel of my palm against my temple, trying to prevent the headache that is sure to arrive at any moment. Blodwen. Here?

"She didn't offer a reason." He sits on the edge of the bed to slide his feet into his boots and pull the laces tight. "There's breakfast on the table when you're ready. We'll be in the safe room." Rolling his shoulders, he stands and leans over to me, pressing his lips against mine in a lingering kiss. He's gone mere heartbeats later.

I'm left to ponder Blodwen's intentions on my own while dressing in my leathers and braiding the long hair on the right of my head. I will need to shave the short stubble on the left soon. It's at that stage where you cannot tell its length from afar. I run my fingers through the thick hair, the cropped patch that always reminds me of the tavern fire, and sigh. Today is going to be one of those days.

I rush through a breakfast of eggs and slices of a green food I have not tasted until now — it's kind of nutty, but delicious — wondering if Blodwen merely wishes to spend more time with her son. With war demanding sacrifice, and stealing lives that do not deserve to be lost, I wonder if Torin's mother is feeling somewhat sentimental.

Her loneliness might be too much after all this time. Living on an island made of nothing but rock, with only the fearsome sea creatures to keep you company, cannot be an easy life to live.

A shudder runs down my spine when I remember *why* Maude banished Blodwen to the island her dilapidated hut rests on. She takes pleasure in *feeding* off the tormented minds of others, even torturing the fae for the desired effect.

That, or she intends to feed from the suffering the Dusk fae endure daily. As I clear away my plate, I decide the latter is the more likely scenario.

Shouts echo through the manor as I walk closer to the terrace-level safe room. The words garbled at first, becoming clearer as I walk towards them.

"You still haven't said why." Torin's tone is one of frustration. "You agreed to come here and discuss payment, yet you haven't given us a reason why we should allow you to stay. We have enough enemies without angering Maude further, and letting you live here will do exactly that."

Blodwen's oily voice prickles the hairs on my nape. "Is it so hard to believe a mother wishes to spend more time with her son?"

"Yes," says Torin.

I slip through the ajar door, closing it softly behind me. It doesn't surprise me to see him with his arms crossed over his chest, those dark eyes narrowed to slits at his mother, nor am I surprised to see Vander standing beside his second, his posture rigid. Wyn's presence, however, is a welcome sight.

Her long hair is tied back in a tight bun at her nape — a strange style for her, given she prefers to leave her ebony locks loose — and her eyes bear the weight of many sleepless nights, but at least she is here. She's taking an interest in the court and trying to fight her demons.

I ease into the room and stand beside Vander, ignoring the wall of shadows in the corner. "Well met, Blodwen. It's lovely to see you again." *Lovely* scalds my tongue.

She limps towards me, those thin lips peeling apart to reveal crooked and missing teeth as she smiles. Her gnarled hands wrap around mine in a vice-like grip. "Bria of Dusk." She closes her eyes, her nostrils flaring as she scents the air. "You have shattered the walls around your power. Did you discover why they were there?"

"No. I'm not interested in knowing. I have access to my magic, and that's all that matters. Though, I'm certain Father is responsible for caging my powers."

She frees my hands, leaving a scorching echo of her touch behind. I clasp them behind my back, discreetly easing the feeling away. "I wonder why," she says, her dark eyes sparking with curiosity. Sunken and haunting, they're eerie to see. "Why mask such power?"

"Jealousy? Anger? Regret? Fear? There are many reasons why Kerym would cage her magic," says Torin. "That's not why we're here. Why do you want to stay with us, Mother? I want the real reason, not some bullshit excuse about wanting to spend more time with me. We both know that's a lie."

She leans against a barrel and sighs. "I heard of the Gloom. Whispers of Maude fighting Dusk reached every corner of Radelea, including my lonely island at the south end of the Deathly Rapids. I don't trust my High Lady will leave me in peace."

"Why?" asks Wyn. It's the first word I have heard her speak in days.

Blodwen's assessing eyes turn to her. "Because I am Torin's mother. She will assume hurting me will hurt him. She would be mistaken to assume as much. Even so, she might use me as collateral."

"Then how about this," says Wyn, stepping towards Blodwen. "You help us now, and we will send guards to watch your poor excuse for a house."

"Wyn," Vander hisses. "That's not how we speak to our guests."

She only shrugs.

"Her words were cutting, but she's right," says Torin. We all turn to him, and he adds, "If Blodwen's worried about Maude taking advantage of her, why shouldn't we send guards to protect her? She knows about Bria's powers and the cages that were around them, and now she knows about this." He uncrosses his arms and waves a hand at the shadows veiling the iron cage, and Tohminic within.

Although Blodwen has not seen him, and he's so silent he might as well not be there, there is no denying we're hiding something here. If Maude were to capture her and use her mind control gift to sift through Blodwen's recent memories... That is not something we can risk.

"I agree," I say, though my voice is quiet.

Vander startles. *"You want us to waste resources protecting her?"*

"Yes. If Maude discovers the strength of my powers, she'll stop at nothing to capture me. I've lived through captivity once, Van. I refuse to do it again."

"Those guards would be better suited patrolling our borders or guarding the ward relic." He pauses, his brow furrowing. *"But*

you're right. Blodwen is vulnerable, and she knows too many of our secrets."

"If you two are quite done speaking mind to mind, let's continue the debate." The glint in Blodwen's eyes is a sure sign she was eavesdropping on our private conversation.

"Will you do this for us if we send guards to your island?" asks Vander.

Blodwen opens her mouth to speak, but I rush to add, "And if things are looking too dangerous for you, we'll bring you here. With your history, we're not comfortable giving you free rein to use your gifts in Dusk. This is the only compromise we will consider."

The hope pulling Torin's eyebrows higher is unmistakable. He sags into a wooden chair and says, "It's the best outcome we can hope for. You help us, and we protect you."

Blodwen taps a crooked finger against her chin. "I would require no less than three guards. All male. And an escape route, should I need it."

"Would a rowboat suffice?" asks Vander.

She smiles a crooked smile. "Yes. Yes, I think it would."

"Then we have a deal." Vander extends a hand, his light brown skin in contrast to the sickly pale of Blodwen's too-thin fingers when she accepts the gesture. "Don't double-cross us, Blodwen. It won't end well for you."

She takes the threat in her stride. "I would not dream of it. Explain how you need my help."

Vander jerks his chin at me, then at the swirling shadows.

Though the shadows are Ruith's doing, I can remove and replace them whenever I see fit. As much as my entire being protests at the notion of freeing Tohminic from his cage, I gather my Winter-born power in my palms and take hold of the darkness.

Slither by slither, I lift the shadows, sucking them into my soul where they shrink and writhe with my three other powers. They feel foreign at first, but settle after a heartbeat and meld with my magic. My stepfather's power is substantially stronger than mine, causing the tips of my fingers to tingle with energy. It's a high I doubt I will feel again.

First, the single wheel and the lopsided base of the cage come into view, followed by the grid of iron bars that track up each of the four sides. Beyond the dark metal, a male figure rocks back and forth, his hands a mess of angry red blisters.

"Put them back," Tohminic whimpers. "Put them back. Please."

"How very curious," says Blodwen, stepping closer.

I close my eyes against the sight of Tohminic so broken and focus on drawing on the threads of my metal bending magic. The silver writhes in my palms, eager to bend and contort. I wonder if they'll stop fighting my every command given time, but push the thought aside to concentrate.

I wrap the threads around the iron pin that bolts the door closed and lift it free. It clinks against its holster, the thick chain securing it to the cage tinkling with every movement, clanging louder when I let the pin fall free. The door creaks as I swing it open with my magic.

"Help me. Please, help me. She will not stop." Tohminic repeats the same words he spoke when Ruith brought him here. Over and over, each syllable growing quieter as his words turn into more of a chant. "Help me. Please, put them back." He scampers into the corner, gripping his head in his hands with so much force, the tips of his fingers turn white.

While Torin and Vander pull him free, I draw my magic back inside and secure the hatch in my mind, sealing off my magical signature before Blodwen can taste the true strength of my powers.

"No, no." Tohminic's panic is too heart-wrenching to be a ruse. Sweat beads on his forehead and upper lip as he thrashes for freedom. He lunges for the bars of the cage and tries to pull himself back into the scorching confines of the iron.

The acrid stench of burning flesh fills the safe room when his palms wrap around the bars, the scent threatening to bring me to my knees. Memories flash and flicker; a trident piercing my torso, a blazing desert, and an undead guard.

"Breathe, Princess," Vander says through our bond, even while wrangling a desperate Summer Lord.

I slam my eyes closed, trying to rid myself of the horrific memories. Air hisses through my nostrils as I take a sharp breath and let it out through parted lips. *I am not in the cage. I am free. This is not a disgusting trap.* The words repeat in my mind until I believe them.

By the time I'm calm enough to pry my eyes open, Torin and Vander have Tohminic pinned, and Blodwen is kneeling beside him, her hands pressed against his temples.

His wide eyes dart around the room, his head thrashing from side to side. His breaths are ragged and harsh, and tears track to the worn fur rug covering the floor. "Please, please."

I cannot recall how many times the same word slipped from my lips, only to go unanswered by him, by Xaler, and by the Mother Star. Tohminic showed me no mercy then, and I will show him no mercy now.

"Shut up!" My tone is a venomous whip, my shout so loud it causes everyone to freeze. "We will not help you if you keep screaming," I add in a softer tone.

Tohminic sags into the floor. Though his screams are no longer piercing our ears, he continues to whimper.

Wyn scoffs. "I have better things to do than to watch this." She leaves before any of us can stop her. I cannot blame her for not wanting to be here — she was a victim of the Summer Lord's depravity, too. The Mother Star, wherever she is, knows I do not want to witness this, either.

"That's better," murmurs Blodwen. She hums as she closes her eyes. "Ah. I'm going to need five guards, not three. And a regular delivery of food."

"Why? What did you find?" Torin asks.

She silences her son with a scathing look before piercing Tohminic's mind with her magic once more.

He shudders, his chest vibrating with the onslaught of power to his mind. His eyes widen further, the white surrounding the amber too bright, too riddled with crimson veins.

Blodwen tenses her fingers and grunts.

Tohminic screams, an agonising, tormented sound.

"That should do it." Blodwen sits back on her heels, her chest heaving. "I have placed wards around his mind. They should hold."

"What was wrong with him?" asks Vander.

"It is for the High Lord to decide if he will talk about it. For now, I have done as you asked. I expect the guards by the time the crescent moon rises." Blodwen flits from the safe room, her long black robe billowing behind her.

I turn to Tohminic, frowning. "What did she mean?"

He slowly sits, then moves to his hands and knees and crawls towards me. "Bria. Oh, Bria. I am so sorry." He moves to grasp my legs, but I jerk back. "Please forgive me."

I look first at Torin, who wears an expression of shock, then to Vander, who is murderous; His hands are clenched, one of them over the wooden handle of his axe, the other at his side. His upper lip trembles before forming a silent snarl.

I look back to Tohminic, who is still reaching for me. "I can't hear this."

No one protests when I flee. The door cracks against its frame when I slam it closed, my back thudding against the outside wall when I lean against it, relishing in the support the exposed brick offers.

My breaths seize in my chest. I brace my hands on my knees and hang my head, those three words screaming in my mind. *Please forgive me.* Tears sting my eyes, but I blink them away. I told myself I would not shed another tear because of Tohminic of Summer.

How can I forgive everything he did? Choking me in the Autumn gardens, the taunts and threats, capturing me from the Day forest, and forcing me into that cage. The same cage I just freed *him* from. After Nikolai. I do not know that I'm able to overcome that hill, the jagged mountain that is forgiving him.

Deep voices flow into the hallway from the safe room, reminding me of how close I am to my captor and torturer. The male who put me through so much, so close, and begging for forgiveness. My hands curl into fists. Too close, I am too close and I cannot be near here or I will storm back in and show Tohminic exactly where he can shove his apology.

I jerk upright and peel away from the wall, thudding up the curling staircase. There are only two places I wish to be right now. Since taking Vander to bed is not an option, I settle on the second best choice.

By the time I reach the manor archives on the next floor, I'm calm enough that I stop slamming my feet against the floor. Though I am breathing easier, and I am no longer screwing my face in anger, I am not ready to be around other fae.

After selecting a handful of scrolls and tomes from the shelves, I slide into a hidden alcove along the side of the archives, hidden from view by the statue of an air wielder that leads to the war room. I give my back to the large window, unwilling to stare at the endless night beyond.

I dive into recounts of the first time the Mother Star rose, reading the ancient text of the fae — it's a shame the language is no longer spoken, the looping but harsh letters no longer written — as they recall how it felt when the darkness gave way to light. It was after the six high fae who ruled Radelea shared wine, signed the treaty, and vowed to cease the fighting. It is when they declared court boundaries.

Many think it a coincidence. That it's unbelievable, and the Mother Star's rising cannot be because of a signed length of parchment and a chalice shared between six. Some think the sun is more sentient than we give her credit for and her blessing us for the tentative eons of peace is believable, if not a little far-fetched. The rare few believe she approved of the treaty and rewarded the realm with colour and brightness.

Each recount contradicts the next, with some stating she rose straight after the treaty was signed, and others claiming it was days later. The one thing they all agree on is her appearance was welcome, and something to rejoice. I have to agree. If I could make her blaze from the sky once more, I would give whatever she demanded.

I would offer myself as a sacrifice if I had to.

I set the thick tome on the table, the thud the only sound in the archives except that of a boot scuffing against the floor. My hands freeze, still gripping the ends of the leather cover. I whip my head up just in time to see a vision of black slink from beyond the statue.

If I were a fae from another court, I would not look twice at the statue of a centuries old Dusk fae with the tornado in his palm. But I know better; it's an illusion, a gateway to the war room, and beyond that, the portal to the human realm.

Ebony hair shimmers under the fae lights as Wyn disappears into the hallway. I have a heartbeat to decide whether to follow or leave her alone, and gut instinct has me rising to my feet and spinning to the window, where she's darting towards the northern beach, head slashing back and forth to ensure no one follows.

Hazy mist clings to the land. The bitter cold of morning will linger without the Mother Star to warm the blades of grass and curling leaves.

A lone albatross drifts over the lapping sea, and the tip of the bird's left wing, in a mesmerising onyx, grazes the water. She has to have a wingspan of at least three long swords.

I do not second-guess.

Wrapping the amber threads of my animalistic power around my thoughts, I send pulses of magic towards the albatross, claiming the soul as my own. The core of my being, my mind and soul, soars from the manor and through the open air until I am merging with that of the bird.

Chapter 9

M Y SHARP EYES NARROW on a scrambling crab on the sandy shore, and the bird's instinct is almost powerful enough to override my desire to follow Wyn. I overcome the need to feast on the crustacean and bank towards the west, where Wyn is untethering a small rowboat from the dock.

I emit a clacking bray, my bill snapping together like a pounding heart, and tuck my webbed feet up as I circle overhead, trying to put the pieces together. She must have gone to the war room when she left us with Tohminic, using her memories of Ad'Starrag as an excuse to leave. I feel as if she has disregarded the struggles of anyone who has ever fought some kind of trauma; to use such a thing for your own gain is disgusting. It's clear she is not herself. She would never stoop so low. I'm sure of it.

Wyn leaps into the boat and uses a burst of air magic to push away from the dock. She sets a wrapped package — how did I not notice she was carrying something? — on the seat opposite then splays her hands to the sides, a steady stream of wind propelling her through the dark water.

I soar through the still morning air and follow her north for a while. Just as I am beginning to wonder why she's sailing towards the Winter Court, she turns west. My tiny bird's heart hammers in my chest, and I dip a few sword lengths lower. There is only one court west of Dusk and south of Winter.

The Night Islands.

I sense the air speed through the narrow slits on the sides of my bill and tilt up to catch the drift of the faster air current above. Exploiting the wind's energy means I can travel farther without expending energy of my own. I will use the ebb and flow of the breeze to chase Wyn to her destination and discover what her plan is.

I rise higher still, gliding in the wind current until I reach the peak, then dip. My speed increases, and I cut through the slower air closer to the ocean and gain on the little rowboat which is speeding across the low waves and heading straight for the northern entrance of the Deathly Rapids.

The roughest sea tunnel in Radelea is nothing but sheer cliffs that block the sky with their mammoth size and a raging ocean with currents so strong even the water-wielding Day fae fear them. At one end, the island Blodwen calls home. At this end, the Rapids split into two, where one of the sea corridors opens to the north, and the other towards the east. Towards home.

My wings catch the wind current, and I allow it to propel me closer to the churning water at the entrance of the Rapids before using my downward momentum to catapult back up. Soaring over the cliffs gives me a better view of the rocking boat and the waves crashing against its hull. Although the view is unobstructed, keeping control of the albatross's body while observing my best friend is too difficult.

I veer to the west, aiming for a rocky outcropping. The instinct to land is lacking, so I improvise by angling my wings against the wind and dropping my legs. I slow a little, but not enough, and slide along the slick rock before colliding with the vertical wall of the cliff. Shaking off the daze, I stumble around to face the Deathly Rapids once more, and peer over the edge, expecting to see Wyn still crashing through the water towards Blodwen's island.

Instead, she's tethering the rowboat to a lone, barnacle-covered post and stepping onto a narrow stretch of pebbled shore that I would miss if I did not know it was there. Morning mist swirls around her feet and settles on the tip of her leather boots, the crunch of sand and pebbles beneath her feet too distant to hear. She waits by the boat with her hands clasped before her, looking towards the cliff face a mere sword's length away. The parcel remains in the boat, untouched since she placed it there.

I rustle my wings. This cliff marks the edge of Night's largest island, the mountainous land Maude calls home. Her castle lies somewhere to the west, hidden among the craggy hills, deadened trees, and what remains of the former Night Castle — the haunting temple crumbled when the land broke apart, leaving nothing but the occasional stone wall behind.

Five figures appear down below, folding onto the narrow strip in a tight line. The centre figure can only be the High Lady, with her pale skin and obsidian hair almost glowing in the darkness. Her ice-blue eyes are visible even from here. Pulses of her blood and bone magic ripple up the cliff face, tasting of rust and sounding like the screams of tortured souls.

I puff my chest and ruffle my feathers, instinct declaring her a threat.

Guards flank her on either side, each of them carrying a curved longbow and quiver of iron-tipped arrows, and dressed in black armour that sends a wave of fear coursing through me. The last time I saw that armour was during the Gloom.

"Was your mission successful?" Maude asks.

"I'm sure you're already aware of how it went," says Wyn, surprising me by saying more than three words, which seems to be the norm for her now. She unclasps her hands to gesture to the rowboat. "As requested, My Lady." Her tone drips with disdain.

Maude nods to a guard, and he saunters to the boat to retrieve the parcel. It's as long as his arm. From the bulge of his muscles, I would say it's not as light as it seems, either. He places it at Maude's feet and pulls the twine free, then unfolds the fabric to reveal the contents.

From so high, I cannot see what lies within the canvas and twine. I waddle closer to the edge of the cliff, scuffing my webbed feet against a loose stone. It skitters over the flat surface before tumbling to the ground below, seeming to hit every jutting rock as it bounces to the shore below.

All six faces whip up, and six pairs of eyes narrow at me.

I freeze. Not a single feather twitches while I await my fate. Either they will decide I'm a lowly bird unworthy of their attention, or whatever Wyn has delivered is important enough for this secrecy, and —

The closest guard nocks his bow in the blink of an eye. Before I can react, the bowstring twangs and an arrow whistles towards me. In the time it takes for the iron tip to reach me, two scenarios crash through my mind: I can allow the arrow to hit me and send me careening backwards where I cannot see Wyn, or I can throw myself forwards and tumble to the ground far, far below, still risking the arrow piercing my flesh. Of course, I could send my soul soaring back to the Dusk Court, where my fae body waits in the archives, but then I risk not knowing what this is about.

I jump without thinking about the consequences. If I could just *see* what's in that parcel, I could figure out how to help. Because the Wyn I know and love would never do something like this. It's all I can think of when the arrow sinks into the soft flesh at the base of my wing, causing me to screech in pain.

Gravity claims me as I tumble to the ground, and with every smack of my limp body against the cliff face, I think of Wyn and understand she would not meet with Maude of her own free will, especially after all that occurred during the Gloom. So, what does the Night Lady have over her that would make my best friend turn her back on her court and her brother?

The burning pain in my wing is dull compared to the battering my small body takes as I careen for the rocky shore. I hit jutting rocks and gnarled branches, bouncing from one to the other before slamming to the ground with a sickening crunch.

Pure agony scorches through my other wing, throbbing and stabbing with every ragged breath I take. But all I can do is to beg the Mother Star for mercy. *I'm sorry,* I cry in my mind. *I'm so sorry I sacrificed the life of this creature for my benefit.*

"It is just an albatross," says a gravelly voice. The tip of his boot nudges my heaving chest, sending sparks of pain in every direction. "A dead one soon enough."

I flick my beady eyes around the cove, searching for Wyn, and find her backing towards the rowboat. Her wide silver eyes veil her fear well. I can only see the tightness because I know her so well.

Once I realise she's safe, I scratch my feet against the stones I lie on and twist just enough to see a guard re-wrapping the parcel. I catch a glimpse of something black, its glint dull in the lightless night, before the guard covers it with the beige canvas once more.

"It is astute for a mere bird," says another guard. "I wonder if it is an Autumn fae."

Maude squats beside me. Her bright blue eyes narrow to slits as she peers into my eyes.

I slam a mental shield into place and focus on the pain throbbing in both wings. I make my breaths harsher and force my chest to work harder, trying the only thing I can think of to keep her from using her mind control powers to infiltrate my thoughts.

Her lips thin, and she leans closer. Her nostrils flare when she inhales deeply. She stands and turns to Wyn. "Who is it?"

"I don't know." Wyn continues to back towards her rowboat. She points to the cliff I was spying on them from. "It's just a bird. There's probably a nest up there."

In the heartbeat Maude's face drifts towards the cliff, Wyn widens her eyes at me. She jerks her head to the east and mouths, "Go!"

She's still in there. The Wyn I know, the Wyn who fought for and with me against Tohminic and Father is still there. Although she's urging me to flee, I cannot leave her here with five night fae on her own. I won't.

I turn away from her, my answer in the pained movement. *No. I am not leaving you.*

Her sigh is too audible.

"Kill the bird," says Maude in a lazy yet curious tone as she turns back to Wyn. "Let us see if Wynetta speaks true."

Rough hands snatch me from the ground, sending jolts of pain from my bill to my webbed feet. The guard grips my head so tight my eyes bulge.

Mother Star, show me mercy.

I do not know what will happen to my soul if the animal body I'm controlling dies with me trapped within, and I do not wish to find out. I have no choice but to tug on the threads of my animalistic powers and drag my reluctant soul back to the archives, leaving Wyn to face this battle on her own.

The gasp that tears at my throat is laced with fear. I peel my cheek from the table top and leap to my feet. The wooden chair crashes backwards and collides with a low shelf, knocking tomes and scrolls to the glistening floor. I don't bother to set them right, but tear from the archives and into the hallway.

I push my legs hard, using my arms to gain momentum. It's a miracle the bird's pain did not follow me to this body. I shake my head and clear the thought; I need to concentrate if we're going to get to Wyn in time.

"Vander!" I shout through the mind link I share with him, entwining the words with the turmoil and panic clenching my heart. *"Wyn's in trouble."*

"Where is she?" he growls.

I race through the manor, explaining while dodging fae stumbling from their rooms in search of something to break their fast. *"Meet me at the northern docks. After Tohminic, I found solace in the archives, reading about the first time the Mother star rose. The shelves hid me from view, so Wyn didn't see me when she exited the war room."*

"What was she doing in there?" His voice is strained, as if he's racing from wherever he was to meet me.

I burst through doors, race around the manor to the north, and track straight for the dock Wyn took a boat from not too long ago. *"I don't know. That's why I followed her."* Three figures sprint towards me from the west — there is no time to wonder why Alizeh is with Vander and Torin — and I slow my speed. *"I entered the body of an albatross and tracked her. She went to the Night Islands, Van."*

"Why?" he asks, lunging for the rope securing the second boat to the small dock.

I brace my hands on my knees and pant, nodding an acknowledgement to Alizeh and Torin. Through ragged breaths, I say, "She delivered some kind of parcel to Maude. It was long and heavy. I tried to see what was inside." I go on to tell them how I alerted the guards to my presence on the cliff and everything that followed.

"Are you hurt?" Vander's silver eyes glow brighter than a full moon.

"No. I'm fine. The bird is dead." My chest constricts as I step onto the boat and take the seat beside Alizeh at the rear.

Torin leaps in but remains standing. "There's something we're missing. Wyn would never make a deal with Maude."

Alizeh's bubbling chuckle is a contrast to the heavy conversation. Her form ripples as she sends delicate blasts of wind behind us to propel us through the water.

I raise my brows at Van.

He answers through our bond. *"We were in the village square when you called out to me. Alizeh wants to help. I'm hesitant, but if Maude has captured Wyn, we need all the help we can get."* Out loud, he says, "Where is she?"

"Are there guards?" Torin rubs his hands together in glee. "It's been too long since I stabbed a Night fae."

I roll my eyes at him, then turn to Alizeh. "Enter the Rapids at the northern entrance. There's a small cove on the right not far from the junction."

She sets her jaw, nodding her understanding. Her wind-like hair whips around her face as she pushes more air from her wispy fingers, forcing the rowboat into a speed I'm certain will shatter the wooden hull.

I grip the wooden gunwale, treating the rough sail as I would treat riding Solana and moving with the ebb and flow. Alizeh's wind roars in my ears, and I strain to hear my voice when I turn to Torin and say, "There are four. Five, if you count Maude."

"Four, you say?" he shouts over the raging wind and crashing waves. He doesn't so much as stumble as he stands in the jerking boat.

"Two each," says Vander. "Alizeh can distract Maude. Bria, get Wyn out of there by whatever means necessary. I don't care if you have to knock her out. Just get her home." Our eyes connect, and his emotions flicker along the twin soul bond.

This is where we complement one another. He is willing to injure his sister in order to save her, whereas I'm more inclined to use words as a motivator. Violence isn't always the answer. But for this, for his last blood relative, I will do things his way.

I lift a hand from the gunwale, jolting forwards when an enormous wave collides with the hull, and grip his hand. "We'll get her home, Van. You have my word."

"We're approaching the sea tunnel entrance." Alizeh's voice is a tinkling wind chime. She slows her wind to navigate the vessel through the churning water.

I peer over the edge, frowning at the white swirling on the water's surface. "It wasn't this rough when Wyn came through."

"It's part of their wards," says Torin, peering into the darkness ahead. "The more unwelcome the visitor, the rougher the Rapids."

It's likely why Blodwen lives on a small island at the exit. Anyone brave or foolish enough to decide visiting her is a good idea must endure the rushing water first. It's as good a warning to steer clear as any.

"What's the plan?" Torin asks. "Stab first and ask questions later?"

Alizeh giggles, then twists to the right to change our direction, avoiding a protruding rock, smooth and worn by eons of suffering the water's wrath.

"We've lost the element of surprise. Maude will know we're coming." Vander looks ahead, joining Torin in searching for the narrow stretch of pebbled sand. "I can create an illusion to confuse them. It might give us the advantage we need."

"You can't hold an illusion while fighting two guards. Not without opening yourself to injury," says Torin.

"I can do it."

His dark eyes narrow. "I'm not saying you're not able. I'm saying we can't take risks like that when Wyn's life is on the line."

"My magic is not a risk. I'll do it." The males don't hear me over the raging water, so I clear my throat and speak louder. "I will do it."

They turn to me, both frowning. Vander says, "You don't wield illusions, Princess."

"No. But I have my mother's shadows. They might not be strong enough to blanket the entire cove, but it will be enough to give you two an advantage. I will control them while Alizeh docks, but I'll have to drop the darkness once I have Wyn."

"Will it work?" Torin asks.

Vander searches my eyes, finding nothing but determination and trust in my own abilities, before turning to his second. "She's strong enough. Bria won't let us down."

A weight settles on my shoulders. It pushes me down and threatens to suffocate if I don't get my timing right. Like the waves churning all around us, my stomach tightens and roils. My shadows come naturally, unlike the metal bending power that fights my every command. Even so, I should not overestimate myself. Wyn's life depends on it.

"There." Torin points just ahead. "Slow down, Alizeh." His tongue curls around her name like a caress.

"Are you sure you can do this, Princess?"

I look Vander in the eye when I answer. *"Positive."*

As we near the narrow shore, the fight and determination within me retreats. I strain my eyes to see through the thinning mist, but no matter how hard I squint, the view is the same. The cove is void of anything but the dead albatross. There are no Night guards. There is no sign of High Lady Maude. Wyn and her rowboat are gone.

We're too late.

Chapter 10

"WYN!" VANDER'S SHOUT BOUNCES off the cliff face, creating an endless stream of her name.

I grip his shoulder and force him to face me. "We'll find her, Van. She can't have gone far. It didn't take us too long to reach this cove. Torin will read the memories of the rocks, and we'll go from there."

Alizeh bounds across the narrow stretch of beach, twirling and laughing. "There are remnants of magic here. Folding." She hums deep in the back of her throat. "It tastes of the stars."

Torin ignores her as he steps up to the jagged rock rising high into the sky. He plants both palms against the damp grey and closes his eyes, concentrating on his power to extract memories from objects.

Vander jerks his shoulder from my grasp. "She could be anywhere by now. This isn't enough."

"Then I'll scour the land from above." I trace my eyes over the towering cliffs, searching for any sign of animal life. There's nothing but darkness. Meeting Vander's anxious gaze once more, I say, "I'm going to send pulses of magic along the cliff until I find a bird to meld my soul with. When I do, I will lose control of this body. Keep me safe."

The command has two benefits. He will focus on making sure I remain unharmed, which will take his mind off Wyn's disappearance, and he won't let me fall into the raging Rapids at our backs. I can't count the number of times I have returned to my fae body with bruises and aches from falling the moment my soul leaves in search of an animal.

He sighs and snakes an arm around my waist to keep me upright. "I've got you, Princess. Always."

Warmth spreads from my heart to my fingers and toes. Vander has always had my back, and even while his stomach is clenching with worry about his sister, tonight is no different. He was there after Tohminic first attacked me in the Autumn gardens, there when Father admitted his true feelings about his only daughter, and he was there when I escaped the burning clutches of the Summer fae. He crawled beside me rather than force me to walk because he understood my need to prove myself to the Mother Star.

I press a gentle kiss to the stubble lining his jaw, the small gesture conveying everything I cannot say at this moment. No, those words are for later, when we're alone and lost in one another. Later, when Wyn is safe and Alizeh isn't relishing in the tension.

"She didn't leave with the Night fae," says Torin, looking at us over his shoulder and keeping his palms on the cliff. "Maude and her guards folded, but Wyn took the boat. Can you use your power from the Rapids, Bria? We need to leave *now* if we want to catch up to her."

In answer to his question, I twist from Vander's grip and step into the swaying rowboat. This time, I ensure I am seated beside Vander instead of Alizeh, and lean into his warmth before closing my eyes.

The amber threads of my magic are eager to obey and slip from the hatch with a burst of power. The sweet musk of Solana after a run replaces the brine of the ocean, the firm but soft feel of Vander's thigh beneath my palm fades away, and my fingers skate over coarse fur. A low growl, akin to the hum of a growling pack of dire wolves — native to the Bolbala Ranges and rarely seen — slips through my clenched jaw.

I wrap the ribbons around my soul and send it blazing through the darkness, where I probe every crevice along the cliff face and caress every jutting rock. There are no rodents or small birds or lizards. I find nothing until I reach the highest point.

The raven's mind rebels against my intrusion, but I overcome his instinct to caw and flee within one beat of his fluttering heart.

Blinking my beady eyes open, I assess the five ravens around me, all asleep with their heads hanging low. Their chests rise and fall in soft heaves. As dark as a starless night sky, their feathers blend with the landscape. The raven is the perfect bird for this.

I stretch my wings wide and fall to the side, the long sable feathers catching the current before I have dropped so much as one long sword down. The five comrades of the bird I'm occupying caw into the night, and the rustle of feathers follows me into the dive.

As I tilt into the upstream, I realise the five others are not fol-lowing, but chasing. Being the most intelligent bird in Radelea, it would not surprise me if the gang of ravens know something is amiss with their friend. As it is, the bird's soul I merged with rebels against my presence and fights for control of his body.

The need to make this quick makes my heart pound. I scour the water below, finding nothing but the rowboat I arrived on. Vander holds my limp body tight while Torin trails his fingers through the churning water, reading its memories. Alizeh sends ferocious blasts of air behind them, propelling them through the water with concerning speed. Farther ahead, where the Rapids calm and the linear waves take over, several splashes catch my attention.

The raven steals control of our sleek body and dips into a dive, hurtling for the shoal of silvery fish frolicking at the water's surface. The gang of five trailing behind dive after me, a lone screech piercing the otherwise dark and quiet dawn.

Obey. The single word is enough to ignite my power and command the raven once more. I bank left and pull from the dive in a wide arc before soaring over the ocean's calm depths. Behind and to the west, my friends battle the end of the Deathly Rapids. I cannot afford distractions, so I push all thoughts of Vander and the others from my mind, lest the raven fight me for dominance once more.

I rise higher. The faster wind this high guides my direction as I swivel my head from side to side, searching for a lone boat among the waves and finding her moments later. The bluish glow of a fae light illuminates Wyn's features as she glides across the centre of the ocean, half way between Night and Dusk and almost directly below me.

My caw is resounding and follows me into a dive. I tuck my feet close to my underbelly and retract my wings until they're flat against my sides. Wind, scented with a hint of carrion from the nearby Harpy Barrens, whips at my face and beak. I do not let it deter me.

My speed increases to an eye-watering pace as I hurtle closer to the rowboat. The five ravens still following screech and gurgle and plummet after me. Their determination to save their friend from an imposter reflects my determination to save Wyn. The realisation tears at my insides, and a single tear blurs my eye.

Wyn turns skyward when I grow closer, her wide silver eyes, so alike Vander's and so alike the glittering stars of night, soon narrowing as she watches my approach.

I spread my wings wide and angle my lower half towards her, slowing my descent, then land on the seat opposite with a thud, my talons piercing the aged wood. *Caw.* I tilt my head, assessing the red blotches on her tawny cheeks and the swelling around her red-rimmed eyes.

"What you did was reckless," she says. She wipes her nose with the back of her hand. "Reckless and foolish. She knows who you are and what you can do. You do not care about our court or our safety. Leave me alone."

It's more words than she has said to me since the Gloom, since the Mother Star refused to rise on the first day of darkness. Her tone cuts sharp, like an unfurling whip, and slices into my heart and soul.

Five ravens circle overhead, creating a cacophony of anger and concern. One dives closer, talons extended, but pulls from the dive before those deadly talons pierce my skin.

I twist the other way, looking at Wyn through narrowed eyes. The look alone speaks volumes. *I did it to help you. Because*

I'm worried about you. You risked everything to save me from Summer, and I will do the same for you because I love you.

She scoffs. "Nothing can help me now. Return to your fae body. And tell my brother to stop wasting his time. His efforts are better spent rebuilding the villages and protecting the court." She sends a blast of crisp air behind her, launching the rowboat faster.

Two ravens dive, one of them brushing my head with its wing, and I know I cannot command this bird's body any longer. If Wyn does not use her air magic to send me careening into the ocean's depths, the five ravens dipping and weaving closer will ensure their friend does not suffer any longer.

I hop from the seat and across the bottom of the boat until I'm close enough to nudge Wyn's leg with my beak. *I'm here if you need me,* the caress says. *Come to me when you're ready.*

She sniffs and looks away, towards the glowing fae lights of the looming Dusk Court. Just as I'm tugging on the threads of my animalistic power, she says, in a voice so rough and quiet I have to strain to listen, "She'll retaliate. And not in a way you'll expect. Be prepared for anything. This is all I can offer you right now. Prying further will only fuel her anger."

Fur and musk and growls of warning envelop my soul as it speeds over the ocean. They grow stronger the closer I get to Vander and the rowboat, and they are all I know until I slam back into my fae body. The growls slip past my lips as I bolt upright.

"Princess? Did you find her?" Vander tucks a loose strand of copper behind my ear. His hand remains there, cupping the side of my face. "Is she okay?"

I shake away the remnants of the raven's instincts and sigh. "I believe so. She doesn't want us to follow her. I think she's afraid of what Maude will do."

Alizeh's hands fall to her sides, the wind wraith's form flickering between corporeal and sparkling wind. "She is unharmed?" When I nod, she moans and says, "Well, this day has turned into a real downer. If there is no excitement, I will take my leave."

"Thanks for your help," says Torin.

She offers him a seductive wink. "Come find me tonight, Wind Whisperer. You owe me a night of excitement after this." She's gone in a billow of air, the scents of brandy and lily of the valley chasing her across the sea.

"Why is Wyn afraid of Maude?" Vander asks, more to himself than anyone else.

I answer, regardless of if he wants to hear it. "She seems to think I was reckless in following her —"

"You were," he admonishes.

"— and she said Maude knows what I am. She thinks the High Lady of Night will retaliate for what happened this morning, and not in a way we expect."

Vander's hand falls from my face, landing on his leg with a smack. "Why, though?"

Torin shakes away a shiver. "Isn't it obvious, Van? Wyn's strange behaviour, Tohminic's sudden change of temperament... They can only mean one thing."

I know where he is going with this, and I hope the Mother Star blesses him with being incorrect. But he's right. All the pieces fit. I suspected it when I followed her to the Rapids, and she strengthened that suspicion when I sat as a raven on her boat. Dread settles in my stomach like a leaden weight. It tries to drag me to the ocean floor where I will never have to face this truth and what it means for us… what it means for Radelea.

But if there is one thing I know about the truth, it's that it will *always* reveal itself, no matter how hard and how long you fight it.

"Say it," growls Vander. Rage, at himself and at Maude, stabs along our bond.

Torin's dark eyes glint with malice. "Maude's using her mind control magic on them. She's been controlling Wyn since the Gloom, and I *will* see to it the Night bitch pays for what she has done."

Flashes of lightning illuminate the sky ahead, casting a golden glow over the rooftops of the western village. Thunder rumbles as angry and swollen clouds converge over Dusk Manor.

"I'll fucking kill her," snarls Vander.

"Before we do anything," I say, my tone holding a hint of hesitation, "we have to speak with Tohminic. He's the only one who can confirm our suspicions. Acting without first gathering proof is reckless and foolish."

Vander sends a vicious blast of wind behind us, which sends us jolting over the water towards the Dusk Court. Thunder rolls across the sky as we leap from wave to wave, the bow of the rowboat slamming against the dark water. "Why do we need proof when everything fits? It's a waste of time."

His anger ripples along the bond, twisting and contorting and creating swirls of wrathful clouds overhead. He cannot see past the rage to think clearly.

It's up to me to make him see sense; as the other half of his soul, I will bring calm and reasoning, where he can only see vengeance and brashness. I turn to Torin with raised brows and mouth, "Help?"

He sighs, his lips pulled tight. "Bria's plan has more merit than storming Night with no backup. I say we hear what Tohminic has to say, then take that to the other High fae with everything else we know. Demand aid. We need it. The High Lady of Spring is yet to choose a side in the war. With her nature magic and psychic abilities, Maude doesn't stand a chance."

"Think about it, Van. It makes more sense than running blindly into a fight." I rest a hand on his forearm, where he holds it out to keep the steady stream of air pushing us towards home. "You told me mere moons ago I was allowing my rage to rule my actions. You said I shouldn't let it rule me, but use it to *fuel* my motives and decisions. I have taken that advice to heart and implemented it. Have you?"

He slows the wind, and we bump against the small dock at Dusk's north. "Fine. We talk to the Summer Lord and ask our allies for help." He makes quick work of tying the rowboat to the single post — the rust stains dribbling from the nails scream of a hard life beside the ocean — and leaps onto the sandy beach. "But be warned: I will wait no longer than five moons. After that, regardless of if we've heard from our allies, I storm Night."

"Understood," says Torin.

"Vander," I begin.

He pierces my soul with a glare. "I will do this with our without your help."

Chapter 11
Tohminic

MY NAILS BITE INTO my palms. The distinct tang of blood invades my nose. The flash of pain is miniscule compared to the demons tormenting my mind. I push deeper and relish in the scent and the hurt. I deserve it. The Mother Star knows I deserve to suffer for what I have done.

The pain flares. My sharp intake of breath causes the fae beyond the shadows to quiet. They have been arguing for too long. Their voices have hissed and strained, and still, they argue. I do not care to know the dilemma they debate. I care for the pain. I care for the distraction.

They resume their discussion, and a softer voice joins the chorus of the others. It is a voice I hear during the moments I allow my thoughts to wander. It is a voice that tears at my soul and squeezes my worthless heart until it is all I can see, hear, feel.

I know why she is here. Though my constant whimpers have blocked most of the argument between High Lord Vander Theron, the Wind Whisperer, and the Whisperer's mother — Wynetta Theron has said little since arriving a short time ago — the words pierced my veil of shadows, my sanctuary.

They intend to lift the darkness. They intend to pry into my mind.

I cannot allow them to. I uncurl my fists and grip the bars with what little strength remains. This cannot happen. The iron and the shadows, they are my penance. They cannot take them from me. My arms shake as I drag myself closer to the corner. The scent of burned flesh replaces the sting caused by my fingernails. I grip tighter.

"No, no." My voice is less than a whisper. It is a shadow of what it once was. *I* am a shadow of what I once was.

Unable to hear my pleas, the fae beyond the veil lifts the darkness. First the wheel. Then the base. My eyes widen. This cannot happen. It cannot. I cannot cope.

She will return.

The burning of my palms becomes too much. I tear them from the cage and fist them into my hair. I fall back. *No, no, no. Do not. Please.* Every part of my being aches as I rock back and forth, but I do not stop.

Fae light pierces the shadow. Before I am ready, I am bathed in brightness. It glows beyond my closed eyes. Blazing red sears across my vision. It warms my chilled skin. "Put them back. Put them back. Please."

"How very curious," says the Whisperer's mother. Her feet scuff against the floor when she steps closer. Her voice is a rasp of venom. It is a mocking cackle and a threatening whisper.

The pin holding the cage door closed clangs when *she* removes it with her magic. Such a unique power. A strength she deserves after what I put her through. The squeal of the door rings in my ears. It creates a melody with my whispered chanting.

And the other she is there. In the back of my mind. She is waiting to pounce, to command.

"Help me. Please, help me. She will not stop." I repeat the words. Over and over. Each syllable grows quieter as my strength fades. "Help me. Please, put them back." The iron bites at my already ravaged palms as I scamper into the corner like the rat that I am.

Vander Theron and the Wind Whisperer jerk my feet to the door.

I cannot. They cannot. The shadows. I need them. "No, no." The cool lick of the sweat on my brow and upper lip is unwelcome. I do not deserve the reprieve. I thrash against the grip of the males and lunge for the bars of this torture vessel. I fight to pull my useless body back into the depths of burning iron and haunting memories.

The males win. With my strength depleted, my mind tormented, and my will to fight evaporating, they haul me onto the floor with no mercy. My legs lock into place beneath me. I try to leap to my feet, intent on returning to the cage, but Vander Theron and the Wind Whisperer slam me back down. Both males remain while the Whisperer's mother kneels beside my aching body.

She presses gnarled fingers against my temples and her mind control power pierces into my very soul. It is cold and unwelcome. It is foreign and cruel. She will join the other. They will work together to bring me down.

I thrash against her hold. My head cracks against the floor with every violent twist, sending booms through my skull that cannot hope to drown out her voice.

Tohminic, she taunts. With the same drawn out vowels she often uses. Her venomous tone chokes the air from my lungs.

My breaths turn harsh. Tears stream from my eyes. "Please," I beg. "Please."

I am the vision of a broken male.

"Shut up!" *Her* shout is so loud, everyone in the room freezes. Me included. Those emerald eyes burn through my soul. They are such a vibrant green. So bright. Even her time at Ad'Starrag could not dampen the spark within. "We will not help you if you keep screaming."

Her words writhe through me, like a snake poising to strike. They do not cause the pain they should. Perhaps this is my chance. Perhaps this is the Mother Star's way of telling me I must make amends. The last vestiges of my fight flee, and my entire body sags. I whimper in relief. I whimper in fear.

Wynetta scoffs from her place against the wall. "I have better things to do than to watch this."

"That's better." The Whisperer's mother hums and closes her eyes. Her magic licks over the intrusion in my mind. "Ah. I'm going to need five guards, not three. And a regular delivery of food."

"Why? What did you find?" asks the Wind Whisperer.

She silences her son with a scathing look before piercing my mind with her magic once more. A bone-chilling shudder vibrates my chest. My eyes prickle with pain when they widen impossibly further. She tenses her fingers with a grunt.

I scream through the fresh wave of agony. The sound tears at my throat until the salt and rust of blood coats my tongue.

Tohminic, the voice inside my head taunts. *You will die for this. I will sink my claws into —*

A shield slams over the voice, cutting the words short. There is emptiness for the first time in many moons.

The Whisperer's mother retreats. "That should do it. I have placed wards around his mind. They should hold."

"What was wrong with him?" asks Vander Theron, Lord of Dusk.

"It is for the High Lord to decide if he will talk about it. For now, I have done as you asked. I expect the guards by the time the crescent moon rises." It is the last I hear from the Whisperer's mother.

"What did she mean?" *she* asks, in a voice so soothing I wonder if I imagined torturing her at Ad'Starrag. No. I cannot conjure such a horrific theme. It is not possible. It was too disgusting. Too depraved. It was real.

She endured it. And though I could not control it, I must apologise. My body protests as I push myself up and twist onto my hands and knees. The blisters from the iron flare with pain. I relish in it. *It is my penance.*

I drag myself across the floor. "Bria. Oh, Bria. I am so very sorry." She leaps out of reach when I grope for her legs. "Please forgive me."

"I can't hear this." Her dusk-orange hair whips behind her when she flees the room, leaving me with Vander Theron, who looks to be plotting my demise, and his second, who will help him bury my broken soul with glee.

"What did Blodwen mean?" Vander Theron demands the moment the door thuds closed.

All I can manage is to turn my face towards him. Nothing more.

The Wind Whisperer says, "Let him rest first, Van. He's no good to us in this state. His hands are still shaking."

"Fine. I want a guard stationed at his door at all times." The High Lord of Dusk breezes from the room, the scents of cedar and ocean drifting behind him.

The infirmary at Dusk Manor is equipped with everything their healer could ever need. Father — may the Mother Star bless his soul in the afterlife — could have taken a few pointers from the Dusk fae; Ad'Starrag does not have so much as a dedicated bed for the sick or injured, as if my father abhorred the idea of my denizens being less than perfect.

During my waking hours, I stare at the plain white wall. It does not hold my interest. Rather, it provides a blank canvas for the memories to play out on. From entering the Autumn castle, dressed in the colours of my court to impress High Lord Kerym and his son, only to collide with High Lady Maude. She ran her blood-red nail, which she had sharpened to a deadly point, down my cheek, and whispered my name like a caress.

It is the last free memory I have.

The last unmarred by all I have done.

There is a hollowness in my chest that somehow weighs me down. It presses me into the firm mattress of the bed. My eyes, so gaunt with dark shadows, dip to my hands. These hands have inflicted pain. They have harmed and abused. They have loved, too, but not in any way I would normally enjoy. Not in a way I find enticing or respectable.

A tired memory resurfaces for the umpteenth time since Bria Sutherland lifted the shadows veiling my cage. A memory of my swollen cock stealing the air from Chlora's lungs. Bile burns the back of my throat. The acidic tang coats my tongue and my stomach churns. How could I treat a female with such degradation?

I roll onto my side with a pained groan. The blisters from the iron are yet to heal and throb with every movement. I refused Penna's magic, acknowledging the necessity of natural healing. The white wall becomes a montage of memories, images of naked bodies, abused females, Bria in that disgusting cage, and the severed head of an angler from Day.

My fault. It is all my fault.

This mental torture is my penance.

I cannot bear to see anyone. Fae come and go, all trying to encourage me to eat or wet my tongue. I cannot. The Mother Star granted me freedom from her. I will not throw the sun's blessing away by enjoying my time here. The demons will haunt my mind until they tire. I will endure the pain of those memories. I will endure the horror of what I inflicted on others.

This is my penance.

They come for me an entire day after freeing me from the cage. A moment of hope blossoms within. Hope that Bria will gift me with her shadows, hiding me and my depravity from the realm.

I am not so lucky.

Vander Theron bursts into the infirmary, his leathers soaking from the torrential rain. "Tell me what the fuck is wrong with you."

It is not a question. He spits the statement with such hatred, any self-respecting High Lord would retaliate with the arc of a sword. But I lost all respect for myself when I allowed her to plant seeds of herself in my mind, when they blossomed into thorn-riddled vines and tangled through my thoughts, erasing all sense of Tohminic of Summer. She extirpated him.

"Pardon?" I find myself asking, though I know what Dusk's Lord wants. I saw it in his sister's eyes when she fled the safe room yesterday. The hatred. The haunting. The fear. She suffers, as I once did.

Bria Sutherland's lips curl into a frown when she trails in behind the Wind Whisperer.

He rests a scarred hand on the leather-bound hilt of a dagger and says, "We suspect Maude of Night controls Wyn's mind. We're here to gather proof through your story."

My story. As if such a thing interests anyone.

But if it is a story they wish to hear, then I will accommodate them. Perhaps speaking the horror out loud will lighten the weight on my shoulders.

So I tell them.

I tell them how I have had no control over my words or actions since Rennyn's born day ball. How I was eager to court

Bria of Autumn, but my words were twisted into something of a nightmare. That I convinced Fayeth to poison my father — *my father, by the grace of the Mother Star, did not deserve such a fate* — and told her she was welcome in Summer should she wish.

They listen to my story, the three of them. They listen with varying degrees of disgust and anger.

I tell them how I fought every moment of every day for control of my words and actions. How I retreated into the far reaches of my mind during the rotunda sex parties. How I recoiled when my sword sliced through Nikolai of Day's neck. I tell them how I hate myself.

They ask questions. Useless, senseless questions.

Why did she do it?

What does she want?

I do not have the answers. Her mind control was one way. It was a vicious wall of thorns and commands I could not penetrate, regardless of how hard I fought.

The Wind Whisperer asks why I hid after the Dusk army abandoned the siege at Ad'Starrag.

I tell him it is simple.

Maude retreated. She retreated, and I went with her. I hid in my chambers, refusing company of all description. I hid, and I cried, and I screamed. There was not a time when I was not remorseful. There was not a time when I could stomach to clamber from my bed and prepare for the war Maude started. The war she forced *me* to start.

But then she returned. She returned and ordered my undead army to the shore of this island, ordered my selkies to the north.

Why Xaler returned before his task was complete, I still do not know. I do not care to ask; his return may have saved Dusk.

My voice is hoarse by the time I am finished. But there is a lightness in my chest, a seedling of hope. Hope that Bria may find the strength to forgive me, that she may stop looking at me with such conflicting emotions. Hatred, confusion, indecision. They all cross her face at one point or another.

"I have one thing to ask of you, Tohminic of Summer," says Bria. She does not look at me, but at Vander Theron. "Before I ask this of you, know that I do not think I can ever forgive you. I understand you were not in control, but it's your face I see every time I close my eyes, laughing and taunting while you abuse me and others."

"I understand," I whisper around the emotion clogging my throat.

She turns to me now. There is no emotion on her face or in her voice when she asks, "Are you willing to return to Summer and retake your throne? Will you swear fealty to the Dusk Court and pledge your allegiance to us in this horrid war? Do you vow to send your army to join ours when we march on the Night Court?"

Vander Theron bristles. His steel-silver eyes shine with pride.

The Wind Whisperer murmurs an expletive before asking, "Are you certain? We can make do without the flame fuckers."

Her emerald eyes do not stray from my amber. "I am certain."

"I accept your alliance." I put as much strength into the words as I can manage.

I cannot live with what I have done, with what Maude has made me do. But this, bringing the High Lady of the Night

Islands to her knees for the sake of the realm... I will play my part. I will do it gladly. Returning to Ad'Starrag will be difficult. Memories and horrors will resurface. I must endure it.

It is my penance.

First, I must tell them one more thing. "There is something you do not know. I think it is important. Will you hear it?"

They pause as they begin to file from the infirmary.

"Spit it out, Summer," growls Vander Theron.

Chapter 12

I DO NOT THINK I can stand to be in the same room as Tohminic any longer. Hearing his story and witnessing his horror at all he has inflicted is too much. My mind cannot comprehend such things. I cannot accept this is the same male who tortured me, who bargained with Vander and used my life as leverage. But the hope in his tone causes me to pause and the curiosity thrumming along my bond with Vander makes me turn back to the room.

"Spit it out, Summer." Some may think Vander's word a growl of anger. I know better. He's on edge, impatient to set the pieces back on the board and make a move against Night at long last.

"Chlora is not who you think she is," he says. A droning buzz invades my ears, drowning out the rest of his words.

Tohminic's words crash through my mind, tumbling and shattering everything in their path. I had all but forgotten about the Commander General's daughter with everything that has been happening. *Chlora is not who you think she is.* I search my memories for any instance of the blue-eyed female using her powers, but find nothing.

The only way to prove a fae's heritage is through their magical signature, like the sting of my metal bending power and the crispness of Vander's wind. But Chlora... I do not believe I have experienced hers.

Vander's thumb grazes my knuckles in support, as if I have just received terrible news. I frown at him, wondering why, but he shakes his head. Through our bond, he says, *"You didn't listen."*

"We'll get to that second bombshell of information in a moment," says Torin, stealing my response to Vander before it forms. "Who is Chlora?"

I force myself to listen, to look into the haunted eyes of my once captor and torturer. The amber is dull, though not as lifeless as it was when we entered the infirmary hours ago and he spoke the first words of his story.

"You need only to look at her eyes." And I know. I know his next words before he says them. His amber eyes dip to his hands when he grinds out, "She is the Princess of Night, planted in my court the same night Maude stole my mind."

Everything we know is a lie. Tohminic was not acting of his own accord when he trapped me in that cage. Chlora is not the doting lover I believed her to be. Anyone, and I truly mean any fae in this entire realm, could be under Maude's control.

Chlora is Maude's daughter. This changes everything.

"Fuck." Torin's hiss breaks the silence.

"How is it no one knew of her existence until now?" Vander wonders aloud.

Tohminic shrugs. "Maude is as secretive as they come. It is a trait I think all fae can respect. We all wondered the same thing when you declared yourself High Lord of a court we knew nothing about. Radelea is host to many a secret. This is but one of them."

"None in your court thought to mention the strange female posing as one of you?" I ask. I find it difficult to believe she appeared within Ad'Starrag's walls one day and none of the fire wielders or necromancers cared.

"Maude did her research," answers Tohminic. "Our Commander General *does* have a daughter. Although, she has never stepped foot outside of their village home. When Chlora arrived at the keep claiming to be a noble fae of high standing, we did not wonder why she chose now to reveal herself. Maude decreed my Commander General would step down, to be replaced by Xaler, and he returned home moments before Chlora arrived. He never had the chance to refute her claims."

"This is all just a game of luck and coincidence," I mutter. Louder, I ask, "And the true daughter of your Commander General?"

"I am ashamed to say I do not know of her fate," says Tohminic.

Torin snorts. "She's likely dead."

Tohminic's face crumples. "I hold out hope Maude was kind enough to alter her memories and hide her in another court."

"Then you're more of a fool than I first believed," I snap. "The Night Lady has infiltrated your court. She is responsible for my capture and Wyn's current torment. Only the Mother Star knows who else suffers under her control. She would not go to this much effort to *show kindness*."

Wrath has been my constant since the Gloom, but this, throwing venomous words at a clearly broken male... I am better than this. Air whistles through my nostrils when I inhale a swift breath, releasing it through clenched teeth.

"I am sorry." The words are bitter, scorching my tongue with bile. To apologise to someone who has inflicted such cruelty is wrong. I shake my head. "Perhaps with Maude controlling your mind, you have not seen the things we have, and —"

"I recall everything." There's a familiar grimace on his face, one that pulled at my own features not too long ago, when I would recall my time at Ad'Starrag.

"Then you should realise Maude would not show a shred of kindness to your Commander General's daughter," says Vander. His silver eyes dart to me before he faces Tohminic once more. "Tell us about Autumn."

Ice solidifies every drop of blood in my body. "What do you mean?" My heart pounds against my ribs. My mouth runs dry.

"I believe Maude's control extends to your brother," says Tohminic. He adjusts the pillow behind him, sitting straighter. "The night I ordered the undead to attack your western village, I also sent Chlora with a small tea to Autumn. She never revealed what occurred there, but I suspect she gained control of Rennyn's mind."

"Why?" I demand.

He avoids looking at me. "Why gain control of the two largest courts in Radelea, who could bring the realm to destruction if they worked together? Now it is you who is being foolish."

"No. Why do you believe she controls Ren's mind?"

"She has mentioned things she cannot know. Your mother's identity among them."

I stare at him for the length of two heartbeats. Two heartbeats of silence and stillness. Then I erupt.

I scream as loud as I am able, fisting my hands in my copper locks and pulling until it hurts. My knees give out, but I keep screaming through their failure to hold me upright. They hit the ground with a crack that sends ripples of pain up my spine.

Ruith fought for five and seventy years to keep this information from getting out, to protect Uma from the disgusting tradition of our fae — to force a wrongdoer into walking the path of shame, where the Winter denizens will throw rocks and rotting food at them. It is the worst kind of torture for someone as sweet as my mother.

"*Go, Princess,*" Vander urges. "*Chlora and Maude could reveal that information at any moment. It's best the Winter fae hear it from Uma herself.*"

I stop screaming long enough to ask, "Go?"

"*Yes. Go warn your family. We will plan things here. I will give you until the setting of the moon to return to me.*"

I blink back a wave of tears, and warmth spreads through me at the words. My family. "*You will delay freeing Wyn so I can warn Mother? You would risk that for me?*"

"*I would risk that and more.*"

The western village of Autumn is quiet. The tavern is dark, and no raucous laughter filters into the paved street as I slink through the shadows towards the village homes. I keep my eyes to the right — away from the docks, where too many painful but once exciting memories reside — as I take the steep path up the hill and dart down the first dirt road to my left.

Fae lights once gleamed overhead, lighting the way for late night revellers as they stumbled home after enjoying one too many ales, or for the family provider lugging wares from the market through the streets. Now, there is nothing but darkness, as if the nobles have forgotten their denizens completely.

The wild cat's body is lithe and balance comes naturally as I slink across the low rock wall outside Dey's bedchamber window, hoping to speak with them before any of the Autumn fae realise I am here. Being the only one of my students with the ability to read the thoughts of animals, Dey is my only source of information.

There is no possibility I would risk myself by coming here in my fae body. No, that part of me is likely frost bitten on the peak of Kol, the highest mountain in Winter's Bolbala Ranges.

I mewl at the yellowed glass, nudging the rickety pane with my paw. *Dey? Are you in there?*

It is a risk to come here. I know that. On the chance they could be home, not learning the court's history at the castle, I decided the risk was worth it, if only to gather proof of Tohminic's suspicions.

The whisper of sheets in the chamber beyond causes my ears to twitch, and I headbutt the glass. *Dey!*

"Mother Star, have mercy," Dey whispers. More rustles, then a thud, before the shadow of their figure moves beyond the cracked yellow.

They pause before lifting the window, tilting their head to the side. "Who are you?" they wonder. Never afraid of a challenge, and always itching to learn, Dey hesitates no longer before opening the sliding glass.

It's me, Dey, I think towards them. *It's Bria.*

"Bria? But why are you a cat?" They shake their head. "Never mind. What are you doing here?"

Is it true? Is Rennyn acting himself of late?

"This is about your brother?" I purr, and Dey scratches behind my ears. "No one has seen him for many moons. Not since you last visited with the Dusk fae. I am sorry you are not who you thought you were."

The memory of my last visit to Autumn resurfaces, a reminder of when Father's broken mind, thanks to the mate bond Fayeth severed, loosened his lips and he revealed my link with the Winter Court.

I nudge Dey's hand. *Thank you, but this is not about me. Rennyn hides?*

"He does not hide so much as he refuses to leave the throne room and barks orders at any fae who dares to enter." They lower their voice to a whisper. "Father says the High Lord intends to send our armada to join the Night army."

And Father?

"No one knows where he is. We have not seen Kerym since Rennyn began acting differently. I am so sorry."

Thank you, Dey. You have been so very helpful. I miss you all so much. Perhaps, when the war is over and the Mother Star shines once more, you can all come to Dusk. We can go on that adventure we talked about.

"Do you promise?"

I promise. Until then, promise me you and the rest of the class will hide. Swear it now, Dey. I cannot leave until I know you will be safe.

"I vow it," they say.

Gooseflesh covers me from the tip of my frozen nose to every numb toe as I step into the antechamber to Ruith's private home. A wave of gratitude shudders through me when the warmth from the flames engulfs my frozen flesh. Even with the flickering torches, the antechamber is colder than it was in Dusk.

"Halt." A flash of steel blocks my path forward, the lone word from the overexuberant guard stopping me in my tracks.

I rub my hands together and blow a warm breath over my fingers before greeting her. "Well met. I am here to scc High Lady Uma and High Lord Ruith."

"No one enters the High Lord's private residence. Leave, or suffer the wrath of Winter."

My eyes roll for the sky the Mother Star refuses to grace with her glow. "I don't have time for this."

I pull on a thread of metal bending magic, and before she knows what I'm doing, her dual-pronged spear lies contorted on the cold ground. In the next heartbeat, I wrap dense shadows around my shivering form, elbow the guard in the stomach — the deep grunt and the huff of breath are satisfying — and slip through the door.

She calls after me, but by the time she races along the winding hallway towards me, I'm slipping inside the opulent dining room, where my mother and stepfather are enjoying a plate of colourful fruits. It is easy to imagine them like this every evening, sharing stories and relaxing before turning in for the night.

I jerk a thumb over my shoulder when I enter. "You need better guards. Perhaps someone who doesn't think I'm the scum of Radelea."

"Well met, Bria," says Ruith. He dismisses the panting guard with a jerk of his chin. "To what do we owe the pleasure?"

All of my bravado, courage, and wrath wither, seeping from my pores like gasses as my body sags. "There is no pleasure in this visit, I'm afraid."

"Sit, darling, and have some honeyed mead." The kindness in Uma's tone brings a fresh wave of nausea churning in my stomach for what I am about to do and say.

"I wish I could. We learned something today." I summarise following Wyn, Tohminic's story, and what I learned from Dey. Saving the worst news for last, I finish with, "We have it on good authority that Chlora knows who my mother is. If she has already told Maude..."

"Maude will use it against us at a time best suited to her and her cause," finishes Ruith. He runs his fingers through his dark hair. "This is not an outcome I would have hoped for."

"It has been too long, Ruith. It is time they knew," says Uma, resting a hand against her mate's.

"They will demand you walk the path of shame," he says.

I clear my throat. "I will take her place. She has spent the last five and seventy years hiding while I have lived. She has paid her dues. It's only fair I complete the walk."

Mother gracefully stands, smooths the deep sapphire skirts of her gown that compliment her eyes, and approaches. Her smile is grim. "My dear daughter, I cannot allow you to do that. This is my fight."

I look to Ruith for support, already knowing he will argue for my side. It's not that he does not care about my wellbeing. I am not hurt by the knowledge he would rather I walk the path of shame than Uma. She is his mate. His chosen. He would shatter the entire realm into thousands of pieces if it meant he was protecting her.

Just as I would for Vander, and he for me.

"It is wise to allow Bria this chance," says Ruith. "If our denizens are to welcome her into the court, this is the first step to gaining their trust."

Uma's blue eyes narrow. "I know what the two of you are doing. You have my thanks for your protective nature, Ruith, as do you, darling Bria, but I am a grown female. This was my wrongdoing, and I will face it alone." She cups my cheek, spreading warmth from the tips of her fingers to every pore of my body. "I cannot, in good conscience, allow any harm to come to you."

"I am sorry, Mother, but you don't have a choice. You forget where my stubborn nature comes from. Kerym would never back down, and neither will I. If you are determined to walk the path of shame, then know I will walk it right alongside you."

She does not argue further; the stubborn determination written across the lines of my face leaves no room for debate. Instead, she guides me to her garderobe and orders me to select a tulle gown from the armoire.

By the time we have dressed and joined Ruith at the castle's public entrance, a large crowd of Winter fae has already gathered, all whispering to one another. Some of them even dare to point to the twin crowns. First, to the silver piece atop Uma's carefully pinned hair, then to the lopsided piece clinging to mine.

Uma is spectacular in a gown of glittering silver. It screams of the Winter Court. She blends with the brightest of snow when the fae lights hit the gown, but when there is no light to catch the glittering diamonds stitched into the fine material, she might as well be a statue of marble, the only bursts of colour her copper hair and azure eyes.

In contrast to my mother, I have selected a gown of the deepest black. Where Uma blends with the snow, I am pure night. The black speaks of defiance to their sick tradition, it screams of rebelliousness — the old me would thrive on it, and it brings a semblance of normalcy to this dark day — and I hope it will provide the crowd with an easy target, sparing Mother the pain, humiliation, and suffering.

It's a tulle piece that Uma refers to as a gown, but is little more than a sheer robe. The tie that cinches the onyx fabric around my waist requires constant tightening, though the move is pointless. Every dip and curve of my body is on display, the tulle doing little to hide my figure. The sleeves widen so much at the wrists, the folds of the fabric blend with the bodice, joining the cascade of onyx to the snow-covered ground.

I do everything in my power to block out the High Lord's words as he explains why we are gathered here today. I meet the gaze of whichever fae dares to look my way, I stare at the distant western horizon and wonder when the Mother Star will once again retire for the night and we will have the assurance she will return tomorrow, and I relay messages to Vander through our bond, although when he begins to curse and growl, I block him out, too.

After what seems like an eternity of Ruith speaking in a low but deadly tone, he says, "The females beside me are my family. We understand this necessity, and honour tradition with Uma and Bria walking the path towards forgiveness and absolution."

The path of shame is not a long one. A worn trail of mountainous landscape twists and dips between two rows of obsidian statues, the length only fifty long swords. The ordeal will only last sixty beats of my steady heart.

We take the first step together. I cannot help but think of Father, and how he spent five and seventy years begging Fayeth for forgiveness for straying outside their bond. Ruith forgave Uma decades ago, and even now, he wishes for nothing more than her happiness. I spent my entire life suffering, and I think, even though I have always found this tradition horrific, this way of doing things may be better. The Winter fae will wound us. They will hurl vicious words at us. They will sneer. But the moment we step away from the path, it will be over.

It will not last decades. The bruises will fade within days, rather than eons.

When an elderly male throws the first stone, I cannot prevent myself from reacting. I whip my hand out and smack the rounded rock aside, saving Uma from a nasty bruise to the shoulder.

The crowd gasps.

I repeat the same action with the second, third, all the way to the tenth stone. Rocks hit me from the other side, from behind. I do not recoil. I do not utter a sound. But I keep protecting my mother.

At the halfway mark, between a statue of a dire wolf and one of a female wielding a flurry of snow, the crowd quiets.

"She is worthy," someone behind me says. "She has taken every hit thrown her way, yet continues to defend our High Lady. If that is not a show of bravery, I do not know what is. Let them walk free."

Murmurs follow the words, murmurs of agreement.

There is something inside me, though, that hesitates. Through the thuds of pain, I realise this walk means something to me. With every stone colliding with my body, every bruise, and every rock I stop from hitting Mother, I let go of a little guilt. With every step I take towards absolution, I release a little of the hold the crimson and the wrath have on me.

"No. We will pay our dues as tradition demands," I say, looking at the speaker over my shoulder, surprised to see Tarathiel watching me warmly. I dip my chin in appreciation and repeat, "We will pay our dues."

Uma threads her fingers through mine, leaving me only one hand to protect her with. "We will *both* pay our dues. No more saving me. You and Ruith must both learn I am capable. I can withstand the horrors of life."

A sheepish grin curves across my lips. "As you wish, Mother."

Together, truly this time, we complete the walk of shame, and with every sting of pain, I release more tension. I release the wrath that has been bubbling below the surface since the Gloom. I emerge at the end of the path a new female, with a new goal.

I will end Maude's reign of terror, if it's the last thing I do.

Chapter 13

IT HAS BEEN FIVE and ten days since I walked the path of shame and let go of all my anger. The bruises from the stones have long since faded, the echo of the pain a memory so distant I sometimes think I imagined it.

During those five and ten days, I have spent every free moment reading about the Mother Star and when she first graced Radelea with her golden glow. I always come back to the same conclusion. She will not rise again until there is harmony among the courts.

When I am not reading, I'm training in both magic and combat with Vander. And while we train, we argue. He's frustrated with the wait, angry we could not demand the High fae meet us straight away. He wants nothing more than to force the hand of every leader in the realm, demanding they send their soldiers to aid us in storming the Night Court. Then, when the subject of Wyn arises, our training session is over, and he disappears.

Torin and I believe she needs to be confined to the manor. Vander refuses to cage his sister after everything she has endured. We are at an impasse. Vander refuses to back down and we are hesitant to force his hand.

I had hoped he would at least allow me to sneak into the Autumn Court and capture my brother, but he refuses that idea, too. Rennyn's mind is not his own, and we have the means to help him... if we can convince Blodwen to return. I do not care what the price is, what she will ask of us this time. My brother does not deserve the same fate as Tohminic.

So today, while I cinch the brown leather corset tighter around my waist, I am thankful the meeting with the other High fae has come at last. Things in Dusk are tense, and securing alliances with Dawn, Day, Winter, Summer, and Spring will ease a lot of Vander's tension. Perhaps, when his mind is at ease knowing we are not alone in this, he will see sense and detain both Wyn and Rennyn.

The fabric of my simple gown shimmers, flickering between the calm colour of sea foam green and the welcoming hue of fern leaves. There is little I can do or say to sway our only undecided ally — Nyana and the Court of Blooms are yet to pledge an alliance either way — but I am a firm believer in the power of colour. Soothing tones may work wonders on High Lady Nyana. Better than Vander's harsh black leathers, at least.

I peer at him over my shoulder. "Are you almost ready? I'm certain Torin is itching to go."

Van slides the last dagger, the twelfth, into its sheath along his thigh. "Torin is itching to see Nyana again." He snorts. "Her rejection of him when he hand delivered our request to meet is the most spectacular story I have heard."

Rather than send a messenger, we decided requesting a treaty meeting face to face would be the better way to approach this. It gives us an opportunity to demand an answer on the spot, with an assurance of the message only reaching the intended parties. If they had not done so, we would not be meeting with five of the other seven leaders in Dawn tonight.

I am thankful to Jonik for offering us a neutral place to meet. His secluded residence among the north-eastern mountains provides both sanctuary and privacy.

"I hope he asks her again," I say, sliding a pin into the braid curling around my brow. "I'm certain he believes himself to be the Mother Star's gift to female kind."

His eyes brighten. "You never fell for his charms."

"My heart's desire lies elsewhere." I hesitate before adding, "Do you regret it at all? Allowing me into your heart?"

"No. If there is anything I regret, it's not claiming you as my own sooner. I wasted too much time fearing loss. I won't make the mistake of wasting time again."

"It's why you were so determined to storm Night, instead of waiting for proof and allies?" I ask as we exit the manor.

He dips his chin. It is the only answer I will receive with Torin all but bouncing before us.

"About time. What took you so long?" He narrows those dark eyes at my hair. "Typical female."

"Actually, you can blame Van. He thought cleaning and sharpening his knives was necessary for a *meeting*." I still do not understand why he has decided to use intimidation rather than pleasantries. He has even strapped vambraces to his arms and a shield to his back.

Wyn stands rigid beside Torin, her moonlight eyes downcast. "Shall we go?"

"She shouldn't be coming with us," I tell Vander for the tenth time today. *"What if she relays everything back to Maude? What if Night's Lady is already listening?"*

"It's a risk we must take. If Nyana thinks we're not a united force, she will not join our plight. Spring would be an advantageous ally with their control of nature and their psychic abilities." His frustration at the repeated argument lingers in his words. He's right, after all. The Court of Blooms would be a welcome addition to our side of this fight.

"She will know no different if you claim Wyn has remained in Dusk to protect our fae. Please. This is a bad idea."

He searches my eyes, the glimmering silver of his irises deepening to a harsh steel. *"I want her close, so I can monitor her."*

Over Van's shoulder, Torin is growing impatient. He rolls his eyes when he spots me watching him, then widens them as if telling me to get a move on.

"So bring her," I say, *"but don't allow her to take part in the meeting. She can remain in her hut while we convince Nyana to join us. You know this is the best choice. If anything we say during the meeting makes it back to Maude... We might as well invite her, too."*

He sighs, and I know I have won. He turns to Wyn, and with a wince, says, "When we're in Dawn, I can't have you near the meeting. I love you, and I want to help you, but right now, we don't trust you."

"Bria doesn't trust me," she says, pinning me with a glare.

"You're mistaken." I step towards her. "I trust Wyn with my life. It's you I don't trust, Maude. Kindly get the fuck out of my friend's head."

Her upper lip hitches into a snarl.

Torin splutters. "Since when do you speak like that?"

"Since I spend so much time with you, Wind Whisperer." I offer him a wink so he knows I'm jesting.

"Let's go before Torin gets started on the jokes. We don't have time for his immaturity," says Vander, though his lips twitch.

Much to my delight and Vander's amusement, Torin spews a string of jokes about females who use vulgar language, many of them including several other magical beasts and me entering a tavern. He's still rattling off nonsensical words when we fold from the Dusk shore to the Dawn mountains and still laughing when we approach a forked valley between three low mountains.

I tune him out when we reach an arc of small huts to take in the magnificent landscape.

The trio of dark mountains is a breathtaking backdrop, with veins of bitter white snaking from their peaks to halfway down their slopes. Dense mist clings to the summits, rolling in waves of glittering alabaster and drifting into the night sky to obstruct my view of the stars.

The swollen moon, full just last night, casts a silver glow on the valley before me, illuminating a dozen burgundy huts, their gauzy, bone white curtains swishing in a citrusy breeze. Notes of evergreens and some kind of subtle pine tickle my senses, sweet and damp and welcoming.

Bursts of ruby, scarlet, bronze, and carrot orange frame the valley. The sigh of the maples creates a melody with bubbling water and the chirp of a distant kitsune — the small hound-like creature with nine tails keeps to the Dawn mountains, never venturing close to civilisation.

The grass beneath my feet is as soft as pillows of moss as I approach Jonik and Leilani. Dressed in a quilted surcoat of the deepest blue, Jonik is as handsome as I have ever seen him. His mate complements him perfectly in her pale blue kirtle, with the ivory sleeves of her chemise tight at the wrists but trumpeting at the shoulder.

"Well met, Dusk friends," says Jonik.

We repeat the sentiment before dipping our chins in greeting to the others gathered in the clearing. The crackling fire at the heart throws hues of amber and gold over Tasar and Larrad, who are in matching suede jerkins and beige pants.

Zentha, Elmon, and Kyra smile, their genuine warmth soothing whatever nerves remain.

Guards flank Ruith and Uma on either side, one of them Tarathiel, and the other Vacon, Tarathiel's lover and Ruith's second.

Nyana's slight dip of the chin is forced, and her smile tight. The loose curls of her fire-orange hair hang to her petite waist and ripple with her every breath. Beside her, a trio of fae I am yet to meet.

"High Lady Nyana and her consort, Lady Imala." Jonik gestures to the female closest to Nyana. Her strawberry blonde hair shimmers in the moonlight, seeming to have a magic of its own.

"Her second and sometimes consort, Darcel," continues Jonik, nodding towards a male with mahogany hair and warm brown skin. The male glares, ignoring his introduction.

The second male beside Nyana, who has pale green skin and bark-like fingers, goes by Argi. He is also her consort, and according to Jonik, he is a wood nymph, born of the forest to Spring's west.

"You know everyone else, I believe," says Jonik. "Shall we begin?"

Vander leans closer to Dawn's High Lord and whispers in his ear.

Jonik's brows rise, but he calls Leilani forward. "My dear, would you be so kind as to show Wyn to her lodgings? I am afraid the journey has proven too much for her after such worrying times."

As I move to my seat between Vander and Torin, I keep my gaze locked on the crackling fire, determined not to observe Nyana's reaction to the news that Wyn will not be a part of the meeting. To our right, Ruith and Uma sip from stemless gold chalices. Mother's smile as she brings the chalice to her lips is one of contentedness and peace. I realise this may be the first time since she brought me into this world that she has attended something so public.

I offer her a reassuring smile as I take my seat. This is an enormous step from hiding in your bedchambers. But if the way she carries herself is anything to go by, my mother is happy. She is at peace with her world and delighted to be among fae from other courts after being alone for so long.

"Tell us why we are gathered here tonight, High Lord Vander," says Nyana, her voice a tinkling of bells and a seductive caress. "You gave us no option but to agree to meet, yet gave us no insight into why. I will wait no longer."

Zentha's click of the tongue is audible over the popping flames. She leans forward, the lilac silk of her gown rustling. "You have remained neutral in this war thus far, Nyana. Do not be so foolish as to believe you can remain so. The Mother Star has turned away from us. Are you not concerned about the fate of the realm?"

"I am not. The sun will grace my lands with her rays when she feels the time is right."

"Your *lands* rely on the Mother Star more than any other court," I hiss. I cannot believe I once thought I belonged to the Court of Blooms. "I would hope, as High Lady of the nature fae, you would show a little more interest."

Argi and Darcel bristle, shuffling closer to Nyana and resting their hands on twin short swords.

Torin's snort is one of humour and challenge, and is thankfully drowned out by the crackling fire.

"Insulting her won't get you far, Princess," Vander warns. Out loud, he says, "We have not come here to insult your ways, but to beg you to reconsider an alliance."

Nyana tosses her curls over one shoulder. "My answer remains the same. Unless you have more to offer?"

Before Vander can answer, Tasar chuckles and says, "Is it not enough that Maude controlled the mind of a fellow leader? Is it not enough that the Night fae attack us with human weapons? I have always believed the Spring fae to be alluring and kind, not daft enough to bury their heads in the sand."

"*Son.*" Jonik's reprimand is a serpent's hiss. "You will treat our guests with respect."

"We will treat her with respect when she stops making eyes at her lover and opens them to the destruction Maude is wreaking on Radelea, *Father*," says Larrad.

Leilani returns, slipping between Tasar and Jonik with grace. "That is enough, my sons. Perhaps explaining the details will encourage the Lady of Spring to see things differently."

I snatch a chalice from the tray before me to give my hands something to do other than clench and unclench. To give my lips a task other than spewing insults at Nyana until she agrees to aid us in this war.

Jonik leans forward, resting his elbows on his knees and facing Nyana. "The Dusk fae came to me seven and ten moons ago. They brought with them a female wounded beyond repair." He pulls a small jar from his pocket and holds it in the light of the fire. Inside which rests the iron bullet that is a dark stain on our history. "This is what killed her. A bullet made of iron. It pierced her heart, killing Erthana in an instant."

Darcel crosses the clearing and takes the jar from Jonik, handing it to Nyana upon his return to her cushioned seat.

She inspects the small piece of metal, a crease forming between her brows. "What does it do?"

Vander explains everything. He tells her about the human realm and how the Dusk Court has sacrificed everything to protect it. How they use weapons of unfathomable destruction against one another, and how Nyree — I scowl at the reminder of the Ill-fated leader and her betrayal — would sneak into Earth and steal such horrific weapons.

"You want me to pledge alliance to a court that has kept such a secret for so long?" Nyana asks. "How can I trust you are telling the entire truth now?"

"Because Maude uses the human weapons against us," says Ruith, speaking for the first time. "She controlled Lord Tohminic's mind. We fear she controls the mind of High Lord Rennyn, as well. We do not know what she wants, or why she is subjecting the realm to such horrors. What we know is that no one is safe. We have to stop her."

"I thought this war started because the Dusk island appeared. I thought *her* search for a mate only added to the tension." She jerks her chin at me. "This does not add up."

"It does not add up because you are too foolish to pay attention," says Larrad. "The only reason there has been tension at all is because Maude was controlling Tohminic's mind. She incited it. We just do not know why."

"It is not enough." She sets the jar holding the bullet on the ground and stands, smoothing the skirts of her sapphire gown. "Come to me when you have proof, and I will reconsider. Until then, I wish you luck."

No one stops her from retreating to her cabin. We do not stop Argi, Darcel, or Imala from following their High Lady. We're all stunned. Even with the proof we have already provided her, it is not enough to sway her to our side.

Her refusal to acknowledge the truth may be the turning point in the war. It may be the turning point Maude needs to gain the advantage.

Chapter 14

"T HAT DIDN'T QUITE GO how we had planned." Torin frowns at the cabin Nyana and Imala disappeared into, where the sheer curtains flutter in the breeze and an amber glow shines within. "She must know something we don't."

"Such as?" asks Tasar.

Torin turns to him. "Such as the outcome of this war. If the Lady of Blooms believed we would win, she would have already declared an alliance."

I drag my eyes from the fire to the silhouettes within Nyana's cabin, the two females clearly naked as they move towards one another. There was nothing in Nyana's words or actions that lead me to believe she knows the fate of our realm. If, like Torin believes, she is choosing which side to fight for based on the truths her visions show her, I think she would already have declared her choice.

That she is here tonight, and did not refuse our request to meet, speaks volumes. If we are destined to lose this war, she would simply decline any messengers. But she is here, and it can only mean one thing.

"Perhaps the future is not yet determined," offers Jonik, speaking my thoughts out loud, "and Nyana is being cautious.

Choosing who to fight with is no small task. I do not believe she would keep it from us if she knew the outcome."

"She has to know something. She has the power to see the threads of the future," says Larrad. He takes a casual drink from his chalice, as if the topic of conversation is not one that could sway the war.

Zentha crosses her ankles, tucks them beneath her stool, and says, "It is not our place to demand answers. The Spring fae do not take kindly to prying. Best we plan for battle without Nyana. We can amend those plans if she joins us."

"I agree," says Ruith. He whispers something to Tarathiel and Vacon, who leave without acknowledging the rest of us. I suppose with Nyana and her trio of guards no longer lingering by the fire, Stepfather has no use of his guards.

Leilani stands. "High Lady Uma, would you care to join me in my cabin for a nightcap? Bria and Kyra, you are more than welcome to accompany us."

Uma accepts with a wide smile, having not enjoyed the company of a fellow Lady in five and seventy years. The kiss she plants on Ruith's forehead is sweet, comforting. It's a quick press of the lips, a gesture born from years of habit.

The hint is clear. We are to leave the High fae to their debate, leave the males to the planning. I ignore it. I will not be overlooked here like I was in the Autumn Court by my father. "Thank you for the offer, but I think I'll stay here."

Kyra also declines, instead dragging her soon-to-be mate, Elmon, into their cabin.

My heart clenches as I watch the two Day fae walk away. Tohminic's attacks ruined their mating ceremony. Sending hordes of undead to Dusk, Day, and Dawn while the celebrations had us distracted was a disgusting, cowardly move. Mate bonds are not complete until the Mother Star blesses the union with the first rays of dawn light. Without her warming glow, the two are not truly mated. It is no wonder they have not spoken tonight, no wonder their heads hang low.

While Tasar, Torin, and Larrad move our seats closer together, forming a tighter circle for us to converse and plan, I move to Zentha's side and ask, "Are they okay? They seem downcast."

Her honey eyes tighten, smoothing the golden brown skin of her brow. "They will work through it. Kyra believes the Mother Star does not approve of their mating and wishes to return to her family in our east."

"The Mother Star abandoned us because we disgraced her, not because she rejects a mated pair." My eyes stray to Vander, and I wonder if he and I will ever perform a mating ceremony and be blessed by her light. It is a question I must ask him at some point, but now, while shrouded in darkness, I do not wish to beg the sun for anything other than light and warmth. Anything else is asking too much.

"We do not know why she refuses to rise," says Zentha.

I sigh. "I've been researching her appearance. Reading the tomes in Dusk has provided me with only the basics of our history, but from what I can gather, the Mother Star rose right after the signing of the ancient treaty."

I'm distantly aware of Tasar, Torin, and Larrad arguing how best to confront Nyana and force her into joining our fight. Vander, Ruith, and Jonik watch on with either frustration or bemusement.

"Elmon will be thrilled to hear it." Her smile is warm. "As I am thrilled to see you thrive in the Dusk Court, Bria. Your spirit soars."

"Will the females be joining us, or shall we begin without your input?" Larrad crosses his arms over his chest. "Talking about what gown you will wear tomorrow can wait, can it not?"

Tasar elbows him in the ribs. "Jealous, brother? Do you wish to partake in discussions of gowns and tiaras?"

I cannot prevent my laughter as I take my seat between Torin and Vander. The Dawn princes lost their brother. Despite that, they jest and laugh. Ulakas would often instigate the banter, and I am beyond proud to see the brothers continuing his mantle.

Although, I still believe they should wear different coloured gambesons or jerkins, so I may tell them apart.

Their involvement in the conversation — Vander leads the charge by asking everyone's thoughts on how best to win this war and destroy the Night Court — takes me by surprise. Ordinarily, Tasar and Larrad would leave the gritty details to their father, preferring to indulge in plum wine and make inappropriate comments whenever the opportunity arises.

But Tasar says, "I do not think we can thwart her with strength alone."

Larrad adds, "We have to be smarter than her. Cunning. A difficult feat, considering she can read our minds and authorise counter attacks before we make our first move."

"We need to protect our minds from her," says Ruith. "Only then will we move forward. Is there a way, Wind Whisperer?"

"You can place a mental shield around your thoughts," he says with a one-shouldered shrug. "But keeping it in place during battle is difficult. A lesson Bria learned the hard way when a Night fae used their blood and bone magic on her during the Gloom."

I close my eyes to the memory of my entire body burning, of the stabs of pain emanating from my mind. No matter how hard I had tried, I could not rid my body of the tongues of agony ripping through me. The pain flared, grew hotter and fiercer until Ulakas smothered me with his body and shielded me from harm.

He sacrificed himself in doing so.

A knot forms in my stomach, and it becomes difficult to swallow. I cannot look at Jonik or Tasar or Larrad. They know why and how Ulakas died, and though they do not blame me for his demise, I blame myself. I was weak. My mental shield was not strong enough. I will not make that mistake again.

"You did nothing wrong, Princess." Vander's words are a caress, a soothing lick of cool tones and rough promises. *"You cannot keep blaming yourself."*

I offer him a grimace of a smile, and beg him with my eyes to change the subject.

Fortunately, he takes pity on me. He says, "We can't shield our minds from them without sacrificing our concentration during battle. By shielding our minds, we are weaker. Give all your thoughts to the mental shield, and your magic wanes. Do you understand? There's no winning when it comes to war. Sacrifices are demanded. Choosing between privacy of mind and strength of attack is one of them."

"Perhaps the best way to protect ourselves is to distract," says Zentha. "Keep your thoughts on your movements, on the fae you are locked in combat with, and they cannot pierce through the fog of memories to uncover our plans."

"It is as good a solution as any." Larrad sips from the golden chalice in his hand before adding, "What *is* our plan?"

"We were considering planting spies in Night," says Torin.

Vander runs a hand over his shaved hair and adds, "If we can discover any information about Maude's plans which will further our agenda, Dusk is willing to take that risk."

"And if you are discovered?" Jonik's dark eyes lock on Vander.

"The Night fae will never catch her. She's a wind wraith."

A hum of approval runs through the clearing, but it's Zentha who says, "She is brave beyond measure. Commend her courage on my behalf, and I will pray to the Mother Star she remains unharmed."

"Has Alizeh agreed to this?" I ask Van through our bond, lest the others believe him to be autocratic.

"Torin asked her last night. She's more than willing. In fact, from what he told me, she is eager to dismantle Maude and her court."

The wind wraith is a conundrum. The first time I met her, when Vander took me on a tour of the western village, I believed her to be nothing more than a flirtatious lover of ale. But the more I know her, the more she surprises me with her layers. A crust of desire and flippancy. A second, softer layer of loyalty and kindness. She has layers for her unending hunger for the residual energy of magic, layers for the fae she calls friends, and an inner core of pure savagery.

"We will pray for her in Dawn," says Jonik. "Let us talk about my healers. Shall we construct a trauma station somewhere easily accessible for all allies?"

The conversation sways back and forth with ease. We decide on strengthening the wards around Dawn to protect the healers and altering them to allow injured allies through without issue. We Plan for all kinds of attack — from mind control to protecting our bodies from the dark power that contorts blood and bone — and discuss all plausible scenarios.

Winter will send foot soldiers to aid our army, as well as providing a haven for the vulnerable from Dusk, Day, and Dawn, just as they did during the Gloom.

The healers will be a gift in the darkness, aiding the soldiers from our four courts and healing where they can. Their light-wielding armada will begin sailing south, towards our island, come morning.

Day's water and spirit wielders will take their court's ships and join Dawn's armada, creating the largest fleet of ships Radelea has ever seen.

Dusk is to use their illusions to confuse the Night army. We will be on the front line, using our skill in weaponry to keep the foot soldiers at bay.

If Tohminic is successful in regaining control of the Summer Court, he will send an army of selkies and a horde of undead to aid in our plight, and his horseback cavalry will wield the flames of their court against our enemies.

We debate the advantages and disadvantages of each court, listing them and considering how to use them against Maude's army. There is no plan for protecting ourselves against the human weapons, though we acknowledge our best protection is to have a cavalry of wind wielders whose sole purpose is to send volleys of bullets *back* at the Night fae who fire them.

The plan for the war is coming together detail by infinitesimal detail. We are hours of discussions away from a final plan of attack, but when the moon meets the horizon, and we are all too fatigued to speak any longer, we decide to retire and figure out the finer details tomorrow.

By the time Vander and I are alone in one of the cabins lining the perimeter of the clearing, my bones ache, I'm rubbing invisible sand from my eyes, and my feet are dragging against the wooden floor. I collapse onto the low bed the moment I'm within reach of the furs and cushions.

"It's been a long night." Van kneels at the end of the bed, a wicked gleam in his silver eyes. His deft fingers make quick work of the ribbons of my satin slippers, and he slides them from my feet, discarding them behind him.

I lift my head just enough to see him clearly. "What are you doing?"

"I'm helping you." The curl of his full lips is taunting. "After all that talk of war, alliances, and battle plans, and watching you contribute to the conversation, I'm ready to lose myself in our love. The way you fight for our court, the way your devious little mind works. It's arousing, Princess."

Desire swells at his words. I had wondered why lust pulsed along our bond out there. "My mind is not devious." An image flickers across mind's eye, an image of Vander pushing my skirts up to my hips, his head lowering to my most intimate part. I clench my thighs.

He smirks. "I beg to differ."

"Okay, perhaps it is a little devious." I twist until I'm on my knees and crawl towards him. "You only have yourself to blame, you know." I tug on the zipper of his jacket, revealing the muscular chest beneath.

He lowers his lips to the curve of my neck and grazes his teeth along the sensitive flesh. *"I don't know if we'll win this war. Our plans, while clever and exceptional, may not be enough to beat Maude."*

"Why are you saying this?" I ask into his mind as I throw my head back. My fingers trail down his chiselled abdominals and skim the waistband of his leather pants.

He runs his tongue along my throat. *"Because I'm not sure how many more nights I have left to worship you as you deserve. My only wish is to spend my last night lost in our lust. I don't want to waste a single beat of my heart."*

I crawl closer, relishing in the feel of his bare chest against my swollen nipples when our bodies press together. Desire throbs in my core, dampening my panties before he has even touched me there.

A reverberating clang sounds from the far end of the arced row of cabins, the piercing sound reminiscent of a sword clanging against timber, as if thrown against the floor.

"Fuck!" Torin's shout rings throughout the otherwise quiet night, bouncing off the trio of mountains surrounding us again and again until a chorus of the vulgar human word surrounds us.

A second shout from Vander's second drowns out the echoes of the first. "Incoming attack!"

My stomach turns leaden and settles low and uncomfortable as I rush to slide my feet into the discarded satin slippers.

Vander sprints from the cabin, zipping his leather jacket as he runs. Fear pulses along our bond, growing stronger with every step he takes towards the far side of the clearing.

As soon as my feet are covered, I push my aching legs as hard as I can and tear across the too-soft grass. I pass cabin after cabin, our friends rushing from within to join us.

"What is it?" I ask, skidding to a stop in front of the cabin Torin's sharing with Wyn. From the outside, nothing seems to be amiss, but the darkness is an expert in trickery. The blanket of night hides more than we acknowledge.

Tasar and Larrad carry orbs of light in their palms, their magic flickering in the darkness and throwing long shadows over the scene. The sweet rush of Zentha's water magic fills my ears, the scent of brine and open seas washing over my senses.

Torin points to the star-strewn sky. The rest of us do not need for him to speak the threat aloud. He does so anyway. His whisper sends shivers down my spine. "Harpies."

Chapter 15

T HE HARASSMENT OF HARPIES soaring overhead is so large, it's overwhelming. It cannot be their entire population, but I would wager on the Mother Star's return this is the majority. Only the being we worship knows where the rest of them are.

Gusts of air billow through my copper strands as I tilt my face higher, and the scents of carrion and sulphur bring bile to my mouth. I recall the miasmic atmosphere of the Harpy Barrens. The stench wafted from decaying carcasses that were scattered across the arid land; the hickory-coloured plain was dotted with the loss of life. The scent was overwhelming when we stole the talon from a creature I know to be larger than Vander. Here, when the odour billows from the feathers of those flocking above, nausea roils in my stomach and saliva pools beneath my tongue. Though it is more manageable, it still threatens to bring me to my knees and bring up my dinner.

It is seldom they leave their barren wasteland — they have long lived in the ruins of Night's former castle — where they are shielded by the mountain range that runs along the western border of the islands. They prefer the quiet solitude of the greying branches they perch upon, prefer the peace of the crumbling castle and leafless shrubs. If they are so far from their home, then Maude has offered them a deal they cannot refuse. More freedom, likely.

I step closer to Vander, needing the proximity to soothe the panic racing through my veins. The soft fabric of my gown feels wrong as it slides against the skin of my legs. Wrong for the growing tension, wrong for the darkness and ominous shadows overhead, and wrong for me. I am no longer the female who cowers in fear whenever a threat or problem arises, but one of strength and courage who will move the realm itself to protect the fae she loves. Gowns are not who I am. Not anymore.

The desire to shred the silk and discard it in a raging river builds, but I refrain from leaving Vander's side to find my leathers. Instead, I widen my legs and pull the back hem through to the front, knotting it with the folds of silk there. When I am done, there is a large ball of fabric sitting just above my knees, and my gown is essentially short pants.

Vander pulls his gaze from the harassment overhead and eyes me with suspicion. "You don't mean to fight them?"

"I do." I slide the dagger from the sheath at my thigh. "Better we thin their number now than during a larger battle. I will do it alone if you are unwilling to fight by my side."

Pride thrums along our bond. "I was willing to flee. But you're right. Why wait until we're locked in combat with fae to shoot these bastards from the sky?" He turns to the others, who are all gathered around Torin's cabin. "If anyone does not wish to fight, I suggest you fold now. The first descends."

Tearing my eyes to the sky, I see he's right. A lone harpy with long brown feathers hurtles towards the ground with her legs stretched below her. The moment she is close enough for me to catch the smaller details, I see a deformed claw with one talon missing.

"She's intent on revenge," I murmur.

"She's mine," hisses Torin.

Dread pulses through me as I take stock of the harassment and how they move. Some have long feathers, some short. They are brown or black or russet, with the rare few covered in bright, snow white. Whatever their colour, or however their feathers grow, they are all alike in cruel intention. Their faces twist in anger, their talons, which are longer than my hand, glint in the moonlight, deadly and fearsome. With the torso and face of the most beautiful female and lower bodies stolen from the largest of eagles, the harpies are creatures that clawed from the deepest pits of the underworld.

I am inexperienced with war and battle, which is likely why there is no formation that I can detect. While the harpies circle and dip and dive, they do not do it in any kind of planned order. Everything is chaotic, from the dreadful screeches to the plummeting creatures intent on destroying us.

Vander slides his axe from the holster at his hip, gripping it tight with one hand while the fingers of his other splay wide to create a churning vortex of air.

Beside him, Torin unsheathes both short swords. "Bring it on, you poor excuses for females."

Zentha and Elmon urge Kyra to fold home to Warakoris before bringing orbs of glistening water to their palms. The cool caress of their spirit magic thrums through the clearing.

Jonik, Larrad, and Tasar dash into their cabins, returning with long swords, the curve of which threatens to sever limbs and wings. Jonik urges Leilani to run, to flee to their palace home, never taking his eyes from the nearing harassment while he speaks the words in a rush.

Ruith does not tell Uma to leave. She does so of her own accord after wishing us well and sending a prayer to the Mother Star. The worry smooths from Ruith's brow the moment his mate folds from the clearing, and he grips the hilt of his sword — a style I do not often see in Radelea, with the double-edged blade forming a kind of hooked trumpet at the tip — with so much force, his knuckles turn white.

Noticing my appraisal of his weapon, he says, "A Konda blade. I will have one made for you, should you wish it?"

"It's not to my taste, but thank you for the offer, Father." Even if it were to my taste, I doubt I would have the strength to lift the colossal weapon.

He dips his chin at my use of the title and turns back to the harpies, now so close I can count their feathers. Beside him, Tarathiel and Vacon wield similar blades, the males' arms grazing one another in a last wish for luck.

Nyana, Argi, Darcel, and Imala do not wield swords, but snaking vines and razor-sharp leaves the size of a small shield. Nyana has tied her long, red curls back, and the change in her stature is alarming. Gone is the flirtatious High Lady, replaced by a deadly warrior.

I may have underestimated her.

"They will dive and retreat," says Nyana. "After a time, some will land and slash with their talons. Tasar, protecting Larrad will be your ruin. He will be fine without your interference."

Tasar's bronze skin pales.

Larrad puffs his chest, proud to hear he will walk away from this battle with his life.

"Why are they waiting?" asks Zentha. "Why taunt us from above?"

"I don't know," I murmur. I am the only one to respond, the others choosing to adjust their holds on their weapons instead.

But Vander, he sends the vortex of wind he has been holding straight for the circling harpies, sending them screeching and scattering across the onyx sky. The stars have already begun to retreat, signalling the start of another day of darkness, and I wonder, briefly, when I will ever sleep again.

Something tells me this is just the beginning of our battles. But one of many that are sure to tear our souls in two and fracture what hope remains in our hearts.

Tasar follows Vander's lead by sending two orbs of bright golden light into the air. It grows larger and larger the higher it travels before exploding into thousands of glittering specks that blind the enraged harpies. It is enough to put a stop to the taunting.

The beast with the missing talon lets loose an ear-splitting scream, then tucks her wings tight at her sides and dives for Vander.

I pay no mind to the duel he is about to be locked in, instead twisting to my right to await a plummeting creature, its amber eyes locked on me. Habit has one of my legs sliding backwards to act as an anchor, the other remaining loose and ready to pivot if needed. I tighten my grip on the dagger and rip open the hatch that secures my magic.

My signature bursts forth in a clash of blades, the growl of a feral beast, and the cold lick of shadow as darkness envelops my free hand. Ice crystals crack and spread through the Winter shadows of their own accord, a far cry from the frost that would not leave my fingertips mere moons ago. Blending the two magics together in such a way feels natural, as if they go hand-in-hand.

The harpy screeches and extends her scaled legs, both sets of the deadly claws aiming for the hand in which I hold the dagger.

I feign to the right, whipping my hand out and using her intense concentration on my blade to distract. When the beast moves to snatch the weapon from my grip, I send a blast of ice-riddled shadow at her face, blinding her instantly. A twist back around, and my blade slices through her wing, rendering it useless.

There is no time to ensure she does not return to the skies, not with another harpy careening towards me from above. I wrap a ribbon of metal bending magic around my blade and launch it at the beast's heart, ripping it back out in the same heartbeat. The dagger is back in my hand before the sickening crunch of the harpy hitting land reaches my pointed ears.

To my right, the Dawn males blind with magic and slash with swords, working in a triangle with their backs to one another. They are a unit. A team. They do not need help.

Beyond them, Nyana and her lovers fight with vines and leaves and bursts of suffocating pollen, also defending themselves with ease.

Ruith, Tarathiel, and Vacon move with a grace seldom seen among males. They move as if in a dance, their Kondas slicing through feather and claw as they twirl.

To my left, Torin dips and weaves between two harpies, his short swords showing no mercy. He blurs at the edges at times. His speed is a true marvel.

Beside his second, and working with him to cut through the creatures, Vander wields dense air shaped into spears. His axe hangs from his hip now — the proximity needed to wield such a weapon has put him at a disadvantage for the first time — and his daggers remain sheathed all over his body.

I turn just in time to send a blast of cold-infused shadow at a descending harpy, sending the vile creature tumbling across the clearing. Another is on me before I can recoup, gripping my shoulder with its deadly long talons and lifting me into the air. My scream follows me into the sky, piercing and shrill.

Flailing does little to help. My dagger meets thin air when I attempt to slash at the claws imbedded in my flesh. I tease ribbons of ice magic from the hatch in my mind and send them to my palms with desperation. Gooseflesh races after the magic, prickling the hairs of my arms as my fingers grow numb.

I slam my frost-covered hand against the harpy's foot, ignoring her wail of pain, and hold tight. Ice spreads from my palm and fingers to the rough scales, where it climbs the creature's leg and freezes the feathers once it meets flesh.

The claws retract, and I hurtle to the ground.

"Vander!"

"Cover me, Torin!" he shouts above the clashing of swords and talons.

His alarm prickles along the bond a mere heartbeat before dense air cocoons me. I slow to a liveable pace should I collide with the ground, then slow further until I am hovering above the grass.

"Blessed Mother Star," I huff as he releases me and I land in a crouch. My breaths come in ragged pants, and I hiss in pain when I probe my shoulder with my free hand.

Another is on me before I can so much as wince a second time, another set of talons threatening to slice me from head to toe. I twist out of harm's way just in time, and a scaled claw slams into the grass.

I whip towards it, my arm flinging out in an arc and my dagger slicing clean across the joint.

She screams with such force my ears ring. Her russet wing grazes the top of my head when she retreats into the sky, leaving her severed claw behind.

I leap to my feet and wildly look around the clearing. Vander holds one beast back with a wall of impenetrable air while slashing at another with his axe. Torin is in a similar predicament beside him, both short swords glinting as he wields them with expert precision.

From the corner of my eye, I spot a shimmer of ebony hair disappearing behind the cabins. In the mayhem, I had forgotten she remained hidden. I cast another glance at Vander, torn between helping him and chasing Wyn.

"Go!" shouts Zentha, her golden-brown eyes focused on Vander. "They will be fine."

With a growl of frustration, I turn my back on Van and chase after his sister, slipping into the cabin's shadow and hurtling across the soft grass. Her hair, though as dark as night, gleams like a beacon, as if urging me to move faster.

I chase her along the rear length of the cabins, keeping my feet light so she does not startle and attack. We turn north at the last structure and ascend the mountain, racing through a grove of maples and over jagged grey rock before coming to a second clearing, where a lone harpy with midnight black wings awaits. A silver chain hangs from a collar around her neck, like the leashes we use on hunting hounds.

My best friend in the entire realm, the female I learned to rely on and confide in, does not hesitate as she rushes for the creature. The sting of betrayal that stabs into my heart brings me to my knees.

"Wyn." My voice cracks on that one word, that lone syllable.

She spares me a glance over her shoulder without breaking stride. There is no apology there. No remorse. She wraps her hand around the dangling chain and clambers onto the creature's back in one swift movement, bracing her knees in the divots of the wings. She casts one last silver-eyed look over the small clearing, her eyes tracking to the larger space lower down the mountain, where her brother and friends battle, then smacks her hand against the harpy's side in some kind of signal.

The creature screeches before hunching her legs and leaping into the circling fray above, taking Wyn with it to the Mother Star knows where.

From below, the rest of the harpies shoot into the sky one by one, the beat of their wings cracking across the mountainous landscape like claps of thunder. They bank west before straightening and following in the path of who can only be their leader. And on that leader's back, is Wyn.

"It was a distraction." I fist my hands in my hair, careful of the dagger still gripped in my hand, and watch Wyn disappear into the darkness.

Chapter 16

I DO NOT MOVE for some time. It could be mere heartbeats that I kneel on the ground with aching knees, a throbbing shoulder, and my fists twisted into my hair. It could be days I watch the western horizon, unblinking. Though the view of the Court of Blooms, far in the distance and surrounded by fields of wild flowers, is hindered by a moss-covered mountain, I know the harpies flew in that direction, and I refuse to take my eyes off the dark sky until I am certain Wyn isn't coming back.

Vander calls for me through our bond a few times, and each time, I struggle to keep my inner voice steady enough to tell him I'll return to the larger clearing soon. He does not question me, but his worry pierces through my heartache, deepening the sorrow.

My heart slows to a steady beat, my breaths even out to a slow rise and fall, the stars disappear entirely, and I can no longer deny the truth. Wyn has gone. She fled on the back of a harpy.

I allow my hands to fall to my sides. My fingers prickle with the return of blood flow as I push my fists into the grass and heave to my feet. The move sends stabs of pain through my shoulder that have me wincing. I sheathe my blade and cradle my injured arm with my free hand, then turn my back on that western horizon.

I turn my back on the hope Wyn will return.

An ice-cold anger builds within me. It feeds on my energy like a tsunami pulling every drop of water into its destructive wave, ready and waiting to crash over the land, laying waste to whatever is foolish enough to step into its path. I contain it for now, pushing the wrath to the back of my mind and using it to fuel my exhausted steps rather than letting it rule me, as I have been since the Gloom.

As I draw closer to the larger clearing, passing still maples and inhaling the delicate scent of Dawn's nature, voices pierce through the fog of despair threatening to pull me under.

"It's Wyn," Torin says, and I imagine him shoving a hand into his long blonde hair and looking at Vander with wide eyes. "She's gone."

Vander answers as I round the cabins, the small group coming into view at last. "What do you mean, she's gone?" His tone is low and deadly, laced with the protective instinct of a loving sibling. His hands ball into fists, the right twitching towards the axe at his side. Through the bond, his self-hatred and frustration crash through the last remnants of adrenaline.

I send delicate pulses of reassurance back. Yes, he could have listened and left Wyn back in the Dusk Court, but dwelling on mistakes and oversights does not help anyone. All we can do now is work to find her.

"I mean, she's not here," says Torin. "She must have slipped away while we were distracted with the harpies."

Vander closes his eyes and takes several deep, slow breaths. When he is certain he will not sever Torin's head from his body, he says, "Follow the memories of the cabins. If she folded away, trace the magic. Bria and I will go to the manor. She has to return at some point, and I'm low on blades. I want to be prepared in case they attack again."

Torin presses his palms against the mahogany timber of the cabin he was supposed to share with Wyn, closes his eyes, and cocks his head to the side. He frowns, the expression creating a deep groove across his brow.

"We can help," offers Tasar and Larrad, speaking as one.

Larrad adds, "We know this court better than anyone. If she remains in Dawn, we will find her. You have our word."

"She is not here." My voice cracks through the whisper, as if it, too, is unwilling to voice this betrayal out loud. I move beside Vander and take his hand, my thumb caressing the calloused skin. "She is not in Dawn," I say, louder this time.

"Where is she, then?" Vander's eyes narrow at the blood dribbling from the wound on my shoulder. *"You're injured?"*

"I'm fine. I'll ask Jonik to heal me in a moment." To everyone else, I say, "I saw her sneak from the cabin during the battle. I followed her. She met a black harpy at a higher clearing and climbed upon its back. They flew west."

"Maude's control over Wynetta is growing stronger," says Zentha. "Her spirit rebels against the intrusion, but Maude is too strong."

"Jonik," Vander calls, urging him closer with a crook of a tawny finger.

Jonik, who was kneeling beside Argi and healing a wound on his thigh — Argi's green skin is a sickly pale, his bark-like fingers shaking — uncurls to his feet and shuffles closer. He is unharmed, but it is clear exhaustion weighs him down.

It weighs us all down.

"Are you hurt?" he asks me, brushing a loose strand of long, dark hair from his face with his forearm.

"It's my shoulder."

Vander refuses to let go of me, even for a moment, while Jonik cradles my shoulder with both hands, the bright white of his healing magic glowing through his tan fingers and seeping into the four punctures in my flesh. Tingles spread from the contact, knitting muscle back together and repairing all damage.

When I am healed, Jonik steps back and says, "We can fold to my palace and recoup. I doubt this is the last attack we will endure."

Before Vander or any of the other High fae can agree, a Dawn male appears in the middle of the clearing, followed almost immediately by messengers from Day, Spring, and Winter. They speak as a group, all calling for their High Lord or Lady.

Merging with the clamour of voices, a gust of wind carrying a demand from Alizeh, a plea for us to return home. She warns that what remains of our western village is under attack.

Jonik asks the messengers to speak one at a time. I'm horrified to hear them all repeat the same thing.

A village under attack in Dusk.

Apricity, the cliff-top city in Winter, under siege.

A field of precious wild flowers burns in Spring's south, threatening to destroy Nyana's trade prospects.

The merfolk have surfaced from Dawn's lake to protect the palace from a harassment of harpies.

The spirits of Warakoris, Zentha's palace in Day, scream in agony as the remnants of their minds suffer under the hands of Night fae.

Wyn's fleeing cannot be a coincidence. Five courts are under attack, all by the Night Court, if word is to be believed. With Wyn's mind under Maude's control, I find it difficult to believe it a coincidence that she chose now to attack.

The wrath I have learned to suppress bursts forth. Tongues of shadow whip from my palms and steal what light the few fae lights offer. My shadows blanket the cabins, obscure the sight of every fae, and plunge us into impenetrable onyx.

Gasps of surprise and shouts of alarm float through the darkness. I cannot trace their owner or place their location. The grunting of invisible boars fills our ears, the bitter cold of the Bolbala Ranges numbs our fingers, and the tang of rust coats our tongues. All elements of my magical signature, all proof of my loss of control.

"Breathe." The reminder crashes through my skull. *"Focus."*

My breath rattles as I fill my lungs and hold it there. I count to ten, then release the pent up energy while sucking the shadows of Winter back into my palms. "I am so sorry for losing control."

Vander says, "You reeled it in, Princess."

I may have regained control of my magic this time, but something within me warns I may not be so lucky if this happens again. I cannot keep losing control, cannot keep allowing the rage to affect me so.

One by one, our friends and allies fold away from the mountain clearing. Nyana and her trio of lovers do not so much as bid us farewell when they leave for the Court of Blooms.

Zentha and Elmon leave next, determined to save the spirits who frequent their island home from the torturous hands of Night.

Jonik and his sons follow soon after, orbs of blazing light already glowing in their palms.

Ruith, Tarathiel, and Vacon wish us luck before folding to the bustling city of Apricity to defend the fae who live and trade there.

And we are alone.

Torin swears under his breath. "This was a distraction. Something to keep us occupied while Maude snuck into our homes."

I cannot make sense of it. Why would she attack five courts at once? It is clear Wyn has informed her of the meeting we organised, and Maude is using our absence to her advantage, but there has to be something she can gain from this, something worth angering a powerful alliance.

Torin and Vander argue over which avenue to pursue — Vander wants to defend the village, and Torin thinks we are better suited to finding Wyn — but all I can do is curl my hands into tight fists.

Maude granted us permission to enter her court and collect a talon from a live harpy. She knew *why* we needed the talon, and still, she allowed us entry. Mere moons after we placed the relic that enhanced our wards, Nyree and her Ill-fated followers attacked, fighting to claim it for themselves. When they failed,

Maude sent her army to Dusk, and we fought through the Gloom.

That same harpy being here tonight is telling. It is a threat and taunt. It is a mocking message that Night is everywhere, that they control everything.

I shut my thoughts down before Vander can suspect anything and say, "I will find Wyn while you two protect the village. We can't keep rebuilding."

"Are you sure?" His silver eyes shimmer in the moonlight.

"As much as I would like to fight alongside you and protect our denizens, we can't trust Wyn. We must detain her before she feeds Maude more information. It is all that makes sense."

"What do you mean?" Torin collects his short sword from the ground and slides it onto his back.

I arch a brow. "Maude would only attack five courts at once if she was sure each ruler was distracted. Wyn told her we were here, she urged her to send the harpies."

"Fuck." Torin shakes his head. "This is getting more complicated every damn day. I don't even have the energy to joke about Wyn being a snitch."

Vander growls.

Torin raises both palms. "Sorry, Van. But you know me. Humour is my coping mechanism. It'd be yours too if your mother was as deranged as mine."

"Go," I urge Vander, turning to him and pressing a soft kiss to his lips. I linger there, pushing as much love and assurance as I can into the miniscule point of contact. Mentally, I add, *"Be safe."*

"Find her, Bria. I'm counting on you."

Without peeling my lips away from Vander's, I wrap the magic of the realm around me and fold the Dusk Court closer. I lift my foot from the soft grass of the Dawn mountains, and step onto the cool sand of a familiar and comforting shore.

Sweet lavender and zesty orange surround me, melding with the comforting brine of the ocean. There was once a time when I thought sinking beneath the water's surface and filling my lungs with its salty rush would ease my troubles. I have never had more appreciation for fighting that demon.

Life was bleak then. I had just escaped Ad'Starrag with my life, Summer's selkies were hurtling towards me, and I could not see past the crimson that stained my hands and haunted my soul. I could not see the colours of life. The grey in between. The love.

I trail my fingers through the needle-thin leaves of the she-oaks as I walk through the forest towards the manor. The sense of calm that floods through me from the touch of nature soothes away the last remnants of panic, inviting clarity to my thoughts.

If Maude is indeed after the relic that strengthens our wards, and in turn, protects Earth and the ungrateful humans living there, it is imperative I stop Wyn. Not knowing how long she has been in Dusk — given I am uneducated in how fast a harpy can fly — puts me several steps behind, and I will have to retrace steps to the lone mountain ash tree in the centre of our court, hopefully meeting Wyn along the way.

The sound of a distant battle brings a sheen of sweat to my brow. Images of the Gloom try to overwhelm me, the sounds merging with those etched into my memory. The reverberating clang of swords, the screams, the chaos.

I snag a branch from the nearest she-oak tree and hold it close to my chest, inhaling the subtle scent it emits. I would very much like to race to the western village and blanket the entire space with my shadows, giving the Dusk fae the upper hand, but Wyn needs me. Vander needs me to find her. If she is doing what I fear, then everyone is relying on me. I cannot let them down.

The manor is silent when I reach the base of the hill it rests on. Given the darkness ruling the land, I am unaware if it is dusk or dawn or noontime. The fading of the stars and the aches in my body suggest it sometime in the early morning, which would explain the eerie quiet.

But I know better. The sound of battle still rages from the village. Every fae willing and able to fight would be there, defending their homes and businesses and court. Alizeh is likely cackling while blazing across the village square, feeding off the residual energy, energy that creates a low-hanging haze.

"Is it as bad as we feared?" I ask as I enter the manor and climb the spiralling staircase to our apartment on the third floor.

"No. It won't take us long to rid the court of the Night fae. It's a distraction." He pauses for a moment, a sting of pain flickering along our bond. *"We have to figure out Maude's plan. Why is she trying to keep us occupied?"*

I do not say the words out loud, but all I can think of is the relic. My stomach clenches with the need to hurry. I don't want to miss anything, though, so I take careful steps as I enter Wyn's chambers.

Empty.

Lifeless.

Stale.

She has not slept in the bed. The armoire in the corner sits in silence. The curtains are drawn, shutting out the eastern view. But on the small table beside her bed lies a black device I have only seen one time — during our visit to Earth, hanging from the hip of a human police officer.

"Mother Star," I breathe. "Why does she have a gun?"

All sense of calm and restraint flees my exhausted body. I turn and sprint for the stairs. Wyn has a gun. *She* killed Erthana. She will kill more with the horrid weapon if we give her the freedom to do so.

I cannot allow her to take the relic, leaving Earth vulnerable. If she takes it, she will enter Earth and claim more weapons for herself, for the Night Court. She'll give them to Maude, who will use them against us.

Bile coats my tongue as I call for Vander and tell him what I found and what I fear. He's furious, of course. His anger builds when I say, *"I'm going to the mountain ash. I have to know for certain if she took the relic."*

"Don't you dare go there alone," he growls.

"There's no time to wait for backup." I dart through the open doors of the manor and into the calm darkness. Turning east, I take the rarely used path to the centre of the island and push my legs harder. *"If she pushes her magic into the tree..."*

"Go. I'll be there as soon as I can."

I do not need his permission, but knowing I have it gives me the confidence I need to push myself harder. My satin slippers are more of a hinderance than anything, and I waste precious time stopping to tear them from my feet before racing towards the middle of the island once more.

Chapter 17

T HE TREE LOOMS AHEAD, nothing but a clawing figure of obsidian in the dark. Towering over any building or tree in Radelea, the mountain ash marks the centre of everything. Perhaps that is why it holds so much power.

Ahead, a blur of shadow comes to a stop at the wide base. It is difficult to determine who it is from here, but it can be none other than Wyn. She presses her palms to the peeling bark of the trunk and bows her head.

I am left with no choice but to attack. I do not think of the consequences when I rip open the hatch in my mind and send a blast of shadow towards her. A slither of ice magic bursts free, entwining with my shadows and twisting around the darkness like a snake as my magic hurtles for Wyn's back.

It hits her with so much force she slams into the mountain ash. The crack of bone shattering echoes across the land, drowning out the harsh breaths tearing from my throat.

She turns, too slowly to be natural, and snarls. "I have waited many a moon to face you, Bria of Autumn."

I ignore the taunt in her tone, knowing it is not she who speaks, but Maude. My steps are careful as I move closer. My bare feet offer a soundless advance, though it does me little good with Maude watching my every move through Wyn's silver eyes.

Behind her — it will be difficult to remember this is not Wyn, but a demented High Lady intent on tearing the realm into a thousand pieces — snakes of golden power slither from the hollow in the mountain ash. That she has fed her power into the tree is concerning, but I have no time to wonder about the consequences.

There is no sense in responding to her statement. What do I say in return, anyway? Instead, I ask, "Why?"

She wipes blood from her upper lip with a thumb, then clasps her hands behind her back and echoes, "Why?"

"Why are you doing this?" I continue to move closer, my emerald eyes assessing the lack of weapons strapped to her body and the absence of the typical four guards patrolling this area. "Why spend so much time and energy fighting the rest of us? Why bring war to our realm?"

She seems almost giddy to be asked, as if she has waited decades to answer the question. "My heart beats in time with the drums of vengeance. My fists pound against that drum, their fury calling justice to our lands. And my soul, patient and wise, will not rest until the last dreadful beat."

My head throbs at her admission, my tired thoughts unable to decipher her words. My toes scrape against the still blades of grass as I take yet another step closer. Four long swords of distance is all that separates us, a small expanse of green that does not offer safety. My fingers twitch towards the blade at my thigh, and I force them to still. *Not yet,* I tell myself. First, I must understand why.

"None have heard the war drums since the civil war between Day and Dawn. You speak in riddles, hoping to delay and confuse." I take another step, and this time, she smiles. Even with ice crackling at my palms, spreading through my veins, and sending a shiver of fear dancing down my spine, I do not waver. "Your tactics will not work on me."

"Darling, they already have."

The throbbing in my skull explodes into a searing agony that threatens to split me in two. I fall to my knees, my hands flying to my head and clamping tight. A scream so chilling it scares the birds from their trees rips from my lungs and contorts my face. I slam my eyes closed, but not before watching Maude snatch the relic from within the mountain ash's hollow and sliding it into a small pouch hanging from the hip of Wyn's leathers. She pulls the drawstring tight, cinching the fabric closed.

The grating crack of the wards' faltering magic rings throughout Dusk. It booms in an endless explosion, with showers of golden flecks scattering across the sky before falling over the land and flickering from existence. Flashes of the brightest white race along the eight arcs that join the tree with the remaining ward stones, fracturing the connection as they fade from existence.

"Bria?" Vander calls in my mind. *"Why did our wards fail? What's happening?"*

I cannot risk splitting my focus to respond. If I do, I risk giving Maude full access to my mind. Only the Mother Star knows what damage she could do to the sacred bond Vander and I share. It is not something I will ever sacrifice, no matter the consequence.

She saunters closer with her head cocked to the side and a cruel smile twisting Wyn's full lips. "I did not expect the mind of a bastard to be strong, but this is beyond my expectations. Your brother fought much harder. Such a magnificent specimen, Rennyn. *You*, on the other hand, are weak. Worthless."

The pain expands, spreading to my limbs like a raging wildfire, intent on destroying everything in its path. My arms twist towards my stomach and my legs lock. The screams pulling at my throat fade to whimpers as my fingers knot in my hair, pulling a few strands free from my scalp.

She clicks her tongue and turns to greet four guards as they fold onto the grass before the mountain ash. She unties the pouch from her hip and hands it to a burly male, then orders him to return to the Night Islands at once. "I will join you in a moment," she adds, peering at me over her shoulder.

"I shall remain behind," says a second guard, "to protect you."

Maude whips her face toward him. "Leave. Question me again, Rydel, and you will not live to see the Mother Star rise when this is over."

"Yes, My Lady. Apologies, My Lady."

I pant through the agony tearing through my body and take hold of the only thing I can: the bond I share with Vander. The glowing thread connecting my mind with his hums as I wrap myself around it. It centres me. Grounds me. It gives me something other than the pain to focus on.

He responds in the only way he can, by sending pulses of strength and urgency back towards me. He's coming for me.

And though he is coming fast, I know he will not be here in time to capture Wyn. He cannot save her.

The guards race away, fleeing to secure the relic somewhere within their court, making the Night Islands impossible to invade. I pray to whatever remains of the Mother Star's grace that Maude is unaware of the relic's additional power... But she had Wyn's hands pressed against the bark.

My moans twist into a cry.

She knows how to use the relic to torture any unwanted visitors to her lands.

The guards have run for the beach, where they will fold to Night. Vander will not make it in time. Torin is fighting the Night fae in the village. It is just Maude and Wyn and me now.

I look up into her moon silver eyes as Maude forces her closer. It is debilitating to kneel before her and see the hatred staining her soft face. Pain cracks through my heart, not from the blood and bone magic Maude is using to shred my insides, but from the pure, agonising heartache at seeing my friend like this.

Tears prick at the edges of my eyes. "Wyn," I croak, forcing her name through the lump of emotion clogging my throat, "if you're in there, you have to fight. I know it's hard, and I know it hurts, but you have to fight. You have to."

Something flickers over her features, something akin to recognition and kindness and sorrow. Her steps falter. Her hand twitches.

I push harder. "We all love you, no matter what that bitch has made you do. We love you, and we miss you. Come back to us. *Fight!* You have strength enough for this battle."

Her feet skid across the grass as she fights Maude's control. Her hands grope her head and she falls to her knees. My best friend now a mirror of myself. She screams. The sound is heart-wrenching. It is ravaged. Pained.

"Keep fighting," I urge, as the agony coursing through me lessens enough that I can crawl closer. "Push, Wyn. I am here, and I love you. It's okay. You're okay. Vander is coming."

"I can't!" she shouts before screaming into the sky. Her hands move to her eyes, blocking out the word, and likely every horrific memory since the Gloom.

But she does not realise she just did, for that was *her* voice tainted with tortured agony. I take a tremendous risk and wrap my fingers around Wyn's wrists, pulling them away from her face. "You can. You did."

Her silver eyes spring open.

"You're back," I whisper. My tears fall free, tracking through the blood and dirt caked on my cheeks and falling to the grass beneath my knees.

Wyn tears her wrist from my grip, and I worry Maude has returned, but instead of channelling the High Lady of Night's mind control or blood magic, she throws her arms around me. Her body heaves with sobs. She shakes with such violence I fear for her bones.

I wrap my arms around her, holding her tight and whispering in her ear, "It's okay. You're okay. I'm here." Over and over, I whisper the same words until her sobs ease.

Perhaps we are reckless in wasting precious time. Perhaps we should plan or fight. But comforting her is too important. The demons that must be tormenting her mind... The red staining her hands... I force the thought away, determined to remain well away from that pit of despair. The red, it only haunts me while I slumber now. I am determined to keep it that way.

"She's fighting me," she whimpers.

I am not surprised by her admission. Maude is not the type of fae to relent. She will hammer against the shields in Wyn's mind until Wyn loses the internal battle.

I test the bond, feeling Vander's emotions and determining if he still battles in the western village.

He responds to my probing with, *"I'm almost there, Princess. Hold on."*

"She's back," I whisper through the bond in reply. *"I don't know how long we have until Maude regains control, but it's Wyn. It's truly her."*

"Don't let her leave!"

I pull away from Wyn, but keep my hands on her upper arms. While I need the contact to know she is really here, I'm also scared of what will happen once Maude takes over. "Are you okay?"

She shakes her head and takes a shuddering breath. "I... No." She turns her face to the west, towards home. "I don't know if I can keep fighting."

"Shield your mind. Torin says an imaginary wall of atryxium is the best defence." I cannot use the strongest steel in Radelea in my mind. My metal bending magic bucks and thrashes against the intrusion whenever I try to envision such a thing.

It might not be good advice. I amend. "If you're strong enough to illusion yourself in and out of Ad'Starrag, risking the wrath of Tohminic and Xaler, then you're strong enough to keep fighting. I believe in you. I believe you can do this. Maybe you won't succeed today. Perhaps you will fail tomorrow. But you *will* overcome this."

She nods, though her gaze remains on the west. "Thank you. I needed to hear that." The tone of her voice, so despaired and so unlike the Wyn I know, betrays her doubt.

"Look at me."

She closes her eyes, another shuddering breath slipping past her lips.

"Wyn."

She sighs, turning her face to me at last.

"We might not have much time, so it's imperative you listen." I wait for her to dip her chin in acknowledgement before saying, "You. Can. Do. This. Tohminic found sanctuary from her through the shadows of Winter. She could not pierce the darkness, because she could not find him. I will veil you. I will *protect* you. You can count on me." I would do it now, but I would prefer she gives permission first. Living within the shadows is not something to take lightly.

Tears shimmer in her eyes, building before falling free. It is the first time I have seen Wyn cry. The first time she has lost control of her emotions in such a way. It makes my heart clench with anger and hatred and sadness.

"She won't stop," she whispers. Her bottom lip trembles. "She won't stop until we pay for what we did."

"I don't understand. What did we do?"

She jerks violently, crying for the Mother Star to have mercy. She twists from my grip and leaps to her feet, grasping the sides of her head once more. And I know. I know we are almost out of time.

"Hurry, Van. She's losing the battle."

He does not respond, but I feel him push himself harder. So hard, in fact, I fear he is nearing his limit. Pushing himself any further will cause a magical burnout. Penna will be furious.

"No!" She slams a hand against her head. "Not yet."

I scramble to my feet and cup her face. "Look into my eyes." She does, though hers are lined with tears. "Remember when we met? I was soaking wet after begging Nikolai to flee the court with me. You listened to my story. You were the first to do so. Then you told me about the Dusk Court. Of course, I thought you delusional, but you were so adamant, so filled with courage and confidence, that I could only believe you."

Her lips curl upwards for the first time since the Gloom.

"You gave me hope. After five and seventy years of bearing my jaded crown, I had *hope*. Through the darkness that was my life, I could see specks of light. They grew brighter from there. You, Vander, Torin, you all brought light to my life."

"I still find it hilarious how you thought yourself so defiant. Bria of Autumn would be aghast to hear of Bria of Dusk's adventures." She opens her mouth to say more, but hurried footsteps from the west interrupt her.

I know Vander is close. So close we can hear him. And I am so thankful he has made it in time.

Hope of the siblings reuniting bursts faster than it bloomed. The distraction was too much for Wyn. She staggers backwards with a cry of pain. "I can't hold her back. She's breaking through. I... No. No, I can't!" She thrashes while standing, her tawny hands clamped to her skull. She moves as if fighting to free her head of a heavy crown that is permanently welded to her skull.

The hairs on my nape prickle in warning, and I take a step back. Alarm bells peel in my mind, an urgent chime screaming that this is it. This is where Maude regains control. I grope for my shadows, sloppy in my urgency, and bring the darkness to my palms. They curl around my fingers and stretch towards Wyn in a net-like formation. I have to veil her. Now.

Permission be damned.

She straightens. "I hope you enjoyed your conversation. It is the last you will have with the High Lord's sister."

I am too late.

My entire body cripples. Pain like nothing I have ever endured tears through me, ripping and shredding and deforming. A finger shatters. My right femur snaps in two. Scorching blood rushes to my head, bringing flashes of red and black to my vision.

"Vander!" Instinct has me screaming for him with such a desperate plea, the sound will haunt my nightmares right alongside the red.

Wyn's form turns hazy when Maude wraps the realm's magic around her, able to use Wyn's Dusk heritage to fold now the wards are not as strong. She offers one last smirk, one last shattered bone — this time my left ankle — before folding away from Dusk. Folding away from me.

Oblivion claims me within the same heartbeat, and I sag to the ground, knowing nothing but pain and darkness and Vander's panicked shout.

Chapter 18

I THINK I DREAM. Or it could be a memory. My unconscious mind tries desperately to show me a gusty mountaintop shrouded in mist, but the moment the image forms, it slips from my grasp. During the brief flashes of memory or dream, there is no pain. There is no heartache or anger.

Sometimes I believe it is a shame our fae bodies heal with such rapidity. This is one of those instances.

The oblivion lifts with a sudden rush of cool air; the wind brings pure agony with its delicate caress. I am distantly aware of an uncomfortable throb in my shoulder, though that pain is miniscule compared to the burning torture of my legs and finger. And those flares of pain spreading through my body, they are nothing, *nothing*, compared to the crevasse fracturing my heart.

"Open your eyes, Princess." Vander's urgency is unmistakable.

I would obey only for him. My eyelids protest the movement, but I force them open, my gaze colliding with wide silver eyes.

I bite down a whimper and say, "I am sorry. I am so sorry I failed." Tears fall unbidden from the corners of my eyes.

I failed *everyone*.

"It's not your fault." There is frustration in his tone, but there's kindness, too. "Let's get you to Penna. Can you walk?"

"I doubt it. She broke my leg, ankle, and finger. Although, the latter will do little to aid in walking." I marvel at the strange words coming from my mouth and wonder if the pain is making me delirious. Perhaps my mind is not quite my own.

He frowns. "This might hurt. Brace yourself." He slides one arm around my shoulders and the other beneath my legs.

The pain is instant. It blazes like an undying inferno, scorching my veins and scalding my bones. It sears from ankle to thigh and on to my torso, throbbing and stabbing and forcing a scream from my lungs.

I must lose consciousness again, because the next thing I know, Vander is barging through the doors of the manor. The first time he carried me into our home, I was a broken female with nothing left to lose. Now, I am a strong and courageous warrior with more loved ones than I can count on one hand. Maybe two hands, if I am being honest with myself.

We twist down the curling staircase and burst into the full infirmary. It's full. The last time there were so many fae here was during the Gloom.

"I don't care who you're working on, Penna. Leave them and help us." Vander's tone is laced with an authority he does not often throw at his denizens. He sets me down on the only remaining bed and glares over his shoulder. "Now."

Penna, with her silvery-blue hair and noontime sky eyes, hurries over. She tuts at me with resigned affection. "One day, the Mother Star will bless me with never having to heal you again. What have you done this time?"

"Not me," I grit out through the throbs of pain. "Maude, through Wyn. Leg, ankle, finger."

She feeds me some kind of musk-tasting liquid. "Best you are not awake for this. It is going to hurt."

She hovers her hands over my ankle, the white light of her healing magic emanating from her fingers. The first prickle of pain has me gritting my teeth, but my jaw slackens and my head pushes into the pillow. I do not register the second stab of agony; oblivion claims me.

My bare toes curl over the edge of the cliff, fighting for a purchase they will not find. I stagger backwards. Ferocious winds tear at my knotted gown, the skirts, still tied together from the attack in Dawn, expand and balloon and threaten to lift me into the dark sky.

All around me, there is nothing but glittering mist. Jagged rock scrapes at my feet, though the touch of stone is muted. Soft. The mist forms tiny spirals with every move I make, sometimes clearing enough to reveal the flat apex of the mountain I stand upon.

"How did I get here?" The wind chases my voice into the chasm below, too deep to see the bottom, and I twist to follow the echo of my question as it descends through the blanket of white concealing the view.

"I brought you here."

I spin towards the voice — a voice that sends shivers dancing down my spine — bringing my arms up and crouching into a defensive position. The drop behind me is too large to survive, and now that I am facing the other direction, I can see I stand at the apex of a mountain. It is a flat peak, shaped into a natural crescent of grey rock. The same grey rock I rested upon in the body of an albatross.

Fear flashes through my veins and brings a sheen of sweat to my forehead as I wonder how in the Mother Star's grace I got to the Night Court. It is a concerning turn of events, though less worrisome than the High Lady standing before me.

"Why?" I breathe the lone word aloud, while in my mind I am screaming for Vander, only to be met with a wall of impenetrable obsidian. I cannot reach him through our bond, no matter how hard I slam my thoughts against the shield. It is as if he was never there, as if he does not exist.

But I keep assaulting the wall of black that blocks my mind. I ram it with vulgar curses, spear the shield with prayers to the sun, and scrape my agitated thoughts down its length. I am certain I can demolish the obsidian and contact Vander, and I will continue to attack and claw until I break through.

Maude tuts. "I would not do that if I were you."

"Your word means nothing," I spit at her, then continue slamming against the shield. If she is telling me I should not destroy it, then I will do the opposite. I do not trust a single word she purrs.

"I have a proposition for you." Her blood-red lips curl at the sides more and more with every word. Her ice-blue eyes are stark against her pale skin and seem to glow through the swirling mist.

"There is nothing you can say that I am interested in hearing."

"I beg to differ." Her bright eyes flash with humour. "You know, I thought you were weak when we met in the Dusk Court. You have surprised me with your resilience. Though I am loath to admit it, the way you fought to free Wynetta is admirable."

A crack appears in the obsidian. I ram the wall with my entire mind, and the fracture spreads. It pops and booms as jagged veins of freedom spread along its expanse before the entire thing crumbles and I can feel Vander's soul at last.

Through the fog of healing and potion-induced oblivion, I forget the strange dream. In fact, I do not remember it from the moment I awaken to a frantic Vander demanding an explanation from Penna. Although she is just as confused by my unconscious thrashing and screaming as he is.

With the dream forgotten, and nothing to focus on except healing enough that Penna will release me from the infirmary, I am left with nothing to do except lie in bed and listen to the conversations around the room.

I hear tales of bravery beyond anything I have heard, stories from the fae who were courageous enough to fight in the western village. Many of them sustained vicious wounds, inflicted by the Night fae who foolishly attacked our court, though they are well on the way to healing. I even hear whispers of a messenger from Summer declaring their High Lord a failure; Tohminic will not succeed in reclaiming his throne.

I do not know how long I remain in the infirmary. Time ceases to have meaning while healing. Sometimes I wake and find less fae writhing in pain. Other times, I am pleased to say farewell to the injured, so very glad they have healed enough to return home to their families.

Vander brings me news of Dawn. He says the merfolk had the situation handled before Jonik, Tasar, and Larrad had arrived. The same scenario for Day; Zentha and Elmon were both furious they could not fight for Warakoris, the attack having ceased before they folded onto the docks. Spring and Winter both sustained minimal damage, their respective leaders able to defend their courts with ease.

Everything amounts to one truth: the attacks were a distraction while Maude used Wyn to steal Dusk's relic, and in turn, destroyed our wards. Vander has since replaced the basic magic protecting us, though it is weak in comparison.

He and Torin tried once more to warn the humans and supernaturals of Earth, only to be threatened with an inter-realm war. After everything this court has done and sacrificed for them, it is beyond disheartening to hear of their hatred for the fae. They believe us to be tricksters — Vander only has himself to blame for that, in telling them we cannot lie — and refuse to acknowledge the truth that Maude will come for them if given the chance.

Every piece of knowledge I have involving the war does nothing but feed the wrath bubbling below the surface. Every thought of combat and fear, every injury, and every lost soul... My wrath builds and builds.

In my addled state of healing and anger, I reason that we will have to destroy Maude without aid. Our sacrifices in protecting Earth have been for naught. Our sacrifices in protecting Radelea *will* amount to something. I'll ensure it.

Maude's death will not stain my hands with red, but wash what remains of the crimson from my palms. Her death is the last blood I will spill. And right now, while I am healing from injuries I sustained through her abuse of Wyn, I will be glad to see the red seep from her body and stain the ground.

It is a far cry from the female who shook at the thought of being responsible for ending a life. A far cry from the Bria who thought she could fight in war without killing. But war demands sacrifice. I will sacrifice my morals to end it. And be glad of it.

I spend two moons in the infirmary before Penna declares I am well enough to return home, with a warning to be safe and to continue to rest so I do not overexert myself.

I call for Vander as soon as I am out the doors, and spend the night lost in my love for him. I worship his magnificent body with my hands and my mouth, savouring his taste and committing it to memory.

He ravages my body with kisses and caresses. He brings me to orgasm more times than I can count. In the bed. Against the wall. On the floor. From behind, above, below, and sideways. With his cock or his mouth or his hands, I am delighted to forget the realm around us and spend this day with him, lest a bitter battle falls upon our court and we miss our opportunity to show one another just how deeply our love runs.

We do not leave our bedchamber for an entire day, both of us basking in the rare moment of peace. It is a slither of comfort and bliss in a sea of endless darkness. It is a moment we must take, even with Wyn missing and our court under threat. For if we ignore the need we have for each other, if we only focus on battles and hurt and armies, then Maude wins.

When we surface from bed at last, Vander wastes no time in dragging me to the training field. Apparently, I do not handle combat against two adversaries well, and I am to practice duelling against both him and Torin, much to Torin's delight.

Seven moons later, we find ourselves at the training field once more. I'm tiring of being here every day, but there is little else to do. Our search for Wyn has come up empty, even with Torin following her through the memories of trees and buildings, and we suspect Maude is hiding her in the Night Islands. Our battle plans are set in stone, ready to put into action the moment she makes her next move. All there is to do is train and wait. Wait and train.

And lose myself in Vander, as I do every night.

As Torin loses himself in Alizeh every chance he gets.

As Penna and Xaria lose themselves in one another.

I allow a thought to distract me, the memory of Vander above me, his silver eyes watching me with lust and adoration. The distraction costs me.

Torin jabs the hilt of his short sword into my ribs. "I'd *love* to know where your mind went just now. The look on your face was purely indecent."

I scowl at Torin while rubbing my ribs, sure the resulting bruise will not fade for days.

Vander growls and steps between us, his protective nature thrumming along the bond. "Don't even think about pestering her about it."

Torin throws his hands in the air, smirking. "Oh, I wouldn't dream of it, *My Lord*." He leans around Vander, his smirk growing when he asks me, "Blink once if you were thinking about sex."

I splutter a laugh.

Vander, though, does not see the humour. He lunges for his second, and both males hit the compacted dirt with a thud. They grapple for a moment, both of them grunting but only Torin laughing, before Van has the Wind Whisperer pinned.

"That topic is off limits," Van says.

"Why must you ruin all my fun?" Torin bucks, but he cannot dislodge Vander. "First you tell me I can't sneak into Night to spy, instead sending Alizeh. Then you prohibit me from picking up Wyn's trail. Now you say I can't tease Bria?"

"Her trail is cold." As cold as Vander's voice. He pushes himself up and gracefully leaps to his feet, spinning to face me. "Again."

I groan and bring shadows to my palms. He has me practicing with magic rather than blades, claiming I am better suited to the fighting style. I think he just wants me away from the action —

danger, he calls it — so he knows I'm safe. If I can fight from a distance, there is no chance of injury.

There's also no chance of getting close to Maude.

"No, it isn't." Torin gets to his feet, not bothering to brush the dust from his leathers.

"What do you mean?" Vander asks.

"I mean, I read the memories of Wyn's bedchamber door every morning. She was home last night. Left within the same moment, but home all the same. It's the first time she's been at Dusk Manor since Bria caught her at the mountain ash. Let me follow the lead."

"Why didn't you tell me sooner?"

Torin arches a brow. "I tried. You wouldn't hear it."

"Did she take anything?" Van asks. He does not need to voice his true question; Torin and I both know he's asking if she returned for the gun.

"She took it." Torin's grin is wicked.

Unfortunately for Maude, Vander coated the human weapon with his magic. Magic he can trace, since it is born of his soul.

At long last, we have Wyn in our sights, and this time, she's not getting away.

Chapter 19

V ANDER CLOSES HIS EYES. His brow puckers, his chest rises and falls in a steady rhythm, and wisps of air billow from his palms as he focuses on the small slither of power he imbued the gun with. His lips move of their own accord, stretching around a single word.

"Spring?" I ask, looking at Torin with raised brows.

He ties his long hair back with a length of worn leather. "She said the same thing when she left the manor. Repeated it, as if she knew I'd be tracing the memories of her bedroom."

My eyes widen. "This is intentional. She's leading us to her location."

Vander's voice is an animalistic snarl when he says, "She's in the heart of the Court of Blooms." His tone softens. "Without knowing what we're walking into, I'm hesitant to fold into Spring without weapons. Let's stock up first."

We don't return the metal pipes I was using for training to the field's small wooden storage locker. It will only waste time. But I do collect two of the thinner copper strands and slide them into the holsters on my hips as I dash past. The rest of the metal poles remain scattered over the compacted dirt — the hessian sack they belong in discarded at the side — as we race from the field towards Dusk Manor.

My heart pangs with guilt when we pass the stables. I have neglected my beautiful mare, Solana, these past moons. I know the stable hands are taking excellent care of her, but it is not the same as spending time with her. She must be wondering where I have been, and if I have forgotten her. She does not know or understand war. Any excuse I provide is not good enough. I vow to take the time for a ride after we find Wyn.

It would be good for me, too, to get away for a time. To just enjoy the musky scent of Solana after a hard run and relish in the peace that is riding. Perhaps take her to the apple grove so she may gorge on the fruit.

Vander bursts through the manor doors and leads the way to the terrace level below, where we race along the short hallway and into the weaponry. He barely comes to a stop in front of the wall of daggers before plucking two from their hooks and sliding them in sheathes on his thighs.

I stop beside him, collecting four smaller knives for the sheathes at my ribs and a second, larger blade to match the dagger already on my thigh. Next, I strap leather vambraces to my wrists, while the males find the best swords for their backs. A sense of foreboding floods my body, a realisation that this may be one of many times we suit up for a prospective battle.

In an ideal world, none of us would ever see the sharpened edge of a blade. We would not wear leathers, fearing an attack at any moment, and we certainly would not be apprehensive about entering another court.

We waste no more time and exit the manor within moments. The she-oak forest is dark and silent, as if holding its breath in wait to see if we will capture Wyn. There is not a whisper of wind, not a single chirp of insects or birds.

The sand of the south-eastern shore crunches beneath our feet, soon replaced by billowing grasses of shadow-kissed emerald, purple wildflowers with petals as large as my face, and frantic butterflies searching for an open flower they will not find. With the realm thrown into perpetual night, the flowers in Spring do not spread wide. Many insects and animals are starving without the Mother Star's golden glow.

The butterflies, though beautiful on the outside, are lethal. When provoked, like now when they are on the brink of starvation, they dislodge a fine powder from their wings, a powder with the strength to paralyse.

"Careful of the butterflies," I warn as we pick a path through the long grass.

A familiar forest pierces the horizon ahead, the glittering lake to its right making the edge of Nyana's castle. The last time we were here, we were collecting the abundant blue mock lotus flowers, a bloom with glowing petals that can weaken a fae when prepared correctly. I have experienced the effects myself when Nyree drugged me and left me in the tunnel below Dusk Manor.

We take a wide berth around the blue mocks, treading carefully and pausing every so often to avoid a fluttering ebony and sapphire butterfly, and approach the Spring castle, made of crystal, with too many spires to count reaching for the dark sky. Under the Mother Star's gaze, it would reflect a rainbow of colours. It would be beautiful. Breathtaking.

The closer we walk — we do not dare run, lest we frighten the lethal butterflies — the louder the din of battle becomes. It gets harder to use restraint and not dart through the knee-high grass. The moment we step from the billowing emerald and onto a garden path that leads to the castle, we take off at a run.

The Court of Blooms, beautiful and bright and so lethal it is frightening, has only one city, with Nyana's castle at its centre. We race through the brick-paved streets. Any fae who emerges from their home, we ignore. They ignore us in return, all of them eager to follow us into the heart of the city and help where they can.

When we reach the castle, Vander in the lead with Torin taking up the rear, we do not hesitate to draw our blades. For where there should be thriving gardens and fae flitting in and out of the crystal palace, there are too many Night fae to count, all wielding their signature black blades.

In the heartbeat I take to observe the scene before me, I uncover yet another lie my father has told. The Spring fae do not have red hair. Their hair is rose, marigold, lilac, or a gorgeous lapis lazuli. It is violet or teal or magenta. The only fae with hair resembling mine is Nyana, who fights in the centre of the fray.

For five and seventy years, I believed the lie. I have never been more glad I turned my back on my home court, on my brother and father and everything they represent: the heartache and wrath and bitterness that taints my heart. I do not dwell on the knowledge any longer, but shove it down to assess later, when there are no Night fae torturing Spring denizens. When Wyn is safe.

"Stay by my side, Princess," Vander warns, his voice deepening an octave as his axe collides with the chest of a Night female.

I wreath shadows around my palm, then send them careening across the mayhem, where they wind around the face of a red-skinned male. Crimson skin, with hair and eyes so white they almost glow, is the mark of the most powerful of Night's denizens. The blood wraiths. He is one of Maude's most prized guards. She does not let them off the islands very often.

She must gain something from this. Something she desperately needs.

"Torin!" I shout, then point to the blood wraith.

His eyes track to the shadow-covered male, narrow, then spark with excitement. A heartbeat later, he twists through the battle, cutting through Night fae until he reaches the wraith.

A crack, louder than the closest thunder, shudders through the din.

I whip my eyes to Vander. "Wyn."

Together, we fight our way closer to the palace. We twist and weave, dip and lunge, leap and jab. The scent of blood overrides the sweetness of Spring's blooms. Fear and bile coat my tongue. Flashes of crimson and onyx and every colour of the rainbow flash across my vision as Vander and I move to the heart of the battle. Sweat clings to my skin, dribbling past aching muscles and settling in dips and grooves where it is unwanted.

I fling one of the smaller knives at a male who moves to grab Vander, the blade imbedding in his shoulder. It is concerning to think I once recoiled at the thought of injuring another, yet here I am, slicing and stabbing without remorse. Somewhere along the way, I lost the female I used to be. Bria of old was filled with fear and guilt. Now, I care not that these fae may die. I am changed, and I'm unsure if it's for the better. But it's who I am now. I will not question the will of the Mother Star. Not now. Not after everything.

Hardly any time has passed since the gunshot rung out through the city. And during the moments of combat, I have noticed the Night fae do not wield their blood and bone magic. They don't bother trying to control our minds. They do not so much as injure anyone. Yet again, this is a distraction.

Vander breaks through a line of fae by severing a female's foot from her leg. She tumbles sideways, knocking the guard closest to her down. When the line fractures, we are at last graced with the sight of Wyn.

She stands alone, the lifeless body of a Spring male at her feet seeping blood onto the brick path. Her arms are spread wide, as if she welcomes the destruction before her. But when her silver eyes land on me — I break eye contact for a heartbeat to slash my dagger at a lunging opponent — there is something within them that causes me to pause. For those are tears streaming down her face and apology quivering her lips.

In this moment, with my emerald eyes locked on my best friend while Vander covers me from behind, I understand Wyn's pain. It is a pain I have felt myself, and mere heartbeats ago acknowledged its absence. She does not wish to maim and murder, and doing so is crippling her.

I use the magic from my home court, Autumn, to hurl the two copper rods at Wyn, bending them until they're small circles around her wrists. She does not fight me as I meld them together, locking her arms behind her back. She might be herself right now, though I cannot be certain. Restraining her is a small price to pay; if Maude forces her to inflict more harm, I'm not sure Wyn will come out the other side. It will haunt her until the end of time.

A female with ink-black hair grips my wrist, using my distraction to her advantage.

I use her as an anchor and twist towards her while bringing the bitter cold of Winter to my free hand. My palm slams against her cheek, ice crystals spreading from beneath my fingers across her face.

Her lips turn a sickly blue, frost coats her eyelashes, and she staggers back with an ear-splitting scream.

I turn away to meet the blade of another, and I forget the previous female almost instantly.

Something changes in the Night fae. Many of them whip their faces to the south, satisfied smirks curling their lips before they all turn and run, folding the moment they're free of the wards.

"Harpies," spits Vander. "We should have known and accounted for it. It was clear this was a distraction."

It's seldom I ignore him. But right now, Wyn is more important. I race towards her with my daggers out, ready and willing to defend her against the Spring fae converging at the castle doors, most of them watching Wyn with hatred and distrust.

Torin races towards her from the opposite direction. He mouths, "I've got this," before jerking his chin towards Nyana.

"Get her out." Vander pushes his words to Torin on a gust of air, pulling me to a stop with a hand to my elbow. *"There is more for us to do here."*

"What do you mean? We came here for Wyn."

"They do not understand what just happened. As much as Nyana knows that Maude used this fight as a distraction, she hasn't witnessed the brutality of human weapons before. This might be our only chance to sway her to our side."

I cannot tear my gaze from Wyn, even as Torin reaches her, hauls her over his shoulder, and races back the way we came — towards the blue mock lotus field and the freedom of the wardless plain beyond. Every fibre of my being begs me to follow. My blood hums in my veins, demanding I comfort my friend and ensure her safety. My bones jar with my indecision.

"We need them as an ally, Princess. I'd give anything to go with Torin right now, but duty comes first. Wyn's safe with him."

I relent and allow him to drag me towards Nyana, who is now kneeling beside the only victim Wyn and the Night soldiers left behind.

The bodies of the fae who fell lie broken beyond repair, scattered around the battle site and now ignored, but demand my acknowledgement as we pass them. They did not fight to harm or injure.

We did.

In this, *we* are the monsters. And, surprisingly, I don't mind. It does not bother me that Vander, Torin, and I fought for the Spring fae. It doesn't bring those demons back; the crimson haunting my soul ebbs farther away. But I send a prayer to the

Mother Star for their souls. Their deaths were a waste, a senseless sacrifice on Maude's behalf.

"Well met, Lady Nyana," says Vander, dipping his chin.

"What are you doing here?" She does not take her eyes off the lifeless body before her. "Have you come to gloat?"

I bring my metal bending power to my hands and kneel beside Spring's High Lady, drawing the iron bullet from her denizen's chest. "We are here to beg your alliance." I let the deformed piece of metal hover before her. "I didn't think Maude would target your court, and agreed you were safe in your castle. But she did attack. You may have lost but one of your fae, but one is too many. Side with us. Pledge your allegiance to Dusk, Dawn, Day, and Winter."

She faces me, those bright eyes twisted in anger, and hisses, "You dare you ask this of me *now*, when we are still feeling the ache of battle?"

"I do."

Vander collects the bullet into a pouch and tucks it into the pocket of his leather jacket. "If we don't stop her, she'll lay waste to the entire realm. Did you not realise her harpies flew away with their claws filled with blue mock?"

"How many?" she breathes.

"Ten. They were carrying enough of the plant to incapacitate an army," says Vander. He gestures to the dead fae. "And this... this is just the beginning of the destruction Night can bring to our lands if they get their hands on more human weapons. We're trying our best to keep the portal safe, but we can't be everywhere at once."

"She's already destroyed our stronger wards. Don't let her destroy anything else, I beg of you." My voice is sturdy, concealing the edge of hysteria building inside me at the thought of Night using guns against us in battle.

"Is there nothing we can do?" asks a female standing off to the side. "I saw the weapon used. Is there nothing we can do to prevent such a tragedy?"

"You can ally with us." Vander's tone is growing more frustrated the longer we remain here and not at home with Wyn. "We can bring Maude to her knees. Together."

"As the Mother Star wishes," I say, then explain my theory as to why she abandoned us.

Nyana stands and holds a slim hand out to Vander. "We accept your alliance."

The sighs of the Spring fae surrounding us are unmistakable. They, like us, are relieved their High Lady has agreed to an alliance at last. It is sign enough that the way we select the High fae who lead us is not foolproof. Keeping the title within bloodlines has been our way since the beginning of time. Whether it should always be our way is a problem for another day.

"Come," says Nyana. "Let us discuss the finer details in private."

We follow her into the castle, through an opulent foyer, and into a large throne room at the rear. With the walls made of crystal, offering slices of the gardens beyond, the chamber feels spacious and grand. Two enormous chandeliers hang at either end of the room, their crystal beads catching the glow of the many fae lights hovering overhead. The chandelier farthest from us drapes down and connects with a crystal throne, the ostentatious chair's shape resembling that of the castle — with many spires and reflecting the light.

At noontime, this space would be vibrant; the Mother Star's golden rays would pierce through the crystal walls and create a rainbow of colour over the pure white floor. I wish I could see it like that.

"Is there anything we can do to prevent the effects of the blue mock?" Vander asks once the large oak door swing closed with a thud.

"I am afraid not," says Nyana. "Of course, there are antidotes. But they are only effective *after* a fae has ingested the powder." She does not lower into her designated seat, but leans on the armrest, her ankles crossing. "So, an alliance. What do you need from me? What do I gain from it?"

"We need numbers. The Night Court's power to manipulate blood and bone puts us at a disadvantage. We're hoping to use distractions to our benefit, so they don't have a chance to use their magic," says Vander. "What we want most from you, though, is foresight."

Nyana frees her long curls from their leather bindings, allowing them to cascade over her shoulders. "I figured. I will assign my best seers to the cause."

"Thank you." I pour as much sincerity into the words as I can. "In return, we will station guards around your court. We will offer you protection and sanctuary, should you need it. In return for you fighting alongside us, we rid Radelea of evil and encourage the Mother Star's return."

"Her return is not guaranteed."

"No. It's not. But she first rose after the ancient treaty was signed. She'll rise again when we sign a new one," says Vander. "Bria has spent many a moon researching. We are confident in this theory."

I add, "She wants us all to work together. I'm sure of it."

"It is a good theory," says Nyana. She smooths the freckled skin of her brow with her thumb and forefinger. "I will research myself, of course, but what you say makes sense."

"You're still willing to join this alliance?" Vander's impatience is clear in his tone; his need to see Wyn for himself burns strong along our bond.

"I am. Give me two days. When the moon sets on the second day, I will come to you with whatever we discover in our visions." She turns towards a hidden door on the side wall and beckons someone closer.

It is as clear a dismissal as we will get.

Chapter 20

V ANDER AND I WASTE no time in exiting the castle, racing through the city, and exiting into the grassy plains beyond, where we fold the realm around us and step from Spring land onto Dusk's quiet beach.

"Were you harmed during the battle?" he asks as we take the forest path towards the manor.

"No. You?"

"I'm fine. Eager to see Wyn and glad Nyana has seen sense at last."

I take his hand in mine and thread our fingers together. "We have to be careful from now on. The theft of the blue mock flowers is a disadvantage we didn't prepare for."

He hums low in his chest. "I will send messengers to Ruith, Jonik, and Zentha. They should know about this. The battle at the castle was a distraction."

"It seems to be Maude's preferred method of attack," I say as we break through the last of the trees. I belatedly realise this is the first time I have not needed to pause and feel the touch of nature. I didn't snap a branch from a she-oak tree to caress or even so much as inhale the woodsy scent.

"Something to keep in mind." He holds the manor doors open, allowing me to enter before him. "Vigilance is key when considering her next move. The harpies have not left the Barrens for millennia. I believe she'll use them again."

"Perhaps not until the ending battle, if there is to be one."

We descend the curling staircase, heading towards the safe room. Vander says, "I disagree. She'll use them as a distraction, sending them to villages all around Radelea to spread us out. Then, once our numbers are thinned, and we are exhausted from combat, she'll strike where it hurts the most."

"We agree to disagree, then." I pause before the door.

This is one aspect of the twin soul bond that I adore. Disagreeing may be contradictory to the love we share, but our differences make us unique. The differences between Vander and I mean we can see things from different perspectives, and act accordingly. He will plan for harpy attacks throughout the realm, but he'll listen to my thoughts, too, and have plans in place for the possibility I'm right.

I continue, "Thus far, Maude is unpredictable. She relies on that and prays we will see patterns where there are none. Keeping us on our toes works to her advantage. If we do not know her next move, if we cannot see beyond the moves she has made in the past, then she retains the element of surprise."

"Then what do you think her next move will be?"

"I think you're right in saying she'll hit where it hurts the most. She has already targeted Wyn, and for what? There's no sense to it other than to cause us pain." I pause for a moment, considering everything we already know, and the questions we have no answers for. A sense of confidence I don't often feel thrums through me when I say, "She's going to target us. Laying waste to our island makes sense. It'll scatter our forces, destroy our base, and bring a frantic edge to the leaders of her opposition. If we can just lead her away from Dusk and make her chase us to a battleground that suits us…"

"Then we gain the upper hand," he finishes for me. "Good thinking, Princess."

"The question is where. Where in Radelea will we have the advantage?" I mutter to myself, though audible enough for Vander to hear, while I consider our options.

The Bolbala Ranges are the obvious choice. The Night fae are longtime enemies of the Winter Court, and do not cope well with the frost-licked mountains; they do not handle the cold. But in saying that, none of us do. And the mountainous landscape will work in Maude's favour, given her string of islands consists of sheer cliffs and endless crevasses.

Autumn's many creeks and rivers, snaking into the land from the south, disadvantage both parties. The southern location offers a sanctuary for the armada sailing from Day and Dawn, though it's close to Night. The naval warfare would be as destructive as it would be beneficial. I don't much fancy stumbling across Baba Yaga or any of her ogre offspring during battle, either.

Summer is too hot. No one could withstand the heat, even with the blanket of darkness bringing a colder climate to the court of fire and necromancy. We have not heard more from Tohminic, so best we don't settle on any plans involving his court just yet.

Spring's many fields, mostly flat with the occasional hill, would give us clarity and ease of movement. The only city, which is in the central north, would remain unharmed if we chose our location carefully.

Night is out of the question. We're not desperate or foolish enough to give them an advantage *that* good.

Dawn is *not* an option. We can't risk the healers of Radelea. We won't risk their infirmary, our centre of healing, during these harsh times.

Day... Day is a possibility. Warakoris will be safe, given none can access the island town without water magic. Being the smallest of Radelea's courts leaves us with few locations, though. And wherever we choose, the Dullahan is sure to find. A shiver runs down my spine at the thought. The headless rider has long since starred in my nightmares.

"I think Autumn and Spring are our best options. Autumn's undulating land will be an asset if we arrive there first. We can claim the hilltops for ourselves, leaving the marshy ground at their bases for Night. Covering the marsh with illusions, so our enemies are none the wiser, will benefit us, too."

Vander's brows flick to his shaved hairline. "When did you develop a mind for war?"

"When I had little else to do but read." My tone is flat. "You know my life was dull before we met. The only excitement I found was between the pages of history tomes."

He cups my face, his calloused thumb smoothing the frown from my lips. "You're not that fae anymore, Princess. And though it may pain you to hear me say it, I *hope* life is dull for you once more."

My frown returns.

He says, "If life is dull, then we have survived. A dull life is a life without fear. It's a life without war."

I smile now. "Then I share that hope. I will gladly return to a monotonous life if it means we're safe and without conflict." I tilt my head towards the safe room door. "Shall we?"

"About time you two got here," Torin grits out the moment we enter. Sweat beads on his forehead, and his jaw flutters with strain as he holds Wyn in a choke hold. "Maude has taken complete control. She won't stop fighting."

I reach for my shadows, pulling from deeper within myself than I have ever attempted, and throw the room into impenetrable darkness. It lacks Ruith's finesse — covering only Wyn would be the best option — but it is enough for now. "Close the door."

A muted thud follows my order, followed by two sighs of relief. Torin's is more of a groan, while Wyn's is tainted with sadness.

"Thank you," Wyn whispers. "You can let go of me now, Torin. I'm myself again."

"How can we trust your word?" he asks.

A pause, then, "I guess you can't."

"It's her," I say. I step closer, voicing an observation I'm not sure the Dusk fae have noticed. "Throughout Radelea, only the so-called lesser fae contract their words. Even when Maude was speaking through Wyn, she never used contractions. The Dusk fae are unique in this aspect, having spent time on Earth while the rest of us have not."

"You use contractions," Torin points out.

"Because I have spent so much time with you all. I've adapted. In my mind, though, I don't use them all that often. You can release her now."

"Are you certain?" Vander asks. I feel his hesitancy and echo his concern. We have a lot to lose if I'm wrong.

"I'm certain."

Vander gives Torin the order to release his sister, under the caveat the copper bands around her wrists remain. At least until he's sure Maude isn't waiting just below the surface, listening and stealing information we don't want her to have.

A rustle. A footstep. The thud of Wyn collapsing to the floor. She says, with a voice thick with emotion, "I had to do it. You have to understand. If I didn't target Spring now, Nyana would never agree to the alliance."

I kneel beside her, my tone soft. "We understand. You don't have to explain yourself to us."

"She was furious. I wasn't supposed to go with the Night fae when they attacked. Instead, she wanted me to target Day. But I had to. I had to help the best I could. Killing an innocent fae so Nyana understands what's at stake was all I could do."

"Why did she want to target them?" Torin asks.

"To cause heartache. My target was Kyra."

Mother Star, have mercy. Erthana is one thing, but Kyra, the soon-to-be mate of Day's heir? It's beyond comprehensible. Why Maude would need to bring such pain to Zentha and Elmon is... Actually, I understand her motives. It would push the Day Court past the point of restraint, fracturing the alliance if pushed far enough.

Maude's actions, while random, are a clever work of art. Each stroke of her brush leaves smears of black that obscure the vibrancy of what lies beneath. She defaces an artwork of friendship and kindness, replacing it with terror and tension.

Vander's emotions flicker from concern to anger and into frustration before settling on concern once more. While we should use Wyn's lucidity to gather as much information as we can, he cannot prevent himself from asking, "Where have you been these past days?"

"Hiding on the central island of Night. And before you ask, no. I can't give you any information about the layout or defences. I was blindfolded the entire time."

"Fuck," breathes Torin. "There are better uses for a blindfold. Just say the word, Wyn, and I would be happy to show you."

"Bite me."

I feel Vander squat beside me. "How can we help you? Can you break free from her on your own?"

Her breath hitches. "I don't think I can. She's too strong. Growing stronger the longer she's in my fucking head." She ends her words with a shout. If she could move her arms, I think she would shove her hands into her long, ebony hair.

"Then we free you." There's no room in my tone for anyone to argue when I say, "We leave for Night at once."

"To what gain?" asks Torin, though there's a resignation in his voice that tells me he knows what I'm planning.

I stand, brushing unseen dust from my leathers. "We're bringing Blodwen to Dusk. Permanently."

"No."

I spin towards Torin's voice. "We have to. I know you and your mother have issues, but we *have* to free Wyn's mind."

"Then we take Wyn to her, not the other way around," he says.

"We can't. If Blodwen's here, then we can use her to free Rennyn, too. Besides, the moment I lift the shadows, Maude will regain control."

He scoffs. "So not only do you want to sneak into Night and kidnap my mother, but you want to organise some kind of rescue mission into Autumn? You're delusional if you think you can step foot onto your home land without Maude knowing. My whispers have told me she freed the ogres, gave them a freedom they've been long awaiting."

A bitter cold spreads from my toes to my head. Father banished the ogres to the southern forest for a reason. They were too vicious, too hungry for the flesh of our younglings to be allowed anywhere near the villages and the castle.

"The order came from Rennyn," Torin adds, as if the knowledge will sway my decision.

"He has given himself over to her completely," I mutter. Louder, I say, "All the more reason to free his mind. Once he has control of himself again, he will send the ogres back to their forest home and fight alongside us."

"I thought you didn't want anything to do with Kerym and Rennyn?" asks Torin. "After everything they put you through, the taunting and concealing, the lies, I thought you were done with them? Isn't that why you shaved the side of your hair?"

Vander growls from beside me. "Watch yourself, Wind Whisperer."

I trail my hand through the darkness until his forearm is beneath my palm. "It's okay. I can fight my own battles." To Torin, I say, "I know you don't like it, and I'm sorry you have to keep doing this, but you know it's the right choice. Wyn can't free herself from Maude's control. What if there's information she can't say right now, even with my shadows protecting her from the Night bitch?"

He snorts at that, and I know I'm winning him over. There's nothing like well-placed profanity to make him see sense. He asks Wyn, "Is there more you're not telling us, more you *can't* tell us right now?"

Wyn makes a choking sound in the back of her throat.

It's answer enough.

Torin groans. "Fine. We bring Blodwen here. First sign of her feeding off a Dusk fae, and she's gone. I don't care if she hasn't broken through Maude's control yet. And I'm not leaving until I've eaten. No one should visit my mother on an empty stomach."

"That's fair," I say. "Is there a way to guarantee she doesn't feed off our denizens?"

"Of course there is. We threaten her."

Vander, speaking at last, asks, "With?"

"There is only one thing she fears. Maude's wrath."

We spend too long discussing the best way to collect Blodwen from her lonely island in the south-west. We have taken a rowboat there one time, and it was enough for me to know I have no interest in doing it again. But this is my idea, and if I back down because I'm frightened of the Deathly Rapids and the silvery-white fish below the water's churning surface, then

I might as well walk around with a sign hanging from my neck declaring me a coward.

In the end, we settle on the same plan as last time. With the obvious condition that on this occasion, we will not have a boat filled with five undead bobbing behind us.

I stay with Wyn and Vander while Torin folds to Winter in search of Ruith. Though I am confident in my ability to cast shadows, I have not tested the range in which I can control them. There are no assurances I will be able to leave Dusk, let alone the manor, without the shadows protecting Wyn following.

The moment Torin leaves the safe room, I ask, "Why didn't you step in when Torin and I were arguing?"

"To begin with, I didn't agree with your plan. Easy, Princess," he says when I start to explain the benefits of bringing Blodwen to Dusk. "After hearing your points, I agree. We can't risk Maude regaining control of Wyn." His emotions soften, both of us listening to the soft and even breathing coming from the fur-covered floor. With the dense shadow covering us all, we can only assume Wyn has fallen asleep.

I am grateful she is able to. How her mind must be tormenting her with the memories of all she has done since the Gloom. Rest is the best thing for her right now.

Vander continues, "The other reason I stood back and let you handle it? I trust you. You were standing your ground, making valid points, and you weren't letting yourself be overcome with emotion. Torin can be a right pain in the arse at times, and you handled it well."

"Thank you," I whisper, glad he cannot see the heat creeping over my cheeks.

Torin and Ruith arrive not long later, my stepfather eager to contribute in any way he can. I withdraw my shadows from the room — and blink rapidly at the onslaught of fae lights trying to blind me with their amber glow — leaving Wyn's mind exposed for less than a heartbeat before Ruith covers her in his own blanket of darkness.

I ache to learn the finesse he has over the shadows. Now is not the time, though I make a mental note to beg him to train me. I still struggle, especially when I'm exhausted, like now.

We're quiet while we climb the spiral staircase, a kind of tension brewing beneath the surface while I help Vander prepare a stew for dinner.

Torin disappears into his bedchamber, where Alizeh is waiting after returning from spying on the Night Court. She discovered nothing of importance, unfortunately. The moaning begins before I have so much as angled a knife over the carrot in my hand. I make sure to chop extra loud, doing everything I can to drown out the noise.

Nothing seems to help. So, instead of trying to make as much noise as possible, I hasten my pace until the stew is over the fire, bubbling away, and the mouth-watering scents of meat and root vegetables waft through the kitchen. To get away from Torin's grunts and Alizeh's squeals of delight, I disappear downstairs to clean my blades and make sure I have enough to get me in and out of the Night Court unscathed.

By the time I have armed myself and returned to the upstairs apartment, Vander has ladled the stew into five bowls, sliced whatever bread he could find, and set three places at the over-sized dining table.

"Why only three?" I ask as I enter.

"Don't get mad," he says, setting two bowls on a tray, "but I'm staying here. I can't leave Wyn when she's like this."

"She's asleep."

He looks at me now, those beautiful eyes so reminiscent of the moon's silver glow dripping with fear. "And I want to be here when she wakes. I missed this. I was so wrapped up in everything else that I didn't realise my *sister* was being controlled. This is... She's all I have left of my family."

I close the distance between us, pulling his face down until our lips collide. With our mouths connected, and in turn, our hearts, I speak into his mind. *"I'm sorry I questioned you. Of course you should stay. Torin and I will be okay. And if anything goes wrong, you're just a mind link away."*

"Promise me you'll be careful."

"I promise." No hesitation. I can give him this. It's an easy gift to give, the gift of peace of mind.

He pries my lips apart, his tongue sliding into my mouth and claiming all that I am. He tastes of warmed bread and gravy with undertones of ale. He tastes of fear. Of uncertainty and indecision.

I lean into his embrace and trail my hands over the curve of his shoulders.

Torin, always with impeccable timing, clears his throat. "I'm starved. Let's eat, then get out of here. The sooner we do this, the sooner I can return to Alizeh."

"Return?" Alizeh's voice is a tinkle of bells. "I'm coming with you."

I pull away from Vander to face the wind wraith. "Are you certain? It will be dangerous."

She flicks her wind-like hair over her shoulder. "I'm not leaving him to deal with his mother on his own." She looks at Torin with a kind of adoration I do not often see since the Gloom. "And if she so much as looks at him the wrong way, I'll wrap her in a tornado and send her hurtling across the realm." Wisps of compacted air unfurl in whispers from her palms, hair, and chest.

"Oh." Surprise flits through me.

Torin, a hybrid Dusk and Night male who enjoys the company of many females, finding himself in a different bed most evenings, and Alizeh, a wind wraith who is just as sexual as the male she's looking at with such adoration... they're in love.

It's an unexpected yet pleasant turn of events. It's funny how war affects us. For me, I am more determined than ever to fight for what I have earned. I no longer fear the red staining my hands, and I have welcomed my guilt. Vander continues to fight hard for the court he inherited from his late father, Connak. But for Torin and Alizeh, war has brought them closer together. It has made them realise life is too short to waste time in the beds of fae they do not belong with.

Their love is a precious thing. A jewel in the darkness that is worth protecting. For if their love is to blossom further, the realm must be at peace. We have to end this war, not only for ourselves and our realm, but for moments like these to shine brighter. So terror does not overshadow the happy times.

Chapter 21

"I DON'T RECALL THE Rapids being this vicious." My tone is tight, my voice rough from the constant grunts and suppressed screams.

The churning waters, with their beige foam and endless depths, forced Alizeh to slow our pace the moment we entered. With each crossing I make of the Deathly Rapids, they grow fiercer, more determined to capsize our rowboat, the vessel the only thing standing between me and drowning.

"You don't remember what I told you when we came here the first time?" Torin shouts over the crashing water.

"No." My knuckles whiten further — I did not think it was possible — as I grip the wooden seat.

"The Rapids act as part of Night's wards. If Maude's paying attention to her wards, she would have known we're here the moment our boat met the first crashing wave."

I cast my eyes to the west. It's the only direction I *can* look. Turning to face the way we came makes me shudder. The thought of releasing my grip on the boat is too fearsome to consider. On either side of us, to the north and south, there is nothing but sheer cliffs. Above, glittering stars appear, and the waning crescent moon hangs low in the sky. It's the only sign night is falling. The weak light the moon and stars emit, though incomparable to the Mother Star's shine, makes night brighter than day now.

Alizeh guides us around a tight bend, and we enter the Rapids proper after taking the eastern entrance, which is closest to Dusk's wards. This stretch of the narrow tunnel is rougher. The water here is more determined to claim our lives, eager for our souls to join those of the lost fae shooting beneath the surface of the slate-blue sea.

The rowboat bucks like a wild stallion intent on freedom. It launches skywards before slamming down with brutal force. Again and again. We are thrown sideways, using the low sides of the boat to prevent our fall into the deleterious water. During one such moment, I catch a glimpse of silvery-white deep below. My heart pounds against my chest and fear-tainted sweat clings to my forehead and upper lip as I brace against the frail timber.

The glittering figures spiral around us, growing in both number and size the closer we get to the exit, just as they did when we first came for Blodwen. While it is concerning the figures are surrounding us, forming a spiralling ring, they did not attack last time, and I do not believe they will attack again.

The souls of the damned, Torin once told me, are thirsty for blood to replace the magic they once controlled. If they do attack, I shudder to think about the damage they can cause.

From nowhere, Torin releases a huff of surprise.

"What is it?" I ask, daring a look to the seat behind me, where Torin and Alizeh sit side-by-side.

He frowns. "We're about to pass through the wards."

"And?" It's not like him to be so uncertain.

"And they're the same." He shakes his head. "Maude didn't use the relic to enhance them. I was sure I'd have to scout for the nearest ward and destroy it so we can move forward, but her wards are lacking."

The boat lurches with shocking violence, cutting the rest of the conversation short. There is a kind of unease brewing within me, a warning of sorts. Whatever she has done with the relic she stole, the relic we fought hard to create... Nothing good can come of this.

I send a prayer of thanks to the Mother Star when we crash down for the last time, the water changing from vicious to calm in a single breath. Blodwen's hut looms ahead, just as dilapidated as when I was last here. No lights shine from within her worn hut.

But as the roar of the Rapids fades, other sounds make themselves known. Shouts. Echoing clangs. A lone scream.

"Faster," Torin urges.

Alizeh releases her most powerful gust of wind yet, cackling while she does, and sends us hurtling over the water's surface as if skating on ice. We reach the lone barnacle-covered post within three beats of my thundering heart, and tie the rowboat to it within the next, while our hands tremble with the need to draw our blades and cut through the four Night guards backing Blodwen against the crumbling wall of her home. Five Dusk guards lie dead around the island.

As soon as the boat is secure, Torin and I leap onto the pebbled shore. We do not so much as formulate a plan of attack. We just run.

Alizeh, still cackling, breezes past us, nothing more than a gust of wind.

Torin moves fast, drawing both short swords while he races for his mother. He doesn't break stride as he slices his blades through the air, severing a hand from the arm of one guard and slicing across the midsection of another.

I pull on the threads of my metal bending magic and send three long swords and a handful of arrows into the sea at my back before palming two daggers and lunging towards the handless fae.

Beside me, Blodwen stands immobile with her arms stretched wide. Between ducking the obsidian blade arcing towards my face and jabbing a dagger towards my assailant, I catch a glimpse of burgundy mist seeping from the pores of Blodwen's target.

A shiver runs down my spine. Ice crackles in my veins.

I twist towards my opponent before I can think about what Blodwen's doing. Before I raise my hands to defend myself against the Night female's lethal blade, Torin spears his sword through her throat from behind.

Alizeh twirls and somersaults above, taking far too much pleasure in the chaos and remnants of magic. It is a side of her I doubt I will ever grow accustomed to.

"That's the last of them." Torin's dark eyes drink in the scene. "She knows we're here. If we don't leave *now*, we're dead."

"We?" asks Blodwen, wiping a speck of burgundy from the curve of her lip with a gnarled finger and popping it into her mouth.

He sheathes one of his swords, keeping the other in his dominant hand. "Yes, Mother. *We*. You're coming back to Dusk with us."

"What do I get out of it?"

Torin snorts. "Your life. You're welcome to refuse and stay here, of course. But looks to me like Maude's finished with you. You're a liability now."

"If I am a liability, it is because you lot thought it acceptable to come here. My life was simple until you stuck your nose where it does not belong," she hisses.

"We came because we need you," I say as I sheath both daggers.

Blodwen's dark eyes slide to me. "Realised the Theron female is not quite herself, have you? It took you long enough."

Wrath scorches through my veins. It widens my eyes and brings a desire for revenge into my tight fists. My pulse slams against my throat as I jab a finger at Blodwen's chest. "You best send your last prayers to the Mother Star if you're saying what I think you're saying."

Alizeh stops cackling. She hovers at shoulder height, her misty figure near invisible in the darkness.

Torin freezes. "You knew?"

"Of course I knew," Blodwen sneers. "I would have told you if you had asked."

Red shutters over my vision. "You best pull me away, Torin. I'm about to do something I'll regret if you don't."

The rage is all-consuming. The finger stabbing into Blodwen's sternum trembles. If Blodwen had been kind enough to tell us Wyn's troubles back when she freed Tohminic from Maude's control, we could have prevented so much pain.

Torin's muscular arms haul me backwards, lifting my feet from the pebbled shore and turning me away from his mother. "Take your revenge later," he whispers. "We still need her to free Wyn. If you attack her now, she'll never agree. Get in the boat and let me deal with this."

I nod, but he holds me for a few moments longer, until my breaths even out and my hands unclench.

"Are you good?"

I force my jaw to unclench. "Yes. Hurry, please. Maude could be here at any moment."

Alizeh glides over us, then settles at the stern, ready to lurch us forward with her air magic. Though she is ready to set sail, she does not take her eyes from Blodwen, and mutters a continuous string of insults under her breath about deranged fae females and war-forced sacrifices.

While Torin spends precious moments convincing his mother — desperately, which is a surprising change from the anger he often displays around her — to join us in Dusk, I untie the rowboat from the salt-licked post, coiling the thick rope between the seats. I tune out their conversation while I hold the vessel steady, using both hands to grip the post so Alizeh and I don't drift out to sea. Or back into the Rapids.

I am more surprised than anyone when Blodwen leaps into the boat with the agility and grace of a youngling. It's a stark contrast to her hobbling walk and gnarled fingers.

"Let's go." There is something in Torin's tone, a hesitancy. When I raise my brows at him, he shakes his head. "I'll explain — Fuck!"

I release my hands from the docking post and twist to follow his line of sight. All the blood drains from my face and plummets into my stomach, where it settles with the weight of an anvil.

Blotting out the stars on the northern horizon, where the Night mountains don't pierce the dark sky, and flying straight for us... hundreds of harpies. Hundreds.

"Blessed Mother Star, have mercy on us," I breathe. "Get us into the Rapids, Alizeh. As fast as you can!" I stand and face the harassment, using whatever strength my legs possess to brace against the violent rocking of the boat.

They come hard and fast, with their wings tucked close to their sides, their scaled legs hidden amongst the downy feathers of their underbellies, and rage contorting their faces. The ebony leader, the same harpy Wyn clambered atop and fled the Dawn Court on screeches a long, ear-splitting cry.

Alizeh, in all her billowing and powerful glory, guides us into the Rapids in record time. The towering cliffs, too close together for the harpies to come any closer, provide a safety net I never thought possible. Having spent my life fearing this stretch of Radelea's seas, I find it a strange comfort to thank the sheer rock face.

One harpy, either foolish or brave, dips into a dive. She hurtles towards us with more speed than I thought possible, only just fitting between the jagged rocks on either side of the sea tunnel. But the cliffs are closer together this far down, and the beast screeches as she becomes wedged between them.

A horrible way to die. Her comrades will leave her there to starve. Her bones will be a horrific reminder of the dangers of going rogue.

My thighs scream their thanks as I lower back to the seat and grip the edge of the boat with one hand, while my dominant hand strays to the handle of the dagger at my ribs. Maude knows we're here, and I don't believe she will allow us to leave so easily. Sending the entire population of harpies after us is proof enough.

The Rapids, so rough now that sprays of white water have us drenched within moments, throw us into the dark night air and have us slamming back down with thunderous cracks and shuddering booms that have me fearing for the boat's structure. The roar of the wrathful water drowns out everything from Blodwen's shouts of alarm to Torin's words of encouragement for Alizeh.

Whirlpools fight to drag us under, spinning us with dizzying ferocity before spewing us out in whichever direction they can. Gone is the slate-grey, replaced by growing mounds of sea foam that obscure the glittery silver souls circling the boat.

"They grow restless. I have never seen them so hungry."

I don't know how I hear Blodwen's warning over the raging water, but her words send prickles of terror dancing down my spine.

"You'd know," shouts Torin. "Half of them are trapped there because of you."

"I never claimed to be perfect."

I lean over the side of the boat, holding tight so I don't fall into the churning water, and observe the damned souls of the Night fae who are unfortunate enough to be trapped in the Rapids. A lone fish — I recognise it as a small salmon from my many adventures to see Nikolai at the Autumn docks — darts between the circling souls. The poor thing only makes it past two before the entire group descends on it. Within two beats of my pounding heart, the souls decimate the salmon, leaving only bone behind.

I jerk away from the water, snatching my hands from the gunwale of the boat, where the tips of my fingers are frighteningly close to the vicious spirits, and grip the seat to keep steady. I am not interested in becoming a discarded skeleton at the bottom of the Rapids, never to be seen or heard from again.

For the rest of the trip back to Dusk, I sit in silent fear of the hungry souls beneath the water. I make a vow to myself to never enter the Deathly Rapids again. Even if my closest friends need me to rescue them. This is a kind of terror I do not wish to endure.

With everything I have lived through, there has always been a niggling thought in the back of my mind that there's a way out. With the taunts and disrespect in Autumn, I held onto the notion that I could one day escape and live a simple life with my mother in Spring. When Tohminic held me captive in Ad'Starrag, then again, when he forced me into the iron cage, there was always the hope that Vander and Torin would come to my rescue. When we fought alongside one another during the Gloom, I did not so much as consider our army falling.

Hope. It is the one thing that can drag us through the darkest of times. It is the light at the end of the tunnel, a promise of simplicity and easier times. Looking back, I realise I have always had hope, even if I did not wish to name it as such during those hardships.

But now, with the ocean fighting to capsize our boat, and the hungry souls circling in wait, I cannot find it within myself to find hope of making it home alive, of making it back to Vander alive.

The hopelessness subsides when we break through the end of the Rapids at long last. The island I call home, the Dusk Court, emerges on the horizon.

I cannot help but think bringing Blodwen home is the beginning of something big. A glance over my shoulder reveals a raging storm brewing over the Night Islands; Maude knows we were within her grasp and escaped yet again. I turn back to Dusk. Whatever her next move, we will face it as one.

Chapter 22

BLODWEN PRESSES HER GNARLED fingers to Wyn's temples, and the room falls into a tense silence. The only sound is the swish and thump of Torin's pacing against the far wall.

Alizeh watches Torin, her misty eyes tracking him as he walks back and forth. She struggles to rein in her power and small tendrils of her gale-force winds slither through the safe room from where she stands by the door, clearly uncomfortable yet unable to drag herself away from a newfound love.

Ruith, having lifted the shadows veiling Wyn, watches Blodwen with a kind of curiosity I have not seen since teaching my students the history of the Autumn ogres. Dey's furious scribbling as I spoke of the High Lady refusing to relinquish her hold on the animalistic magic coursing through her is something I will forever hold dear. That they believed the words I spoke to be worthy of writing down... Dey was my favourite for that reason alone. They were the first fae to show me interest and to *listen* to what I had to say.

Vander is tense beside me. His hand trembles where I hold it with both of mine, the pulses of fear fluttering along our bond revealing just how scared he is for his sister.

"Are you okay?" I ask.

"What if it doesn't work?"

I watch as Blodwen closes her eyes and wisps of inky black magic unfurl from her fingers and seep into Wyn's pores. *"It worked with Tohminic. There is no reason it won't work with Wyn, too. Have faith, Van. We're getting her back."*

He only nods, his words evading him as Wyn screams, the sound so tormented and riddled with pain that it echoes through my bones.

Wyn's entire body shudders. Her chest vibrates from the onslaught of Blodwen's power. Her eyes spring open, the whites around the moonlight silver too bright in the dim room. Blodwen grunts, and Wyn screams once more, tormented and agonised, before sagging into the worn fur rug beneath her.

"The wards I have placed around her mind should hold," says Blodwen. "If she does not welcome Maude back on her own."

"Why would she do such a thing?" I ask.

Blodwen's dark eyes assess me from across the room. "Having your mind controlled for so long causes untold damage. Many become reliant on the presence within them. Time will tell how she handles being herself once more. Now, where do you keep the food?"

"Alizeh, could you show her to the apartment upstairs, please?" I do not take my eyes from Wyn's limp form, but I know Alizeh will leap at the chance to leave. These emotional scenes are not something she enjoys.

"With pleasure." Her voice is a tinkle of bells, hiding the undercurrent of contempt she has for Torin's mother. "Come, Blodwen. I will show you to your new lodgings."

She means my old bedchamber. Given I have spent more time in Vander's chambers than my own, it makes sense for me to allow Blodwen the comfort of having her own space. A space that is close enough to Vander, Torin, and me that we will know if she breaks her promise of not feeding on the Dusk fae.

The moment the heavy door thuds closed behind them, Vander sinks to his knees beside Wyn. "Are you okay?"

Since Blodwen placed the shields within her mind, she has remained lying on the floor, limp and staring. No emotion has flickered across her face. She has shown no sign she's aware of what has happened.

Until I free her wrists of the copper restraints.

She lunges for Vander and wraps her arms around his neck, speaking through ragged sobs. "I thought I'd be forced to live with her inside my mind forever."

He holds her tight. "She's gone. You don't have to endure it any longer. You're free."

I have not known Wyn for long. In fact, it has only been five moon cycles since she appeared in my chambers in the Autumn castle dressed in that maid's gown and clearly uncomfortable. Although it is a mere heartbeat of time for a fae, I believe I know her very well. Well enough to understand her dislike of deep and meaningful moments.

With this in mind, and knowing Vander is not likely to release his sister any time soon without my prodding, I kneel beside the Theron siblings and say, "We need information. Freeing you from Maude's clutches will not go unnoticed. We must act before she does."

She pulls away from Vander — he releases her, though with obvious reluctance — and wipes the tears from her eyes. "What do you want to know?" When Vander is not looking, she mouths, "Thank you."

I dip my chin in acknowledgement. "When she confronted me at the mountain ash, I asked her why she's doing this. Her answer was perplexing." I recite what is burned into my mind, where the words have taunted me since Maude stole the relic. "*My heart beats in time with the drums of vengeance. My fists pound against that drum, their fury calling justice to our lands. And my soul, patient and wise, will not rest until the last dreadful beat.*"

"Drums of vengeance?" Torin scoffs. "Who talks like that?"

"Maude," Wyn and I say together. My lips twitch into a smile.

Ruith paces, walking along the same path Torin walked when Blodwen was here. "She does not speak of the literal drum, but of the way her heart pounds with the need for revenge. She claims her own hands will deal the justice she seeks. But for what reason?"

Wyn leans against the leg of the nearest chair. "You can all thank Bria for this information. I only know it because she had the brains to ask." She closes her eyes, as if dredging a memory from the depths of her mind. Opening them once more, she says, "Maude has waited three hundred years to take her revenge on the Theron family. She never has and never will forgive our father for inciting war within her court. His death was the catalyst she needed to make her move. She wants me and Vander dead."

"She's held a grudge for *that* long?" Torin's aghast. He shakes his head in disbelief, long strands of golden blonde falling free of their leather binding. "No wonder she's such a bitch."

When Lord Connak died, and the veil illusioning this island lifted, revealing the Dusk Court after centuries of hiding, that should have been enough. Maude should have thanked the Mother Star for dealing the justice she desperately sought. Instead, she used it as an excuse to bring war to our realm.

Wyn continues, "She doesn't care that the original Night Court fractured, or that we formed a court of our own. It's the fact that we won. We beat her. She'll never forgive us, and she won't rest until we pay the price for our betrayal."

"We know why she chose now. Father's death was an opportunity she couldn't let go to waste," says Vander. "But why not just attack the moment he died, when we were vulnerable? Why drag this war out? Why risk losing so many fae?"

"A question we would all like answered," says Ruith, who has stopped pacing and is now watching Wyn with keen interest.

Wyn sighs. "She wants us to endure as much pain as possible, so we know how she has felt all these years. Everything that's happened since Father died is because of her."

"Everything?" A stone settles in my stomach, and I already know I will not like the answer to this.

Her eyes flutter closed. "Every court sent ships to surround Dusk after you announced our unveiling, Bria. Your father's ship anchored beside Maude's. She took his mind then. She needed all of Radelea's nobles in one place so she could determine who would best suit her vile plans. I doubt Kerym would have agreed to Fayeth's idea — forcing you to find a mate — if Maude was not present in his thoughts."

I take a grounding breath and fight the bubbling rage within. Why did I shun my family? Because I was too foolish to see their actions were not their own. I have known for some time that Ren is being controlled by Night, but Father... Revealing how he truly felt about me, and in the presence of Vander and Torin, was out of character. Refusing to rescue his only daughter from the horrors of Ad'Starrag, again, out of character. Everything he has said and done since we sailed to Dusk has been out of character. I hang my head in shame as heat crawls over my cheeks.

"You didn't know, Princess."

"I should have. He's my father, and Rennyn my brother. We have to help them. I was ignorant and blinded by selfishness; I could not see the truth, even if it smacked me in the face."

"We will. We'll help them."

To distract myself from that pain, I ask, "What was in the package? The one I saw you with in the Deathly Rapids?"

Wyn smirks. "That was when I had *some* control over my actions. She had ordered me to steal weapons from Earth. I'm pretty sure she meant guns, but I stole their tasers."

"Tasers?" asks Ruith.

"They're small devices that deliver low-energy electrical pulses. The pulses render the target useless for a small time. They're battery powered."

Torin snorts. "And Maude doesn't know human electronics don't work here? That the magic in Radelea short circuits them?"

"She does now," says Wyn. "Her tantrum was nothing short of comical. She killed four of her guards."

"Tell us the rest." Torin leans against the wall, bracing one foot at the base and crossing his arms in a faux casual stance. "We have to know everything if we're going to take her down."

Wyn pushes to her feet, looks us each in the eye, then says, "She infiltrated Tohminic's mind at Rennyn's born day ball. Everything he has done since then was because of her. Chlora gained control of Fayeth's mind not long after, forced her to kill High Lord Iker, and coerced her into severing the bond she shared with Kerym. Maude and Chlora control the selkies, the Autumn Court, and the harpies." She points to me and cocks an eyebrow. "That's why you couldn't use your animalistic magic on them. Their minds were fae."

"With all we know," says Ruith, "I think it safe to assume Lord Tohminic will fail in regaining control of the Summer Court. We should plan for his extraction at the earliest convenience."

"I doubt we'll have the chance," says Wyn.

"What do you mean?" Vander tenses beside me.

Her eyes spark with anger. They flare with the need for revenge, then narrow with grim persistence. "She knows you saved me. Knows you took Blodwen. It's the final provocation she needed."

I stand, dragging Vander with me. "Say what you mean to say. What is she planning?"

"She will have us surrounded before the moon sets."

Chapter
23

MY BARE TOES CURL over nothing, fighting for a purchase they will not find and sending small rocks tumbling into the mist-shrouded darkness. Ferocious winds tear at my loose copper hair as I stagger back from the edge. The carrion-scented gusts try to pull me back towards the cliff, and I dig my toes into the cold stone.

All around me, there is nothing but a glittering white mist. Jagged rock scrapes at my bare feet, though the touch of stone is muted. Soft. The mist forms tiny spirals with every step I take to the centre of the mesa, sometimes clearing enough to reveal the flat apex of the mountain I stand upon.

The mesa, a crescent-shaped surface of grey rock, is the same grey rock I rested upon in the body of an albatross. It's the same grey rock I dreamed of nine moons ago. I had forgotten the dream; my mind dredges it up from where I had buried it deep, where it taunts and rejoices — the memory, so muddy and difficult to grasp, elates in its ability to hide from me for all this time.

"I've been here before." The wind chases my voice into the chasm below, too deep to see the bottom, and I twist to follow the echo of my question as it descends through the blanket of white concealing the view. The sense of déjà vu is overwhelming.

"You have indeed."

Ice prickles the hairs on my nape as I spin towards the voice and crouch into a defensive position. I probe my body for a weapon, finding every holster empty of my favoured knives. Fear flashes through my veins and brings a sheen of sweat to my forehead as I wonder how in the Mother Star's grace I got to the Night Court yet again. It is a concerning turn of events, though less worrisome than the High Lady standing before me. Less worrisome than folding through Radelea without intending to, for a second time.

"Why?" I breathe the lone word aloud while screaming for Vander across our bond, only to be met with a wall of impenetrable obsidian. I cannot reach him through our bond, no matter how hard I slam my thoughts against the shield.

But I keep assaulting the wall of black that is blocking my mind, ramming it with vulgar curses, spearing the shield with prayers to the sun, and scraping my agitated thoughts down its length. I am certain I can demolish the obsidian and contact Vander, and I will continue to attack and claw until I break through. I have succeeded once, and I will succeed again.

Maude tuts. "I would not do that if I were you."

"Your word means nothing," I spit at her, then continue slamming against the shield.

"I have a proposition for you." Her blood-red lips curl at the sides more and more with every word. Her ice-blue eyes are stark against her pale skin, seeming to glow through the swirling mist. "Before you tell me there is nothing I can say that you are interested in hearing, know this: I beg to differ. I told you once how impressed I was with your resilience. Again, I marvel at your loyalty to your loved ones. Freeing Wynetta was an obstacle I was unprepared for. You angered me."

"And you bore me." The obsidian cracks. I slam against it with all my mental strength.

"I assume Wynetta told you everything?" she asks, those bright eyes flashing with humour.

A second crack appears in the obsidian. I ram the wall with my entire mind, and the fracture spreads. It pops and booms as jagged veins of freedom spread along its expanse.

"I have brought you here to offer you a way out. Hand over the Theron siblings, and I will release your father from my control."

Everything within me stutters to a halt.

"Bring them to me," Maude continues, "and I will order my armada to retreat. They move on Dusk as we speak. Come morning, my army will have your pathetic joke of a court surrounded."

"You have my father?" I recall Dey claiming none in Autumn knew where he was, that none had seen him since he revealed my mother's identity.

Her smirk is cruel. "Your darling of a brother did not care when I entered your home court and took Kerym. In fact, I think I may have broken Rennyn. He is not quite right. Did you know he destroyed his own village?" She clicks her tongue. "Such a tragedy."

"You're lying." She has to be lying, playing on my fears to get what she wants. Ren would never attack an Autumn village, even under Maude's control. He'd fight.

"I tire of your denial. This is the last time I will come to you with such a generous offer. Give me the Theron siblings. In return, I will give you Kerym, *and* my army will retreat. The war will end. In handing me Vander and Wynetta, you save hundreds of thousands of lives. You will save the entire Dusk Court."

Her offer is tempting. But I'm a selfish fae. I had a taste of life without the ballgowns, tiaras, and title I was born into. I tasted freedom and friendship and love, and I will *not* give that up. Especially not for a male who regrets my birth, one whose mind is not his own. Father's madness will not abate simply because the war ends. His torment will last until his final breath.

With as much vehemence as I can muster, I spit, "I decline your offer and look forward to facing you on the battlefield." I crash against the wall of obsidian in my mind, and the cracks deepen. A second attack, and it shatters altogether. I grasp the bond I share with Vander and *tug* as hard as I can.

The last thing I hear before I return to my body is Maude's sigh of disappointment, followed by a deadly, "You will regret this, Bria of Dusk."

❦

I bolt upright with a gasp and grip my face in my hands. My head throbs in time with my rapid pulse, slamming a thunderous rhythm.

"Bria?" Vander groans and rolls over to face me, sleep still clinging to his voice. "What's wrong?"

The longer I sit and wallow, the longer I am awake, the more the dream slips away. I'm not certain it could be called that, though. A dream.

"I think..." I start, but shake my head. It's not possible. I would know.

Vander's leathers — we have both taken to sleeping in them, lest a battle rages we're not prepared for — crinkle as he kneels in front of me and pulls my hands away from my face. "Tell me."

Terrified emerald clashes with concerned silver. I speak more to myself than to Van when I say, "Maude was in my head. It's the only thing to make sense. To dream of it twice now... Breaking through the shield in my mind. The mist. There's no other explanation."

"Come." He takes my hand and drags me through the upstairs apartment until we're in the spacious sitting room.

We both ignore Torin, asleep in one of the leather chairs while he waits for Alizeh to return from spying on Night, but he wakes regardless of our attempt to be silent.

Vander fills two crystal cups with amber liquid and hands one to me. "Explain."

"What's happening?" Torin rubs sleep from his eyes before stretching his arms above his head. "I'll have one of those."

Vander hands a cup to his second, pours himself another, then repeats, "Explain."

One sip of the multi-flavoured liquid and warmth spreads throughout my body. Fruit and flowers and oak coat my tongue, the zesty burst bringing a pleasant wave of courage. "I dreamed

I was in the Night Islands." I give every detail I can recall of my time on that mountain, what she said, how I reacted, and how I broke through the wall of obsidian in my mind, then finish with, "She was in my head, wasn't she?"

Torin tosses his head back, emptying his cup in one mouthful. He leans forward with a groan of appreciation. "Sounds like it. Why did you refuse the deal?"

I cannot keep the confusion from my face. "Why would I accept it? My father has lost his mind. He's not who he once was and will never be that male again. Saving him and sacrificing Wyn and Vander doesn't make sense. Not to mention, Maude was likely lying. There is no reason for her to yield in this war, not with her so close to getting what she wants."

"Bria would be foolish to accept anything from Maude," says Vander.

I take another sip of brandy to soothe my frayed nerves. There is no way to determine if I have made the right choice, not until it's too late. But I think Father would be proud. He is not the type of fae to accept trades such as these. I am certain he would not have considered it if the roles were reversed, if Maude tried trading me for Rennyn. He would have laughed and told her to shove her deal where the Mother Star cannot have a hope of shining.

"We should send a team to extract Kerym and Rennyn," says Torin. "I'm happy to volunteer."

I shake my head. "She'll expect that and will have plans in place for such an occurrence. We'd be walking into a trap."

"A fair point." He peels himself from the seat and pours another finger of brandy. He drinks it in one. "So, what do we do?"

"I don't think there's anything left but to flee," says Vander. "Wyn said the Night army will surround us come morning. Maude said as much to Bria. We're defenceless here. What we need is to gain the upper hand."

Alizeh breezes into the room without a word, darting straight to the window.

"Then we go to Spring." Both males look at me in shock. I shrug. "Autumn is out of the question, with Night controlling Rennyn and the ogres loose in the villages. If we're to gain an advantage, we must beat Night to the fields of wildflowers, where we can claim the best battle grounds. Can we get everyone out in time?"

Torin meanders to the floor-to-ceiling window, wraps his arm around Alizeh's waist, and looks out over the northern view, towards Spring. "No. I'm afraid we can't. Van, you're going to want to see this. Bring the brandy. Whole bottle."

Vander does as instructed, handing Torin what remains of the amber liquid. He tenses beside his second, breathing a string of expletives that make me lurch to my feet and join them.

Where there should be a blanket of dark ocean, there are hundreds of ships. Fae lights bob in the water, from the masts, and from the decks. Wisps of blood and bone magic snake over the calm waves and probe our weakened ward.

We race from the manor, not pausing for anything until we reach the mountain ash tree, where we face a terrifying sight. From this vantage point, we can see the entire coast of Dusk.

From this vantage point, we can see the thousands of Night, Autumn, and Summer ships surrounding the island.

"Look over there." Vander points towards the south-east. "What *is* that?"

"A selkie," offers Alizeh.

I turn and squint at a dark patch among the just as dark water. A dim fae light illuminates some kind of object. "A crate?"

"No," says Torin. "Not a crate. It's a rowboat. And that isn't a fae light, but a flame. That's High Lord Tohminic, with one other. A female. Mother Star, grant me the absolute delight of that female being Chlora."

Alizeh cackles. The two are clearly made for one another.

"Is he injured?" Vander asks.

I wonder the same; the bundle of fabric on the bottom of the boat is not moving. At least, I cannot tell if it is moving from such a distance. I cannot even see there are two fae, like Torin claims.

"Not sure," says Torin. "Let's go find out."

Vander leads the way down the gentle slope, heading towards a fork in the worn path. "Bria and I will go. You two should begin evacuating the denizens. Get the vulnerable to the Bolbala Ranges and those willing to fight to the battle grounds in Spring." When Torin nods and picks up his pace to a jog, taking the northern path, Vander calls out, "Keep it quiet. We don't know if she's listening."

"You got it." He salutes us both before jogging to the manor, where he'll begin slowly making his way through the court, waking fae and sending them to either Spring or Winter.

Alizeh floats after him. Her laughter is absent for once.

I would give anything to let the denizens continue resting in peace. To be woken by such devastating news... It would cause anyone to panic. Especially with Torin's colourful way of dealing with things.

"Wyn is still sleeping," I say while we jog towards the shore. "After everything she's been through, I don't think letting Torin wake her with this news will be good for her."

He pulls to a stop, torn between helping his sister and rescuing Tohminic and whoever sails with him.

"I'll go. We'll meet you at the beach."

He breathes a sigh of relief. "Are you sure?" I nod. He presses a soft kiss on my temple. *"Thank you, Princess."*

I turn in the opposite direction and race towards the manor. The backdrop of stars, so beautiful it makes my heart ache, and the crescent moon, waning and almost gone, seem to mock me from their perch in the dark sky. Their beauty is a contrast to the tension holding me in its grip. I roll my shoulders to ease the discomfort, though it does little to calm the churning of my stomach.

As I climb the hill of Dusk Manor, perhaps for the last time, I cannot help but wonder if this is it. This is the beginning of the ultimate battle, which will determine the fate of Radelea. The beginning of the end. Come tomorrow — or the next full moon or after two and ten moons, depending on how long this draws out — Radelea will not be the same.

No fae within the realm will be the same.

All because of Maude and her foolish desire for revenge.

I dash through the manor as fast as I can, passing sleep-stricken and panicked fae. Many of them beg me to explain why we're forcing them to leave their home. Guilt tears through me when I can only offer them three words. "We're under siege."

To my surprise, I almost collide with Wyn on the stairs. She's still buckling her leathers when she slams to a stop. "What's all the commotion about? Are we under attack?"

"Siege." I lead the way outside, explaining Tohminic and whoever he's sailing with. "We're evacuating everyone. Every single fae. Vulnerable to Winter and soldiers to Spring."

"I thought we'd have longer," she says as we burst through the front doors. "I thought you and I would have time to drink too much wine and forget our worries."

I'd love nothing more than to drown my sorrows with Wyn. It has been too long since we spent time together, one on one, as friends do.

I throw a glance towards the stables, and my heart shatters. Trying to get Solana out of Dusk is too risky. I don't have the experience folding with animals, and I'm not brave enough to try it when the entire court is relying on us getting them to safety.

Wyn, noticing my pained expression, says, "Go help Vander. I'll find Torin. He can get the horses out while I take over evacuating everyone."

"Are you certain?"

"I'm okay. My mind is my own and I'm ready to fight back. Go," she urges. "I'll see you in Spring."

Leaving her feels wrong on so many levels, but there's no other choice. War demands sacrifice. I've said it once and I'll say it many times before it's over. This is one I have to pay. Vander may not agree, and he may not forgive me for leaving her, but I couldn't live with myself if anything happened to Solana or the rest of the horses.

So I race for the she-oak forest and the sandy shore beyond, turning my back on Wyn and the manor. And in this moment, it feels like I'm turning my back on everything that makes me who I am. My morals, my guilt, and my desperate yearning to make it through the war without sacrificing a part of myself.

I race away from Dusk Manor, and race away from my benevolence. Maude wants a fight. I, Bria of Dusk, will give her everything she wants and more.

Chapter 24

I MAKE IT TO the edge of the forest within heartbeats. It's a marvel that I do not stop to bask in the glory of nature, to caress the needle-like branches of the she-oaks and calm my frayed nerves.

The trees thin, offering a view of the dark south-eastern ocean, obscured only by a frantic Yaryn — it is surprising how lucid Iker's mate is, given he died a gruesome death in front of everyone — and Vander kneeling over a bloodied body.

I cannot determine characteristics from here. There is a face, so swollen and beaten it could belong to anyone. There is a torso so viciously attacked there are more gashes and punctures than intact skin. And there are legs so broken they twist at unnatural angles, as well as an arm that ends in a stump at the wrist rather than a hand. It's a true miracle the fae is alive, which is proven by the shuddering rise and fall of their chest.

Vander looks up as I approach. His eyes skate over me, looking for his sister among the oaks and pines bordering the beach.

"She's gone to help with the evacuation," I say, my tone timid. "And we have asked Torin to save the horses. What happened here?"

He turns back to who must be Tohminic and continues wrapping torn lengths of fabric around the stump of the Summer Lord's left arm. "We knew he was failing in his fight to regain control of his court, but this is beyond anything I envisioned." He secures the makeshift bandage with a knot and sits back on his heels. "Chlora and Xaler have taken over Summer."

"It was a ploy," says Yaryn. "They led Tohm to believe they were on his side and willing to fight against Night with him. When he was sure they were acting true to their word, they attacked and left him to die."

"You're too sane for a female who lost her mate." I am unable to prevent the words from spilling forth. Perhaps I am bitter. Perhaps there is something deep within me that is saddened by the fact Father endures the madness Yaryn does not.

She scoffs. "Our mateship was a ruse. We never completed the ceremony. I was already carrying Tohminic when I met Iker."

"Who is his father?" I wonder out loud.

"A lesser fae from the village who took what he wished." Her tone is just as bitter as mine. I cannot blame her. "Iker has no true heir. We would very much like this to remain unknown throughout Radelea. You understand. If anyone were to discover the High Lord has no claim to the title, the moniker would pass to Iker's brother."

Vander brushes sand from his legs as he stands. "I didn't know he had a brother."

"He is not worth knowing." She takes her place at Tohminic's side, brushing strands of overgrown mouse-brown hair from his bloodied forehead. He doesn't react. "You mentioned an evacuation?"

"We don't have a choice. We're surrounded." The anger tainting Vander's words is a mirror of my own. He lifts his face and narrows his eyes at the ships bobbing in the ocean.

"Has your healer left?"

"I doubt it," I say. "Penna will remain in the infirmary until the last possible moment. She will not leave the fae she is responsible for until she has to."

Vander grimaces. "I don't think he'll survive the trip up to the manor. Best we bring Penna here to heal him."

We both sacrifice a dagger to Yaryn, so she can defend her son if necessary, and leave the Summer fae to return to the manor.

We're just in time; Penna is preparing to fold to the Dawn Court to help her fellow healers when we arrive, and hurries off to heal Tohminic as best she can before folding with him and Yaryn. We offer to escort her to the beach, but she declines, instead telling us to evacuate our denizens. We can't argue with her logic. There's nothing we can do for Tohminic short of getting in Penna's way, and the Dusk fae are more important than a Summer Lord on the brink of death.

War. Sacrifice. This is but one of them.

We spend a lot of time going from house to house, from business to business, in the western village. I am thankful to pass Wyn along the dusty streets and offer her reassuring smiles at every given opportunity.

A messenger finds Vander while we're clearing the metal smith in the town square, who informs us of Penna's safe arrival in Dawn. He has no update on Tohminic's injuries, but assures us he was alive when Penna folded.

Torin joins us after we evacuate the last of the village. "Horses are safe in Spring's west. The few huts around the south and east are clear, too."

"Thank you, Torin, for saving the horses."

The sincerity in my tone makes him uneasy, and he runs a scarred hand over his head and laughs it off.

With no one left in the western village to evacuate, we move to the destroyed village in the north. The village where Maude took control of Wyn's mind, using the selkies as a distraction. In hindsight, we should have guessed she and Summer we were working together back then.

The moment Vander utters the words, "We're under siege and evacuating to Spring and Winter," to the few who linger in the village, the first cannon fires from the Night ships anchored offshore.

The cannonball, a hollow orb of glass filled with iron powder, misses its mark. Instead of crashing through the group surrounding us, it collides with what remains of the small village's stores. The sound booms across the court. The ground shudders ever so slightly. Debris careens through the air.

A second attack follows soon after.

I whip around, facing the armada looming closer than before, to see hundreds of shadows moving within the water. They grow larger the longer I look, and as they close in on the sandy beach that marks the northern perimeter of Dusk, their details become clear.

A head breaks through the rippling water, followed by skeletal shoulders, the skin seeming to hang from the emaciated frame. The body is so decayed that nausea churns in my stomach. Their appearance has nothing on the ripe odour of carrion they bring. I wonder how we ever thought the fae Nyree controlled were undead. The lack of scent alone should have been enough for us to realise they were alive.

One by one, members of Summer's undead army stagger onto the beach.

The few younglings — who were waiting for instructions from their parents in silence — scream and race for shelter. It breaks my heart to see such terror contorting their faces.

"We're out of time!" Torin draws both swords from the sheaths on his back. "We'll never make it beyond the wards. You have to lift them, Vander."

"I don't have the energy," Vander growls. "Not to lift all of them."

"Then I'll help," I offer.

More of the gruesome undead clamber onto Dusk land, their haunting growls reminiscent of a cornered animal.

"Do it now!"

Torin's shout is all it takes for Vander to drag me towards him and press his forehead against mine. I place my hands on either side of his face, my thumbs soothing away his worry with small, gentle motions. He mirrors the action.

I open the hatch that keeps my magic from bursting out. The threads of silver, amber, onyx, and pearly white flow through me, spreading both warmth and cold as they seek the connection between us. The magic seeps from beneath my fingers and snakes into Vander's mind, where it melds with his illusions and wind.

I'm a visitor in his mind, a magical conduit offering him more magic as he sends ripples of power through the void, where it flickers around eight shining beacons. The detail in the wards is mesmerising. Gold and white and blue all at once, but not at all. Solid yet not, and pulsing with dizzying energy.

One by one, Vander's mind wraps around each of the eight ward stones and unlocks the magic pulsing within. They stutter from the trio of colours to black, then disappear altogether.

When the last ward has been deactivated, he releases his hold on both my magic and my face. "You're free to fold off the island." He sends the whisper on a gust of wind to every fae within the court. A bone deep worry pierces through our bond, and so low only I can hear, he says, "I hate this. Handing Dusk over to the undead and Night fae is wrong."

"We don't have the capacity to defend it. The Mother Star knows I wish we did, but we just don't. We don't have the numbers, and we don't have the protections. Fleeing to a safer court ensures our survival."

"This is my home." His voice breaks on the last word.

An iron-filled cannonball hurtles overhead, the wind whistling in its wake. It crashes hard into a crumbling building just south of us, and though bitter fear settles in my stomach like a lead weight, I do not run or fold. Vander needs to hear this before we leave.

"If my life has taught me anything, it's that home is not a place, but a feeling. It's where you can be yourself, where you can show vulnerability. Home is peace and safety." I press my palm to his chest, right over his heart. "This is home. This is where you feel all those things. Where I am. Where Wyn, Torin, and even Alizeh are. *We* are your home. It will hurt to lose this place, but losing us would hurt more. Use that knowledge to keep fighting."

A lone tear builds, then falls to the dirt at our feet. "The manor holds so many memories. Good and bad."

Behind him, Wyn approaches, Vander's sadness mirrored on her face. My words are not just for him, but for her as well.

I slide my hand from his heart to his temple. "You hold those memories. The manor may trigger them, but you control them."

"Enough of the emotional crap," shouts Torin, racing towards us. "Unless you want to take on *that*, I suggest we get the fuck out of here."

When I turn towards the advancing horde of undead — a brief flicker of relief steals a huff of breath when I realise no fae remain in the village, all having folded to their ordered stations — expecting their blackened and decayed hands to be groping for us, every one of them staggers to a halt.

"What the..." Torin's hands, still gripping his short swords, lower to his sides.

A lone rowboat approaches from beyond the hundreds of undead standing along our shore. It glides atop the water like a stone skittering over ice. I do not realise until the boat is almost to shore that two selkies tow the vessel with thick ropes.

Two fae stand in the rowboat. The first, a female with midnight black hair pulled back in a harsh bun. The other, a male I would recognise from his magical signature alone, if not for his silver hair and emerald eyes. His magic is dense, like thick clay.

It is suffocating clouds of dust. It is calm, like a humble mare. I used to think of it as the feeling of home, of comfort and safety.

The longer I look, the more details I take in. From Maude's blood-red lips and the way they curl into the cruellest of smiles, to Kerym's too-thin body, then on to the gleaming black blade pressed against his pale throat.

I lurch forward. "Father?"

Vander's hand shoots out and tightly grips my elbow, preventing me from following an instinct to protect someone I once called family. "You'll never break through the wall of undead."

His words bring a worrying realisation. Because he is right. The undead are not here to attack, but to prevent us from reaching my father in time.

Wyn moves to stand between Torin and me, her hands twitching for her blades.

Those two strangely realistic dreams crash to the forefront of my mind, teasing, taunting, mocking. For they were not dreams at all. It *was* Maude. She *was* in my head. I rush to secure my thoughts behind a mental wall of obsidian, impenetrable to the Night fae and their mind control.

The High Lady laughs. She throws her head back and graces the stars with her high-pitched cackle. The sound echoes throughout the entire realm, bouncing off the mountains in Winter, Dawn, and Night. Her laugh races across the seas of Day. It dips with the undulating hills of Summer and Autumn and rustles the coloured petals in Spring. Her laugh is the beating drums of war, reverberating around Radelea.

It is the beginning of the end.

She drags her face back down and pins me under her ice-blue glare. "I am disappointed it took you so long to realise. If you had a shred of self-preservation, you would have understood the implications of your *dream* the first time I entered your mind. If you were not the selfish female you are, you would have understood the ramifications before I held a blade to your father's throat."

"Release him," I growl, low and venomous.

"I will not. When we last met on the mountains in the Night Islands, I told you I would not come back to you with such a generous offer. You declined, Bria, and I warned you that you would come to regret that decision. You could have saved Radelea from so much pain. Instead, you chose the path of selfishness."

"What is she talking about?" Wyn asks.

My eyes flutter closed as I answer her. "I thought they were only dreams, but Maude must have been inside my head. She told me she would order her soldiers to retreat if I handed over you and Vander, then threatened me with ending my father's life if I didn't do what she wanted."

Wyn spits at Maude, "I hope the Mother Star smites you where you stand."

The Night Lady laughs again.

When Maude gave me the opportunity to end the war, I believed my father's mind to be lost to the madness caused by losing his mate. Looking at him now, there's a stark difference in the way he is acting compared to the last time I saw him in the Autumn court, when he spoke in nothing but the indecipherable ramblings of madness.

Father's eyes are sharp as he takes in the scene before him, the backs of the undead lining our beach, and how I stand with Vander, Wyn, and Torin to face Maude and her army. His emerald irises, so alike mine in colour and shape, blaze with sparks of anger and frustration. His back is rigid. He shows no fear. At this moment, I realise Maude has control of his mind. How else is the madness gone?

It's a moment of reprieve for the once respected High Lord of Autumn. In the time before his death, the Mother Star has granted him lucidity, where he may acknowledge his downfalls, his mistakes, and his shortcomings, and beg her forgiveness. It is a moment of sanity where he can remember how his life and choices impacted others. He can remember the good times, the smiles, the fights he so bravely won. He may take these memories into death, where he will cherish them from his resting place among the stars forevermore.

A knot twists in my stomach as emotion clogs my throat and tears build in my eyes. I blink them away and take a shuddering breath. "You claim to understand who I am as a fae, but what you do not realise is the hardships I have faced have shaped who I am today. If you had come to me when the Dusk Court first emerged, I would be riddled with fear at hearing your threat. Now, after enduring so much at your hand, I am not willing to play your games. Kill him if you must."

"You would sacrifice your father's life for that of the Theron siblings?"

I offer her nothing but a slight dip of my chin. There is no saving him, not from Maude and not from the madness she holds at bay for this moment.

"Very well," she says, her lips curling into a smirk. "Have you any last words?"

I swipe at the tears streaming down my face with rage-fuelled movements and look Father in the eye. "Throughout my life, you allowed your denizens to treat me like a pariah. You watched while Fayeth chipped away at my soul, piece by piece, until I was nothing more than a husk of the fae I should be. You were not kind, and you certainly did not show me love." I take a shuddering breath, and as I release it, I let go of all the anger. "I forgive you."

He hangs his head in shame. "Bria," he croaks. "You are strong. Stronger than I could have ever dreamed. I regret how I treated you. And I am so very sorry. Let the realm bear witness to the last words of High Lord Kerym Sutherland." He raises his head. His eyes lock with mine, and not a slither of fear shines within the emerald. "I love you, my brave, darling daughter."

Maude drags her obsidian blade across Father's throat with deliberate slowness. His death begins as a single drop of blood that builds before darting to the stained tunic hanging from his lean frame. Another soon joins that crimson line, then another as the blade slices from one side to the other. Soon after, the lone blood track is gone, hidden beyond a veil of crimson.

Father, ever stoic and stubborn, does not so much as flinch. His gaze does not leave my face as the life drains from his body and soul. Even while he sags in Maude's cruel arms.

And I watch. I watch until the blood no longer cascades down his chest, until his eyes roll back and he loses his fight to remain conscious. I watch until Kerym Sutherland is no more. Then, with Vander and Wyn by my side, I fold away from the

Dusk Court for the last time, with wrath scorching my veins and the deep yearning for vengeance curling my hands into fists.

Chapter 25

T HE MOMENT MY FEET touch the soft grass of the Court of Blooms, I stop fighting the onslaught of debilitating emotion. My heart grows so heavy it steals my breath away. It drags me down. I fall to my knees, fighting to drag precious air into my lungs and pressing the heel of my palm against my chest as if the motion alone can rid me of the pain.

I blink against the dry ache of my eyes, seeing the sea of canvas before me but not registering what it means. A deafening *whoosh* in my ears silences Vander's, Wyn's, and Torin's murmurs. My heavy heart sinks lower, settling in the pit of my stomach and refusing to cease the slow beats of anguish pulsing through me.

My father is dead.

I did not think it would hurt so badly. After everything he has said and done, I did not think this would affect me so.

The tears I expected — the tears I allowed to fall free with Maude as my witness — do not come. Perhaps they have deserted me, having fallen free too often in recent times. Their absence irritates me; I press my hands against my eyes and whimper. Am I so broken I cannot mourn my father as he deserves?

I ignore the muted thud of Vander kneeling beside me. There is nothing he can say that will ease the grief. At least, that is what I believe until he speaks.

"Your father was a strong fae. He was beloved by the Autumn denizens and respected by his peers. We will remember his vibrancy and his courage for millennia to come. For such a male to lose his mate and suffer such madness is heartbreaking." Van peels my hands away from my face, crooks a finger beneath my chin, and forces me to look at him. "He's in a better place. I know it's one of those things we say to ease grief, and more often than not, the sentiment does little to soothe the pain, but in this instance, it's a truth you can't overlook. Kerym wouldn't have wanted to live with the madness. He's at peace now."

At first, his words only anger me. He cannot have peace if he's dead. He cannot have anything. There is no better place than the living realm.

Then I realise he's right. Father cannot have peace without his mate. As much as I despised Fayeth, reuniting with her in the afterlife can only benefit Father's soul. The madness will flee, leaving him to rest in peace for eternity.

I lower my hands to the damp ground, disturbing the mildew clinging to the blades of moss-green grass. There's a distinct lack of energy pulling at my core and my limbs, but I push the exhaustion aside. Father's death is a pain I will not overcome within a handful of moments. It is an everlasting sorrow that will follow me until I leave this world.

I cannot do anything about it right now, and dwelling on my heartache will not win this war. Father will find peace in his passing, and I will find solace in that knowledge.

"Thank you." I somehow force the words out through my emotion-clogged throat.

"Do you need some time alone?" Vander asks. "Tell me what you need, and I'll give it to you."

"Sit with me for a while."

I take comfort in his presence while I look out, unseeing, over the sea of canvas before me. In the time we sit in silence, I remember Kerym and all he lived for: Rennyn, Fayeth, his denizens, the Autumn Court. He did not make my life easy, and he did not offer me the same chances he offered my brother, but he *does* deserve this moment of remembrance.

When I run out of memories to offer the Mother Star, I begin to see things more clearly. Like Wyn and Torin's absence. Like the canvas, which is not a sea of beige, but many small tents, all pitched in an enormous field that once held wildflowers. There are wooden racks laden with weapons and shields, a long line of catapults to the side, and pillars of smoke curling to the sky, where I notice the lack of stars and startle at the thought of night having passed — we have been sitting here for much longer than I thought.

The sight before me... it's a war camp of epic proportions. It's a reminder of why we're here, and of why Father is no longer with us. Kerym will not be the only fae to fall because of this war, and the air of tension lingering over the camp is enough to slam me back to reality.

"I'm ready," I say, my legs protesting as I clamber to my feet. "There will be time to mourn after we win this war."

We approach the war camp with our hands joined, fingers threaded together, strolling so we may take in everything from the identical tents that can fit four fae at most to the four watch towers marking the corners of the camp.

Each of the towers — they are wooden and rickety, but serve their purpose well — is host to five sentries, one from each court fighting on this side of the war. The towers loom over the camp and pierce the dark morning sky, and if I didn't know the Dusk sentry in each was casting an illusion to hide our camp from Night, Summer, and Autumn, I would fear Maude finding us from their height alone.

We enter at the south-eastern end of camp, where the Day fae have marked their tents with blue banners adorned with a lone drop of water. The aromatic scents of grilled fish, lemon, and thyme anger my growling stomach. Zentha's tent, a canvas of the deepest blue and twice as large as the others, is empty when we pass.

The camp is silent, with our soldiers taking the time for some much needed rest. We do not know when Maude will next strike with her hand of vengeance. Fae wander between the tents in search of food, and others sit beside small fires sharpening their blades or adjusting their armour. Everyone is morose. Quiet. Melancholy.

"When did you find the time to organise all of this?" I ask.

"I left Torin in charge." He pulls me from the path of a Dawn male as we pass one of the many healing tents. He points to a burgundy tent in the centre of the war camp. "Since our army is the smallest, we're in the middle of all this."

I note the banners for each of our allies and where they are positioned. After Day, we pass through Dawn, with the golden sun shining from their banners and bright white canvas tents with the healer's insignia on their sides. Far ahead, the silver tornado of Dusk, and the snowflake of our neighbours, the Winter fae. At the far end of camp, Spring's green leaf, which I am hardly able to see from here.

Torin chose this location wisely, with the forest and mountains of Dawn to our east, fields of grass and the expanse of the ocean to our north and south, and the Bolbala Ranges in the far west. There are few disadvantages. But then again, this is not the battlefield.

I am just about to ask where we intend to fight when Vander pulls me inside the grand burgundy tent in the centre of camp.

Inside is not as spacious as I had assumed. With four wooden posts preventing the canvas ceiling from falling on top of us, an open flame in the middle, and a scattering of low, backless stools, it's a space not intended for comfort. Though there is a lone table by the door covered with fruits, cheese, and sliced meat, plus two carafes of wine.

With the cramped space, it is difficult to offer each fae within a smile. Six and ten fae do not fit well, but we make do. Nyana and her trio of lovers crowd around the only table, picking at plump grapes and crumbling cheese. Zentha and Elmon stand by the door, the first to greet us with tight smiles. Jonik, Larrad, and Tasar do not fit the atmosphere with their laughs, mirrored by Torin. Ruith whispers instructions to Tarathiel and Vacon. Wyn stands alone, with her back to the fire, watching the entrance and waiting for us.

A hushed round of "Well met" flows through the tent, the Dawn males' laughter dies down, and everyone waits for someone else to speak.

They've been waiting for Vander and me for a while, it seems.

In such trying times, it is hard to find the words. They come after a time, and I say, "It is with pain clenching my heart that I must tell you my father, High Lord Kerym Sutherland, is dead by Maude's own hand. The Mother Star granted him a reprieve from the madness in his final moments, where he spoke his last words." I cannot clear my throat, and the tears that abandoned me in the field flow down my cheeks. The sorrow flares once more. "He loved me."

Zentha sniffs before wrapping me in her warm embrace. "Of course he did, darling Bria. Of course he did." She pulls back with tears shimmering in her golden-brown eyes. "I am so sorry for your loss."

"Thank you, Zentha." I repeat the sentiment to everyone after they offer their condolences before steering the conversation away from my heartache. "Nyana, have your seers seen the future? Do you have any insight for us?"

Her lips thin. "Maude has blocked her mind from my seers. I cannot see when she will attack, only how we are affected. It will be bloody." She offers no more on the matter, and none of us dare to press her further.

Wyn asks, "Do we have a plan?"

"It does not matter how much thought we put to it," says Ruith. "War cannot be planned."

"I beg to differ. Plans will be our salvation," scoffs Tasar.

Larrad says, "A good offence may turn the tides in our favour. We need to have *something* in place. Even if it is just a formation for our armies."

"Our armies are busy fighting skirmishes all over the realm," says Darcel, Nyana's second and consort. His warm brown skin reflects the amber glow of the fire, as if a mirror. It's bewildering and magical and intriguing. "We defended our western forest twice just yesterday."

"Not to mention the attack at the lake," adds Argi, running his bark-like fingers over the pale green skin of his arms, trying to find warmth.

Torin nudges Argi aside and pours himself a chalice of deep red wine. "There are battles raging all over Radelea. I believe them to be distractions."

"For?" Vacon's tone drips with distaste.

Torin turns, gulps down wine, then says, "For whatever diabolic attack Maude's planning."

Ruith narrows his eyes at his second. "A draft of selkies attempted to force their way through the wards at the Caves of Apricity. Both the form of attack and location make little sense. The Wind Whisperer is correct. Maude is trying to distract us."

"Should we just let them attack these pointless locations, then?" asks Elmon. "Focus on what truly matters?"

Wyn spins to face him. "And return home to destroyed villages? We've already sacrificed our entire court. You can't expect us to just *let* her cause so much destruction?"

"I do not believe that is what he is suggesting," says Jonik.

"Nor do I," adds Nyana. The rose gold armour covering her from head to toe suits her. "Radelea will not mourn the loss of a cave system or a forest. Elmon means for us to protect the villages and strongholds, rather than spend energy defending nature. I admire Maude's tenacity, but we are too smart to fall for this. I agree with pulling our forces from where they are not required."

Many agree, including myself. Why waste precious energy and magic fighting Maude's distractions when we should prepare for the real thing?

But those who do not — Wyn, Vander, Ruith, Jonik, Zentha, Imala, and Darcel — present valid arguments. If we win the war, but do not defend the natural wonders of Radelea, there will be nothing to celebrate. What good is decimating the Night, Autumn, and Summer Courts if we lose everything in return?

The arguing continues well into the day. It's a continual back and forth, and no one can seem to agree on a single detail. Vacon grows more agitated. As head of Winter's army, which is focusing on protecting the weak and vulnerable in the Bolbala Ranges, he's determined to pull his soldiers from where they guard the mountain ranges and station them here, where they will be in the thick of the action.

After what seems like hours, someone suggests only sending those willing to defend to the vulnerable and worshiped locations; letting the soldiers decide for themselves is just. And by the Mother Star's grace, we all agree.

Each High fae disappears to relay the orders. And by the time the stars are appearing, everyone is well and truly exhausted. Ruith, who I have always admired for keeping a clear head in trying times, orders everyone to bed.

If we were not so bone tired, and not so riddled with tension, most of us would have argued. But given war looms closer than ever before, I think we are all thankful to spend our last peaceful moments with those we love.

Which is why, when Vander and I slip into our small tent at long last, I do not waste precious time.

I cinch the opening closed, run my eyes over the small space — there is enough room for a pile of furs and cushions, two wooden mannequins supporting our armour, and a slither of grass for our boots — then settle my gaze on Vander. "This may be the last chance we have."

He eases himself to the makeshift bed and shucks off his boots. "The last chance for what?" He looks up at me through tired eyes, his lashes framing the silver and casting long shadows over his tawny cheeks.

One by one, I unbuckle the clasps of my leathers, then peel them away from my upper body as slowly as I can. He moves to drag me closer, but I click my tongue at him and shake my head. "Patience is a virtue."

I shimmy the leathers down my legs, disposing of both the black fabric and my boots before standing naked in front of him. We are twin souls, with a bond blessed by the Mother Star herself. He completes me, and I am not ashamed to stand naked before him, but the way he is looking at me, with lust and re-spect and need shining from his eyes, makes me feel vulnerable. Perhaps it is because I, too, feel those things. Perhaps it's because my entire being is aching for him in every sense of the word.

My greedy eyes drink in every dip and curve of Vander's body while he undresses with deliberate slowness. His muscular arms, which are so loving in their embrace during the hardest of times. The way his powerful thighs ripple when he stands reminds me of the time he crawled for me. His defined abdominals reveal the strength in his body. The strength of a male who has fought many battles for the ones he loves.

"Do you ever think about completing our bond?" The thought has been playing on my mind since I heard of Kyra's hesitation in mating with Elmon. And I feel that not asking this before the war is a disservice to our connection.

He stills. "Every day."

"Please don't feel like I'm rejecting you when I say this, but I don't want to cement our bond before the Mother Star."

This time, when he reaches for me, I allow him to drag me down to the pile of furs and cushions. He asks me to explain, while lowering me into his lap and running his hands up and down my spine.

It's difficult to speak through the building desire. Somehow, I find coherency. "Our bond is not like that of chosen mates. We didn't have to declare our love for each other before friends and family, with the rising sun offering us her blessing. Our bond is complete, stronger than that of chosen mates. I think... I don't need the Mother Star's blessing. We know how we feel, and that's enough for me."

He leans forward to slide his lips along the curve of my throat. *"This is ours, Princess. No one else's. We don't need a crowd of fae to know we are right for one another. If you don't want a mating ceremony, then we won't have one. Simple."*

"You would do that for me?"

He lifts me with one hand, using his other to slide his erection through the wetness building between my legs before sinking inside me. *"I would do anything for you."*

I grip his face between my hands and drag his mouth to mine. His lips, full and tasting of plum wine, meld with mine with a perfection I marvel at every time. My tongue slides into his mouth, tasting and devouring as I rotate my hips.

His hands slip to my hips and hold me in place. He's deep. So deep that he is all I can feel. He pulls back, his silver eyes locking with mine, and growls, "I want to see you, Princess."

I grind against him. The move sends currents of bliss rocketing through my body, from my clitoris to my fingers and toes. I'm a current of power. I am a single nerve ending, sizzling with ecstasy. The desire builds as I grind once more, somehow taking Vander impossibly deeper. A breathy moan flutters through my parted lips.

He releases his hold on my hips to trail his palms over my waist, up the curve of my stomach, and to cup my breasts. He rolls my hardened nipple between his thumb and forefinger, the action only adding to the blazing inferno roiling inside.

I push myself up before slamming back down, and bite my lip to withhold the cry of delight. My hands rove over his chest, their movements disjointed as I continue to rise and fall, each thrust down sending ripples of desire sizzling throughout my body.

We find a steady rhythm. Our eyes never drift.

We do not leave the tent for an entire day, and we are not the only fae to do so. We lose ourselves in one another, revering these last moments of peace before war tears everything we know and love from our flailing grasp.

Chapter 26

THE BONE-CHILLING DRONE OF a war horn blasts across the camp, rousing the army to a mist-shrouded morning. The long note, so low I feel it in my bones, ends with a high-pitched stutter. My breath catches. Two short blasts of the bronze horn, played by a sentry in one of the watchtowers, wake whoever did not jolt from their bed after the first note.

My heart stutters as I untangle from the furs and race to pull on my leathers. Another long, low note spreads through the war camp, this time wrapping around my stomach and dragging it into my throat, where I'm certain it will remain until we either emerge victorious, or I die. Three short, deep blasts of the horn send a trickle of ice down my spine, signalling the last notes of the traditional fae horn.

The instrument, which is as tall as those who dare to press their lips to the cold bronze, and is shaped into an elongated S, has only been heard once in Radelea's history. At the onset of the bloody war that raged for three moon cycles before the ancient leaders came together to sign the treaty and the Mother Star rose for the first time.

Remembering the horn's history sends ripples of understanding through my mind, and I spin to Vander, pausing in the action of buckling my golden armour. "I know how to make her rise."

He cinches the leather bindings of his vambrace together, moving to the other while saying, "This isn't the time. We can talk about it after the war."

"I think this will *end* the war, Van. We need to tell the others."

After securing his greaves, he turns me around to finish buckling my chest plate. "Are you certain? We can't spend precious time discussing a *theory* when Maude's army marches towards us."

"Trust me." I snatch my plated helmet from the wooden mannequin and slide it over my braided hair. My vision is mostly unobscured, with the golden strip covering the bridge of my nose the only glimmer of metal distracting me.

I turn to help Vander with his charcoal-coloured visor, threading the chin strap tight, then looking into his silver eyes. I commit the colour to memory. Moonlight. A glint of steel. Home, if it's a shade at all. "I love you. Please don't get yourself killed out there."

Our helmets clang when he rests his forehead against mine. We take a moment, perhaps the last moment we can, to breathe. "I love you, too," he says, his voice terse.

We work together to place my vambraces and greaves — which are uncomfortable, heavy, and cumbersome — then burst from the tent and into the chilled morning air, to the beginning notes of the war drums.

Two slow, reverberating strikes of the drums succeed three rapid booms. My heart beats in time with the blasts, two slow and three fast. Over and over. I find my feet trying to move in time with the beat, too. The booms will continue until the drummer falls.

The western horizon, so dark it seems to absorb every fae light flickering in the camp, ripples. I squint against the darkness, and the outlines of hundreds of harpies form, a little disfigured, as if they carry something in their lethal claws.

Fae from every court in our alliance race from their tents, some still buckling their armour tight, others pausing at the weapon stands to arm themselves against the Night, Autumn, and Summer fae. It will not only be fae we face on this dreadful day, but selkies, undead, and harpies, too. It is a battle we may not win.

But we will try. The Mother Star knows we will try.

Vander nods to Torin and Wyn as they exit their own tents, both dressed in charcoal-coloured armour identical to his. "Are you ready?"

"No," they say in unison.

Wyn adds, "No one can ever be ready for war."

The four of us race into the large burgundy tent to find everyone else already there, most of them pacing. Even Tohminic has dressed for battle, though he looks like he needs another moon cycle of rest before attempting to fight.

Nyana ties her long curls at her nape before allowing Argi to slide her rose gold helmet on top. "At last." Her tone betrays her nerves. "Your army is ready?"

"Already marching towards the battlefield," says Torin.

Vander clears his throat. "I know we have little time, and our plans are already made, but Bria believes she has insight that may help."

All eyes turn to me. It is not the time to feel afraid or embarrassed, and I spill my theory as fast as I can. "The Mother Star first rose after the ancient treaty was signed. I think we can make her rise once more if we work together."

"How?" asks Ruith. "And why do you think this?"

"It was the war horn that reminded me. The warning notes have not raced across the realm since the first war, when fae from every court worked together to bring down a common enemy: dissonance." I run my eyes over every fae here. "Our sun shines upon every court in Radelea. It's proof enough she wants us in harmony. If one from each court works together to bring down Maude, I believe the Mother Star will once again grace us with her warmth."

Murmurs run through the tent from each High fae, but it is Jonik who says, "Then we will fight together."

"So, what's the plan?" asks Larrad. "Do we just all attack whatever part of Maude we can reach?"

"Or we can form a line and take turns stabbing her?" Tasar's smirk is likely his last before a victor emerges.

I flick my eyes to Vander. I'm not certain this will work, but it's the only option we have. Facing the others once more, I ask, "Have you ever heard of a magical conduit?"

We take the time to check in with Penna, who is in charge of the war camp infirmaries. She has everything under control; she has organised for a younger male to act as go-between, folding from the camp to Dawn's centre of healing, where the grievously injured will be taken.

We do not wish each other luck. We do not say farewell. It is too hard.

Vander and I spend our last silent moments standing atop a watchtower, where we gaze out at the five armies gathering in the east. To the south-east, Dawn and Day ships sway with the waves, their cannons ready for striking as soon as the order is made. To the west, the harassment of harpies grows near, so close now I can discern the unique colours of their feathers.

No matter which direction I look, I cannot see the Night army. There are no Autumn fae, no Summer fire wielders, and no undead. The absence of our opponents is concerning, but it gives us more time to prepare.

The battle grounds lie at the base of the Dawn mountains, spilling over onto Spring territory and filling the forest, which offers us the best defence we can hope for, providing an impenetrable fortress at our backs. Five waterfalls, each in different locations throughout the mountain range, stream water into a rapidly flowing river that cuts across the eastern side of the battleground, offering yet another defence that benefits us.

When the time comes to descend the watchtower and join the others at its base, I offer Van one last look. A look that conveys everything I feel in my heart but cannot speak out loud, for fear of my voice failing.

Vander's gauntlet is cold as he caresses my cheek, his thumb smoothing the worry from my brow. "Be careful."

"I vow it."

Joining the rest of our attack party feels like the beginning of everything. The simple motion of stepping from the watchtower's ladder and onto the grass outside the camp feels weighted. Final. We have a contingency plan set in place for if we are separated — battles are chaotic, and there is no way to determine if we will all come out of it unscathed — yet something inside me recoils at the idea of parting with these fae.

Nyana's hands are covered with sharp leaves. Ruith's shadows snake from his palms. Tohminic wields flames in his only hand, while sparks flicker from the stump of his severed wrist. Cool drops of water splash to the ground at Zentha's feet. Blazing light engulfs Jonik. A harsh wind billows from Vander. Torin stands immobile, reading the memories of the wind with his eyes closed.

At the outskirts of our group, our small team of guards grip weapons tight in their hands. Wyn twists her snake bangle with nervous anticipation. Larrad and Tasar are silent for once. Elmon's warm brown face is pallid, his eyes wide and darting. Tarathiel's Konda glints under the lone fae light above. Darcel cracks his knuckles with menacing intention, his gaze locked on Nyana.

We are a force to be reckoned with, it is certain, as we make the long walk to the battlefield in silence, where we join the thousands-strong army. Five courts, all united on Radelea soil.

At first glance, one would assume there is no set formation to our army. I know better. Their orders, issued by each of the High fae, are to form groups of five. One from each court. They are to protect each other no matter the cost. Looking closer, I can see the small groups huddled together, see their mouths moving with quiet discussions, each of them trying to figure out the best plan of attack. Knowing each other's strengths and weaknesses will benefit them in battle.

The tension is palpable. It brings a metallic taste to my tongue and curls my hands into fists, only to have them splay wide with ice crystals dancing at my fingertips.

"Here." Nyana hands each of us a small vial of shimmering indigo liquid. "We did not have the time to prepare an antidote for every soldier, but we have enough for the best fighters and those in charge."

"This is the antidote for blue mock lotus?" asks Tohminic. His voice sends a shiver of fear along my spine, and I fight hard to suppress it, telling myself he is an ally now. The knowledge does little to erase all I endured at his hand.

"Only take it if you come into contact with the powder. Taking this too soon works against you," says Nyana. She slides her own antidote into a pocket at her breast, within easy reach should she need it.

I do the same, taking comfort in the slight pressure against my collarbone.

A scuffle sounds from the south. A rage-filled shout fills the silence. "Autumn soldiers entering from the river!"

Those around me turn and dart towards the east, where the river rages with fierce anger, as if it knows its water will soon be tinted with red, as if it knows bloodshed is coming.

I draw an atryxium dagger and follow the tight group. I have to shove through several groups of five, but I make it to the river's edge, panting, to see seven younglings with blades at their throats.

"Stop!" I call. "I know them!"

My heart stutters. They cannot be here. Soon enough, this land will be bathed in crimson, some of it theirs if they do not leave.

"They're our enemies, Bria," warns Torin when I step closer. "The Autumn fae are under Maude's control."

"These are my students," I whip at him. "They have been in hiding and are *not* being controlled by Night's High Lady." Turning to Dey, to whom I issued the order to hide, I ask, "Why are you here?"

"We come with news," they say.

Vander steps forward, angling his body in front of me, regardless of my insistence of their innocence. "News of what?"

Mykaela shudders at the venom in his tone. Orli, Hamon, and Mitah shrink closer together. Rhett and Dillon hold hands and stare at the ground.

Dey says, "We hid like you asked, but perhaps not where you would have thought. The walls of the Autumn castle provided sanctuary while we listened and waited for our chance. We know every aspect of their plans. The undead march from the south and will be upon us come noontime. The harpies will release blue mock powder at random intervals, with the Night army finishing what the paralytic cannot. And the Autumn ships —" Their eyes widen at something over my shoulder.

A harpy screeches, as if called by Dey's words, and the first blue mock attack hits the western front. Screams ring through the field and shouts flow from commanders.

Someone cries, "They carry soldiers!"

I order the guards surrounding my students to leave them be, then in a single breath, say, "There are cabins just up the mountain. Hide. For the love of the Mother Star, Dey, take them and *hide*!"

I turn away from my beloved younglings before my fear for their safety gets a choke hold on me. From above, harpies screech and dip low, and the Night fae riding on their backs leap from the security of the feathers and onto the battlefield.

War is not coming.

It is here.

Chapter 27

T HE DRUM BEATS ECHO off the mountains at my back. They boom with every thud of my feet against the cold ground, as if my panic calls to the drummer. We are too far from those hit with the blue mock powder to help. We are too far from the fae dropping from the backs of the harpies to be of any use to those nearest.

Something clicks in my mind. A harsh truth I am not prepared for. Maude's moves thus far have been precise, and always follow some kind of distraction. That I am at the opposite end of the battlefield, along with those sworn as allies to the Dusk Court, is telling.

I risk a glance over my shoulder as I race towards the clash of battle. Dey, who did not flee and hide as I ordered, smirks. A flash of ice-blue shines within their eyes for a heartbeat before Dey's neck twists at an unnatural angle. They collapse to the sodden ground in the same moment. Lifeless.

The guttural roar that pulls from my throat is ravaged and laden with pain. Sorrow fractures my heart, followed by a stab of guilt. If I had not snuck from the court to see Dey, they would not be dead.

I turn back to the fray, now on the very outskirts, and push Dey's death to the back of my mind to dwell on later. Right now, it's imperative that I concentrate.

More blue mock powder rains down from above, glittering like a thousand stars before blanketing those beneath. Cries of shock and pain ring out over the clash of blades when fae fall victim to the paralytic effects of the poison.

I bring tongues of shadow to my left palm while wielding a long dagger in my right, glance at Vander beside me — the others in our group have already dispersed among the battle — then slide along the slick grass to meet my first opponent.

The male is skilled with his short sword. Skilled yet cocksure. The Gloom taught me a lot. It taught me resilience, where to place my trust, and how to endure heartache. It also taught me where the weaknesses are in the Night Court's obsidian armour.

I don't hesitate. My feet move of their own accord, the tiresome training sessions with Vander, Wyn, and Torin paying off at last as I slip into a defensive position. I feign to the left, using my shadows to distract and blind. The moment they cover my opponent's eyes, I strike with my right, the brutal dagger sinking into the soft flesh between his arm and chest. I rip it free straight away, then twist to fend off another male, this one burlier than the first, with less grace in his movements.

Between opponents, I catch glimpses of my allies, notably Blodwen as she feeds from the injured. She was supposed to fold to Winter with the others. Torin will be furious.

Vander remains beside me, wielding his axe with lethal accuracy. He has not yet called upon his powers, his weaponry expertise enough for now.

Alizeh rushes overhead, nothing but a gust of wind, and steals the breath from the Night fae. She ignores their wide eyes and groping hands, moving on to another victim before the first has hit the ground.

Tarathiel moves with such speed around Ruith that he is almost a blur of black armour and translucent skin. His High Lord takes advantage of every opening, his Konda severing limbs and slicing across stomachs with ease.

Beyond them, Wyn and Torin make an excellent team. Wyn uses the power of the wind to push attackers into Torin's deadly path, where they end up either impaled on his short sword or with their throats slashed.

It is gruesome.

The sounds… The sounds are unlike anything I have ever heard. The Gloom, which was horrific in its own right, has nothing on this bloodbath.

A female of Night lunges from my left, her dark brown hands gripping curved daggers that scream of menace. They are not made to kill, but to maim.

I react without thinking and send a blast of shadow and ice towards her. The shadow blankets her face and constricts while the ice numbs and freezes.

As I swing back around, time seems to slow.

Larrad races towards me — No. He races towards *Argi*, screaming a warning that comes too late. Our eyes meet over the green-skinned Spring male for a moment before we both look on in shock.

Blood, red tinted with green to denote his forest-born nature, spills from Argi's eyes, from his mouth and nose and ears. His bark-like fingers contort as he raises them to his head, his mouth open in a silent scream. He sinks to his knees, then tilts sideways and crashes hard to the ground. He does not rise again.

My eyes dart to Larrad, only to find him on his knees as well. Without thinking, I send a blanket of shadow to cover the Dawn prince. I will not lose another of Jonik's sons to the magic of Night. I refuse.

"Cover me, Vander!" I don't wait for Van's response, and sprint across the chaos of the battlefield until I'm skidding to a stop before Larrad.

"Get out," I pant. "I'll cover you until you're gone. See Penna, then return once you are certain you can fight."

He folds away without a word, his face twisted with indescribable pain.

I suck the shadows back inside. The battle has barely begun, and we are already down two of our allies. And I can't help but wonder, as I look at the harassment of harpies circling above... Where is their leader?

The Mother Star offers me no time to ponder the High Lady's whereabouts.

A scream tears across the field, a sound of pure terror, sounding from the southern-most side of the raging battle.

As I look towards the ocean, my stomach twists into a tight knot, for those are Autumn masts slipping between the ships of Day and Dawn. And at the head of their fleet, a larger ship bedecked in amber and bronze. The ship of their High Lord.

The ship of my brother.

Before the ships anchor, the ground begins to shake. It shakes with such violence that fae are thrown into the air. A crevasse forms, shallow at first, but soon splitting the battlefield into two. Iron cannonballs whistle through the air before crashing into the shaking ground and sending sprays of blood and dirt over those close by.

Calls for backup ricochet off the mountains. "Incoming undead! They're crossing the river!" The words of a Dusk fae chase us on the wind.

We have a heartbeat to make our decision. The plan we concocted with the other High fae demands we free Summer and Autumn from Maude's wrath. We believe it will enrage her enough to bring her to the heart of battle. We can free Summer now, or Autumn. Either way, we risk losing one or the other if we do not act fast enough.

One look at Vander is all it takes for me to decide. I failed my father. I will *not* fail my brother, too, regardless of if he failed me time and again throughout my five and seventy years.

We fight our way across the battlefield, slashing and jabbing and twisting from harm's way. We leap over fallen fae, dodge young males who dart between duels to fold away with the injured, and duck below whizzing cannonballs, all while fending off attacks and incapacitating our enemies.

Torin and Wyn join us as we reach the sandy shore of Spring's long beach, where the battle has spilled onto the sand.

"Where are you going?" Wyn shouts as she sends someone staggering backwards with a powerful gust of wind.

"My brother is on that ship." I tease a thread of my metal bending magic free and use it to disarm the female barrelling towards me. "I'm going to free his mind."

Torin ducks beneath the black blade of a long sword, slicing across the female's legs when he straightens. "How?"

"Your mother is here."

"Fuck." His distraction almost costs him his life. If Vander was not paying close attention to his second, Torin's legs would be severed from his body.

He spins, his long blonde hair flailing as he turns and pierces the female in the heart with a grunt. He straightens once more and asks, "What's the plan?"

"Fold onto the ship. Go from there." The words do not sound like they are coming from me, with my ragged pants straining each letter and the harshness coating them foreign.

"Wards?" Wyn asks as we race closer to the lapping water.

"Not on the ships." I gather the realm's magic and wrap it around me, feeling the enormous power of the void, only to let it slip through my grasp when five selkies leap from the depths of the ocean.

A male, who is flanked on both sides, saunters over the sand. Xaler, the leader of the Summer selkies, locks his cruel eyes on me.

My first reaction is to flee. Cold dread spreads from my heart to my fingers, turning them numb. I recall his taunts, his torture, and his depravity. But I remember I'm no longer that female. I am strong.

Vander, feeling my emotions across our bond, twists his palms. A miniature tornado churns between them, growing fiercer with every turn. He slams his hands in Xaler's direction. The tornado tears across the sand, sending the small grains hurtling through the air and leaving a deep groove in its wake, then swallows the selkie leader and his guards. It carries them out to sea and dumps them in the dark water, where they shift into their seal forms.

I rip open the magical hatch in my mind and free my animalistic powers, feeling the coarse fur of dire wolves skate over my palms, hearing the grunt of boars, and scenting the sweet musk of a well-run horse. With a single thought, I wrap the magic around my soul and crash into Xaler's mind so hard we are both stunned for a moment.

I recover first, and with as much strength as I possess, coil my soul around his. I squeeze hard, and continue to squeeze, the coil growing tighter with every frantic beat of his heart. All I can think of is revenge. I can taste the blood on my lips from his assault, feel the flaking skin from dehydration, and echoes of pain ripple throughout as I recall every time he pierced my flesh with his trident. I squeeze and squeeze until his soul shatters completely.

With the selkie's mind now useless, I drag my soul back to my waiting fae body, cradled in Wyn's arms as Vander and Torin guard us on either side.

"He won't be a problem anymore," I rasp. I do not wait for them to acknowledge my words and gather the realm's magic around me once more.

Within an instant, I'm standing on the foredeck of Rennyn's ship. I take a moment to get my bearings. Three anglers and two members of the crew scurry about, providing whatever help they can to the ten soldiers who stand by the cannons along both the port and starboard. In the very centre, a male who makes my blood run cold, standing beside a female who turns that blood to ice. I do not know why Lord Gorred allows Chlora on my brother's ship; I cannot think past the rage scorching my veins to figure it out.

Rennyn is nowhere to be seen.

"Don't disappear like that again, Princess." Vander's tone is wrathful.

"Sorry."

Twin thuds sound from behind me. I do not need to turn to know Wyn and Torin have arrived, but I do turn when I hear a third thump.

Tohminic, dressed in full Summer regalia of gleaming silver armour with flames pressed into the metal, does not pause to greet us. As he passes us, he says, "She is mine."

A hunk of iron replaces his missing hand, its intention clear: bludgeoning. It grazes my armour as he barges through our small group and shouts, "Chlora of Night, I challenge you to a duel!"

Chlora turns. She is so alike her mother that I am ashamed to admit I did not see it before now. Too confident to don armour like the rest of us, her maroon tailcoat is at odds with the chaos of the war raging on the nearby beach. She has pulled her mahogany hair away from her face, with neat curls pinned against her scalp.

Her ice-blue eyes narrow at Tohminic. "Have you returned to beg for more, Tohm? I thought after our last encounter, you would not be so foolish as to face me."

He straightens his shoulders and brings a churning orb of fire to his palm. "I am here to kill you."

Those surrounding her draw their weapons — most of them Summer fae, with only two or three Autumn denizens — and aim them at Tohminic.

Lord Gorred chuckles, his muddy eyes locked on me.

Chlora waves them away. "Stand down, fools. This is not your fight." She sneers at Tohminic. "You have but one hand, and you think you can beat *me*? Do you not know who I am?"

"Your mother cannot save you. She is too weak to fight in a war she started. Her preference to allow others to die on her behalf rather than face this threat herself is despicable. She will not find the courage to rescue you." Tohminic's words are sure, and I have to agree. We have not seen Maude since the battle begun.

Chlora laughs, though the sound is strained. She is not a fighter. In fact, I do not recall seeing her wield magic in the time I have known her. Not when she threatened me in the Autumn Court, not during any of those disgusting sex parties at Ad'Starrag's rotunda, and not during any of the meals I was forced to share with her.

I had always assumed she had the abilities of Summer, with fire and necromancy running in her veins. But to be Maude's daughter… I wonder if she only controls minds like her mother, or if she has the power to manipulate blood and bone like the rest of the Night fae.

"There are five and ten guards," whispers Torin, pulling me from my thoughts. "We can keep them distracted while Tohminic enacts his revenge."

"Ten. The crew will not retaliate. It is not in their nature," I say. The crew and anglers are from Autumn, proven by the burnt orange of their sailing smocks. I know them to be gentle souls, bred for the sea with hands made to haul rope and nets, not weapons.

"Ten against four is not good adds," says Wyn.

"Gorred is mine," snarls Vander. He has not taken his eyes off the abusive lord since he folded onto the ship's deck.

Ahead, Tohminic makes the first move, sending the fireball careening for Chlora. He follows with a second soon after. He does not stop approaching.

Vander sighs and gathers a blustering gust of wind between his palms, then sends it breezing across the deck, where it collides with a trio of Summer fae. They slam into the gunwale, teeter for a moment, then fall to the ocean below. Their screams follow them to their deaths.

"Seven and four. Much better," says Torin. The humour in his tone is clear.

Wyn, who has been dancing from foot to foot, eager to attack the denizens of a court that caused such heartache, palms two daggers and leaps for the nearest Summer guard. She takes him by surprise and her blade slashes across his throat before he even thinks about defending himself. She quickly moves to the next, leaving five remaining for Vander, Torin, and me.

I disarm a slim female with a single thought, my metal bending magic thrumming with pride.

Torin dashes for two at once, each of his short swords making quick work of their enemies.

Vander throws an axe. The curved blade sinks into Gorred's thigh, sending the lord crashing to the deck. He blinds another with an illusion — it is something terrible, by the screams —

then stalks to the male who touched when he was not allowed, who ogled when it was not wanted.

"Please," Gorred begs, like the pathetic male he is.

Vander merely pulls his axe free from Gorred's thigh, readjusts his grip with a lazy confidence, then slashes it across the lord's throat. He uses a strong gust of wind to throw Gorred into the ocean far below.

Chlora screeches as Tohminic advances, and steals a long sword from the nearest fallen guard. It's too heavy for her, and she has to use both hands to wield the glimmering blade. She staggers as she slashes it through the air. That she fights with a weapon speaks volumes; her magic is weak — though her mother is one of the stronger fae I have met — and will do little against Summer's flames.

Tohminic laughs now, and this time when he throws his scorching fire, it caresses the side of Chlora's face with a blistering kiss. He takes the only chance he has and leaps for her, his iron-clad arm swinging in a brutal arc that crashes through her head. Not against. *Through.*

Blood and gore splatter across the ship's deck, glistening under the fae lights like some horrific kind of paint. Nausea churns and bile coats my tongue.

As I expected, the anglers and crew members back away with their palms raised. Though their High Lord is being controlled by Maude, they want no part in this fight. Their will to live is stronger than the loyalty they pledged.

I sheathe my daggers and race forward, with the others close behind. There is only one other place Rennyn could be.

We fight our way across the deck, where Summer and Night fae were hiding behind barrels of mead and crates filled with iron balls. Torin and Vander cut our enemies down before they so much as raise their weapons, and we make it to the captain's quarters within heartbeats.

My eyes pass over the captain as I burst through the door, and land on the familiar harsh panes of Rennyn's face. "Hello, brother. But that is incorrect, is it not?" I take a single step towards him. "You are not Rennyn, but Maude."

Chapter
28

R EN IS THINNER THAN I remember, and his already harsh cheekbones are more prominent. But when he smiles, when Maude forces her cruel smile to curve his lips, his features transform into the youthful softness I always loved. The atryxium sword I gifted him on his born day pokes over his shoulder. His brown hair does not shine as it once did, and his eyes, an alluring golden-brown, hold none of his determination, amiability, or strength. Instead, they hold a glint of malice.

"I wondered if you would fight for his freedom." It is Rennyn's lips that move, and his voice sounding from within, but the words... they are Maude's.

Vander moves to shield me, but I hold out an arm to keep him back. *"Only intervene if needed. Be prepared to follow the trace of my fold. Release your magical signatures."*

The lavender and zesty orange scent of Dusk fills the room, joined by the sweet yet pungent aroma of Vander's illusions, somehow metallic and sweet yet acidic and burning. A ripple of night flows free from Torin, and whispers caress my skin. A suffocating heat swells from behind, and I know Tohminic has also released his signature. Though his sends shivers of fear dancing down my spine, and I fight to suppress a shudder.

To Maude, I say, "I would very much like for you to release him." I am not so foolish as to think she will agree.

She has used distractions to her benefit since the Gloom — before, if I remember Nyree and all she did on Maude's behalf — and it is time she learned how it feels. If I keep her talking, keep her focus on my words rather than my actions, I will pull this off.

It's a battle to keep the concentration from my eyes as I gently open the hatch and free a slither of metal bending magic. I'm counting on the many powerful fae in this room to obscure the rust and bite of my signature.

"I do not think I will." She steps closer, the threat of our signatures likely causing alarm bells to peal in her mind. "I quite like the advantage of having Autumn on my side. Their horseback cavalry is magnificent."

This time, when I step closer, I move to the right, revealing the entire captain's desk. Just as I had hoped, there are many navigational tools, including a brass nautical divider.

"You should not use the horses to further your plans. It is unethical."

She laughs. It is a full body laugh that has her throwing Rennyn's head back.

I use her distraction to my advantage and straighten the divider with my magic before curling it just enough to slip over Rennyn's wrists. Maude laughs for so long that I move two steps closer without her noticing. So close I can touch her.

I lunge for Ren's arms, pulling them behind his back and coiling the disfigured divider around his wrists. Maude's laugh chokes to a stop when I gather the magic of the realm around us and focus on my next location.

This is something I do not know to work, yet I am desperate enough to try it now. I recall every detail of Blodwen: her gnarled fingers, dark eyes, and the slight hook of her nose. I take a step into the void, remembering the slick oil of her voice, and onto grass so drenched with blood it splashes over my greaves.

Cannon blasts chase iron balls over the land. Metal clangs. Screams and groans and grunts are a horrible melody in my ears. The ground lurches beneath my feet.

"Blodwen!" I scream.

"No need to shout. I am here." From right beside me, she helps me to force Ren to the ground, and not needing instruction, presses her fingers to his temples.

"How did you find her so fast, Princess?" Vander asks as soon as he folds beside us.

"Thought of Blodwen rather than a location. I didn't know if it would work. This isn't something we need every fae in Radelea knowing. Let's keep it between us."

"I agree." His voice is strained, and a quick look over my shoulder shows him mid-combat with a willowy male.

Wyn, too, fights to keep me, Ren, and Blodwen safe.

Within moments, Blodwen declares Rennyn's mind free of the Night Lady and flits away to continue feeding on the fallen.

I grip Rennyn's tunic in my hands and drag him close. "Order Autumn's retreat, Ren." I shove him away and leap to my feet. "Your weak mind has done enough damage to our realm. Fix what you broke."

"Bria?" Ren stands as I free his wrists, the blood pooling in the grass trickling down his legs. Realisation crosses his face. "I am so very sorry." Honest pain flickers in his eyes.

Urgent whispers demand my attention, and I turn my back on my brother. I have done my duty in saving him from Maude's control. It is up to him now. He will choose his own path.

"Okay," says Tohminic. "I will regain control of my fae, but you do *not* have my assurance it will work. I am helping to bring her down. Wait for me."

Torin says, "Go now. We'll keep fighting until the last moment."

Tohminic turns and races for the east, where his undead army is crossing the river, Autumn's horseback cavalry behind them. The odour of carrion drifts in his wake as he accesses his necromancy powers.

Now we wait. We fight, and we hope the plan works.

Everything hinges on Tohminic's ability to lead his fae. I never thought I would put so much hope and trust in the Summer Lord, yet here I am, praying for him to succeed. I may not have forgiven him, but I am thankful he is fighting on the right side of the war.

The shadow of a small harpy passes over us, the snap of her wings followed by the tinkle of a clasp that signals the release of the blue mock powder. It flutters down at rapid speed.

I throw myself at the ground and cover my face with my arms. The metal of my vambrace cuts into the exposed part of my cheek, and a hot trickle of blood tracks to my lips. A wrathful wind tears at my helmet and whistles in my ears. I risk a glance, which pays off.

The blue mock powder has moved in two directions, from Wyn and Vander both using their air magic to alter its course. It glimmers from the underbelly of a harpy who tumbles to the ground, landing with a sickening crunch, and shines from the exposed faces of a trio of Night fae who were barrelling towards us.

Vander helps me to my feet, sparing me a wink before pivoting towards another foe.

We fight our way to the centre of the battlefield — to the designated meeting point, where I am praying the others have already gathered — dodging weapons and skidding beneath attacks of magic where we can.

Everywhere I look, fae are locked in combat. A dense haze of residual magic clings to the ground, obscuring the broken and bleeding bodies left to rot. I see vines choking the life from a male, an icicle piercing the chest armour of another, and small tornados ripping across the grass. Spears made of pure flame send blasts of heat over the field, blinding light flashes without rhyme or reason, orbs of water hurtle overhead, and more than one of my allies grip their heads in agony.

The drummer has long since ceased the war rhythm. My heart pangs for the loss of life. War is brutally impartial. Tohminic was right. I *am* a witness to how cruel it can be.

I catch glimpses of fae I know — Xaria, Uma, and Leilani are supposed to be in hiding, they are supposed to be safe — and the urge to fight alongside them burns strong within. But I have a task. One that is more important right now. If we defeat Maude, this will all stop, and my friends will not need my protection any longer.

I can only hope they survive long enough.

Somewhere along the way, the Autumn ships cease their cannon fire and the ground falls still. The cheers that reach the shore from the Day and Dawn fae celebrating my brother's retreat plant a seed of hope in my chest. The Autumn riders who gallop across the river change their aim from us to Night. That seed sprouts when several undead collapse, the magic controlling them having retreated. The sprout blooms when the Summer fae fighting against us turn on the Night fae who were once their allies.

That seed of hope, now a blossoming flower, it is everything. It is encouragement to keep fighting. It's the will to live. But most importantly, it's a dream that we may just win this war.

By the time we make it to the centre of the field, we are all exhausted, ignoring several injuries, but glad to find everyone else already here fighting.

As if she was waiting for our arrival, an ebony harpy descends from above. On her back, smirking with an unknown secret, Maude laughs.

The petals of my flower of hope whither. Only a little, but enough that I move closer to Vander. I yank the gauntlets from my hands — as does everyone within our group — and take his hand.

Tohminic's fingers snake around the knuckles of my free hand. It feels wrong on too many levels, and I force down a bout of nausea as I tighten my grip on his hand. We do not look at one another, both of us aware of the tortured history we share. He twists his face to his left, where Nyana grips the stump of his wrist.

We form a circle, with the solar courts closer to Maude — Zentha, Jonik, Torin, then Vander — and the seasonal courts with the Night army at our backs, Ruith completing the link by taking Zentha's hand.

The harpy lowers to the blood-soaked ground. Her powerful wings send gusts of carrion-scented air over the battle when she flares them wide and lands with a stomach-churning squelch. Her landing is a signal, and every Night fae stills.

We gather our magic in our chests, where it grows bigger and brighter. And then... And then I stop. Beside me, Vander stops. It continues around the circle until all eight of us are no longer gathering our magic.

I turn my wide eyes on Maude. The weight of one thousand suns burns through my entire body, settling with unease in the pit of my stomach. Glowing dimly from her hands as she slides from the harpy's back is an object I have seen before.

I open my mouth to protest, but the order slips from my grasp. No matter what I try, whether it be a spoken word or a simple shuffle of my feet, I cannot control my body.

An evil laugh echoes within my mind. *Form a line.*

We all do, without hesitation.

Maude saunters closer. She tosses the relic in the air, catches it, and tosses it again, all while idly walking the length of our line. She breathes deep, as if she has not a care in the world. "Much better."

In my peripheral, I am alarmed to see every fae standing just as still as me. Wyn, Darcel, Elmon, everyone who swore to protect us while we gathered enough power to defeat Maude stands statue-still. The armies beyond my vision, motionless. Every fae here. We are all under her control.

The flower of hope shrivels and bursts into thousands of broken pieces. We cannot win this war. We *won't*. This is how it ends, with her using the relic's power to control our every action, with us unable to fight back. Defenceless.

The control over my mind tightens to the point that I cannot even *think*, let alone move. All I can do is watch in abject horror as the scene plays out. The bile burning my throat fights for freedom, prevented its desire by Maude's control.

"I am rather enjoying this." Maude continues to walk back and forth along the eight of us while tossing the relic. "In fact, this outcome is much more satisfying." She pauses in front of me. "If you had handed over the Theron siblings when I asked, I would not have found such enjoyment. Thank you."

The harpy behind her rustles her ebony feathers, impatient to return to the skies. Maude clicks her tongue at the beast, granting her permission. Her ebony feathers glimmer under the emerging starlight when she leaps into the sky.

This battle has lasted longer than I thought. The war horns, blown in the early hours of morning, seem a distant memory, yet an immediate one at the same time. How are the stars appearing already?

Maude crosses her arms over her chest. "You, you, and you," she says, jerking her pale chin to me, Vander, and Wyn. "Remain still. Night denizens, you may retreat. The rest of you, fight!"

Her soldiers flee. They run to the outskirts of the battlefield and out of eyesight.

Fae from Day, Dawn, Spring, Dusk, and Winter turn on one another. The Autumn fae change alliances once more. There's even the odd Summer fae who tosses flames at whoever moves near. It is a kind of chaos that makes my blood turn to ice. All our allies... now enemies.

Crippling heartache tears through me as I watch each of my students attacking one another. Mitah is the first to fall by Mykaela's hand. Followed by Orli, Hamon, Rhett, then Mykaela herself, who falls victim to Dillon's blade. They were supposed to hide. They were supposed to be safe.

Dillon does not survive to mourn his friends. Vacon's Konda is all I see as it slices through Dillon's midsection.

My scream lodges in my throat, refusing to surface.

Maude's face brightens. Her ice-blue eyes shine with triumph as friend cuts through friend and ally hurls magic at ally. Her blood-red lips curl at the sides. It is sickening. Despicable.

I can only watch as Elmon defends himself against a Winter female. Can only stare when Darcel uses his vines to bind a Dawn soldier. A Dusk denizen sends blasts of air in every direction. It gets worse with every beat of my heart.

On my left, Nyana sends a trio of lethally sharp leaves cutting through the air. They spin faster than I can track before slicing across Zentha's throat. Blood spurts from the three wounds, so close together I cannot tell them apart. She sags to the ground, her honey-brown eyes wide and searching. She finds her son in the chaos, and her gaze remains there until the light in her eyes fades.

I cannot shed a tear. I cannot move to press my hands against the gaping cuts. My heart aches with the need to cry for Zentha. My father's friend, *my* friend. Gone.

On my right, Tohminic slams his iron bludgeon against Jonik's lower back. I swear I see his mouth move. My eyes have to be playing tricks on me.

Beside Jonik and Tohminic, Wyn hurls gusts of wind at our allies. I blink. She targets Ruith, who stumbles to my side, then Torin, who collapses at Vander's feet, and I realise... No, it cannot be. Is she unaffected? The longer I watch, the clearer everything becomes. Maude ordered Wyn to be still, yet every time Maude looks away from my best friend, she acts, pulling our allies closer with her wind. Then she stops, instead focusing her eyes in one place.

I am almost too slow to watch Blodwen ripple into nothing. She looks like bloodied grass and fallen fae; Wyn's illusion of the battle is almost perfect. Every step Blodwen takes distorts the image.

I drag my eyes back to Tohminic and watch as he chases Nyana to Wyn's side with his flames, then turns to Elmon, his next target.

My heart beats frantically in my chest, and I slam my thoughts against Maude's hold on my mind, hoping to distract her from Blodwen's actions. Distracting her worked once. I can only pray to the Mother Star it works again.

From my feet, Blodwen's oily voice whispers, "Do not move until the time is right." She is silent for a moment before the same words slip through her lips from Vander's side.

The flower of hope bursts free once more. Perhaps... Perhaps we can win.

Chapter 29

Tohminic

THE WIND WHISPERER'S MOTHER severs Maude's control faster than I thought possible. She frees my allies and orders them to remain still until the right moment, just as we had planned before the battle.

The idea of using her in the final battle came to me at the same moment Chlora severed my hand from my arm. I could only think of her bony fingers pressing into my skull, and the relief that followed. I knew Maude would attempt controlling the toughest fae in our alliance, though I did not expect it to this extent, and I knew Blodwen could free them. The plan formed itself, as if planted by the Mother Star. I am merely putting it in action.

Finding her in the Winter Court was a difficulty in its own right, although I am pleased with the outcome. Blodwen was eager for the opportunity to prove herself and took no convincing to join me in battle, especially after I told her Maude cannot control those who have already been freed. Torin may not agree with the plan. His wrath will shatter the realm. It is a shame I will not be here to witness it.

I continue to fight. The path I tread is precarious. Precarious, yet necessary. I work in a circle, defending my allies in the only way I can until Blodwen utters my last order. She moves to the Princess of Autumn and presses her fingers to her temple. As agreed, she is the last to be freed.

I move around the circle, inflicting surface wounds when I must, until I am beside the two females. With my back to *her* — she is stronger than anyone gives her credit for, and deserves thanks for her ingenuity when the war is over — I whisper, "Bria. We are not all required to offer our magic to this cause. As long as one from each court plays a part, the outcome will be the same. You will know when the time is right."

That moment comes in the next beat of my weakened heart.

Blodwen says, loud enough for all to hear, "This is the end."

Maude's eyes whip to Blodwen. She lifts a clenched fist, and as if in slow motion, rotates her wrist. Blodwen's screams ring in my ears as she crashes hard to the ground. It is a shame her life must be wasted, but it is a price she agreed to pay.

I turn until my whole body is facing the High Lady of Night. My heart pounds with frantic beats, as if it knows these will be its last. *This is my penance,* I think to myself. Then I charge at Maude.

Chapter
30

The moment I feel Maude's control slip away, Tohminic's hand brushes against my lower back. He whispers, "Bria. We are not all required to offer our magic to this cause. As long as one from each court plays a part, the outcome will be the same. You will know when the time is right."

"This is the end." Blodwen's words have barely left her lips before she collapses in agony.

The truth in Tohminic's words clatters through my mind, melding with Blodwen's screams. One from each court must contribute to the war's end. I knew that. It is why we ordered the groups of five, with one from each court. But I had assumed we must all work together to bring Maude down by sharing our magic. What he says makes sense. We must all contribute in some way, whether it be using magic to overcome a threat, or freeing the minds of our allies.

Night is accounted for, with Blodwen having worked her magic to free us. Her lifeless body lies at my feet. Those dark eyes, glazed yet dull, are locked on the stars above. I will remember her sacrifice for eternity.

Before I can stop him, Tohminic darts for Maude, a raging fire clinging to his only hand and sending embers trailing behind him. He is a comet blazing through the night.

I want to stare. I want to remain frozen in place to witness what becomes of Summer's High Lord. But Tohminic's signal is clearer than noontime without clouds, and I must play my part. So, with every fibre of my being protesting, I turn away from Tohminic as he charges his tormentor.

"Torin! Wyn!" I shout. "Cover us!"

They obey without question. Darcel, Tarathiel, Tasar, and Larrad — who I am pleased to see recovered — join them. Surprising me are the efforts of Leilani, Uma, Yaryn, and Xaria. They take defensive stances alongside everyone else, their weapons drawn and raised, ready for the Night army marching from the outskirts.

But they are too far from their High Lady. They will not make it in time. I know it as well as I know the lines of my hands.

I snatch Vander's hand from his side. "Form a circle." My words are urgent, filled with a frayed tension that thrums through my veins like a ravaging wind.

He repeats the order to Jonik as they link hands, who speaks the words to Elmon — the tears streaking down his face threaten to bring me to my knees — then on to Nyana and Ruith, whose grip is ice cold as he takes my free hand.

Night's droning war cry joins the screams and shouts from Maude and Tohminic's duel. A glance over my shoulder tells me we are almost out of time. Maude has the Summer Lord on the ground with her red-tipped fingers pressed to his temples.

I rip open the hatch in my mind and free every slither of Autumn magic I can. The metal bending power brings a sour taste to my mouth, and the clang of weapons almost fools me into believing our enemies have reached us too soon. The power I have over animals has fur caressing my face and the scent of tilled dirt ticking my nose. I take comfort in the feeling, and my heart swells as I remember my father.

I push my magic through my hands, where it joins with Ruith's ice and shadow, and Vander's wind and illusions. My body turns rigid as my power races along the circle, where it meets silk petals and churning mist, a kiss of warmth and white light, a whisper of the spirits and cool drip of the ocean.

Our various threads of magic race around the circle and form a single power that pulls at our hands and has our faces tilting towards the sky. An invisible gale whips my helmet from my head and tears at my hair. I stagger back, my arms pulling taut. There is something ancient in the taste of this new power, something fierce in its scent, and something wild in the buzzing melody it creates. It feels indestructible. I do not know how I know it, but there is no mistaking that this is an old magic. It's raw and pure. Brutal. And the sight of it...

The brightest gold I have ever seen blazes from my chest. It's a mirror of the glow shining from beneath Vander's armour. And Jonik, Elmon, Ruith, Nyana. We are six identical pillars of gold. The light, so alluring and deadly, crackles as it races along our circle. It intensifies at each of our joined hands, pulsing and tasting and sending ripples of power over the battle field.

From each link in the circle, a thread of gold arcs over our heads, much like the power of the wards, and joins in the middle. I watch in amazement as more ribbons of gold form. My breath deserts my lungs as the ancient magic creates a shimmering net overhead, the tether keeping it here beginning to fray before it snaps away from my hand with a crack.

I jerk my eyes to Maude. A pang of sadness clenches my heart when I see Tohminic lying lifeless on the ground with his face twisted in pain. But Maude... Gone is the cruel smile I know so well. Gone is the confidence and cunning.

Her ice-blue eyes reflect the golden glow of our joined powers. She turns and runs for her army — they are close enough now that I can see each individual fae — keeping her face towards us and her eyes on the golden net. She does not make it far.

A final crack, and the net pulses once more, the light so blinding I'm certain it would be visible from the height of the stars. A deafening boom rings out over the field. The ancient magic moves with so much speed it disappears for a heartbeat, reappearing over Maude's fleeing form.

It snaps down.

The fighting ceases. Allies look at one another in horror. Guilt and regret and heartache pull at their features as they realise what they have done.

Maude screams. The sound pierces my ears. It tightens the knot in my stomach and sends prickles of ice-cold fear down my spine. I cannot move. Cannot so much as take a breath. I can only watch and wait.

The woven magic covers Maude from her ebony hair to her toes. Her feet refuse to move, and she skids along the blood-soaked ground. She comes to a stop in a small clearing when her limbs lock at unnatural angles. Her chest rises and falls at a rapid pace. The pale ivory of her skin turns a sickly grey.

I see it all in slow motion.

The net constricts. It shrinks in on her body and seeps into every pore. It snakes over her features like golden veins. As if it absorbs her very life force, the gold grows brighter, but her skin... it turns ashen. Grey. It flakes and crumbles and drifts on the breeze. One last flare of that ancient light, and the Night Lady is no more.

Where she stood mere heartbeats ago, a pile of grey ash remains.

I do not dare believe it. My eyes, still wide with shock and amazement, trail over the surrounding area, expecting to see her crawl from beyond one of the broken bodies marking this field as a battleground. Yet she does not surface. The pile of ash shifts, and my attention snaps back to the dull grey. But it is only a breath of wind that rustles the fine powder.

The breath of wind circles our group, cackling, and I realise it is Alizeh. Her breath of air grows into a churning vortex and she blasts through the pile of ash, sending what remains of Maude into the sky.

We are stunned.

Silent.

Vander is the first to recover. He cheers and pumps his fist into the air. All who witnessed Maude's demise soon echo his shout, and the cry of victory surrounds us. We are a group of triumphant fae. We laugh at the absurdity of overcoming an obstacle we all believed would bring about the end of Radelea. Smiles pull at every face. We all cheer. Most of us cry in both happiness and sorrow. Even Alizeh floats to the ground to join the celebration.

Vander hooks an arm around my waist and drags me close, pressing those perfect lips against mine. *"We did it, Princess. We won."*

I hold every one of our allies, thanking them and rejoicing with them. My cheeks ache from the wide smile that refuses to abate.

I am soon passed from Van to Ruith, who holds me so tight I am certain my armour is cutting into his flesh. "It is over, dear daughter. We emerge from the darkness victorious."

"Thank you, Father. Thank you for everything you did to help."

Wyn does not allow Ruith to respond. She steals me from his arms and crushes me to her chest. Tears stream down her face and her body shakes with emotion.

I hold her tight. "We did it. We're free."

She hiccups into my ear.

I am soon pulled from Wyn's hold and find myself engulfed in Dawn. Jonik and his two sons fold me in their embraces, the three of them sporting several cuts and bruises over their faces, and Larrad wincing at the clamour of celebrating fae. They were the first to ally with us. They have been here since the start, have lost a son and brother, played a pivotal role in keeping our soldiers healthy, and they deserve every bit of recognition.

I cannot free my arms to hug them back, but I say, "You have my many thanks for all you offered."

Tasar says, "Our chambers are always open to you, Bria."

"We still believe you would have a lot of fun there," adds Larrad. "Even without Ulakas trying to be the centre of attention."

Jonik chuckles. "She is spoken for, my sons."

I move from the Dawn males to Elmon, who I offer my most sincere condolences. His tears have not yet dried, and I know his smile to be one etched from both sadness and relief this is over.

It is difficult to thank Nyana after holding Elmon through his tears. But I do it. If not for her, many of our soldiers would be paralysed, or dead, from the blue mock powder. She, too, is riddled with grief, her heart aching for Argi.

My mother's hair blinds me when she wraps me in her warm embrace. Ruith soon takes her from me to crush Uma to his chest. I catch whispers of admonishment that are quickly followed by praise and relief.

I turn to wrap my arms around Torin, the last of my friends I wish to hold close. He has been a constant throughout all of this. His laughter and strength have helped me through the toughest of times. He understood my pain when I first stepped foot on Dusk, fresh from the torment of Ad'Starrag. He handed me the branch of a she-oak tree and gave me an outlet for my pain.

I take a step closer, with my arms out wide. His eyes spark with a hint of mischief. Something both vulgar and amusing is about to come out of his mouth. I know it, and I look forward to hearing such a crude joke.

But the joke never comes.

He sputters. His beautiful dark eyes grow wide and track down to where a glint of obsidian spears through his throat. Blood cascades down his chest. It bubbles from his parted lips and stains the already crimson ground. The humour is still etched on his face, and will remain so forevermore.

A raw, grief-stricken scream tears at my throat. "Torin!"

The cheers stop, and without them... Without them, I can hear the din of battle. We were so wrapped up in celebrating Maude's demise that we did not so much as *think* of the advancing Night army. Everywhere I look, weapons clash and magic flares.

I leap for Torin now, catching his fall before he crashes into the mud. With rage-fuelled movements, I discard my gauntlets and vambraces, then pull my friend into my lap. A second wave of battle rages around me. I ignore it. It's not important, not compared to this.

Torin's dark eyes find me in the mayhem, the amusement still shining from within. His hand gropes for my chest plate, and he drags me near.

I brush loose strands of golden blonde from his brow, and do the only thing I can. I do what I know in my heart he would want, what he's asking for in his last moments. I send him into the afterlife with humour. His soul will fade from this world while laughing.

Leaning close, I whisper, "I know you were going to feel me up. Don't even try to deny it. You can't get enough of me." I wink for good measure, though I'm sure the tears falling free detract from the motion.

He tries to laugh, but his chest only heaves and blood dribbles from between his lips.

My voice breaks. "Vander would have had your head for it. I would have cheered him on from the sidelines. I would have delighted in watching him pound your face to a pulp."

He splutters a chuckle and tries to speak. Nothing comes out.

"I know, I know. You think you would have won. You're probably trying to say feeling me up would be worth it."

His eyes brighten. He tries to nod.

"I'll let you in on a secret." Another wink pushes a tear free. "I've the best arse in Radelea."

This time, his laugh sounds clear. His whole body jerks with his amusement.

I do not know if the tears streaming down his face are from humour or sadness or pain. Whatever their cause, I wipe them away. My smile is forced, but I keep it planted on my face while Torin continues to laugh.

In my peripheral, I note the battle beginning to die down. I note fae moving to stand around us. More fae lie dead on the ground.

Wyn and Vander kneel beside me, both forcing a smile, both knowing it's what Torin would want. He wouldn't want us to be sad. He'd want us laughing with him. And that is exactly what we will do.

"She's right," says Vander. "I would have kicked your arse."

Wyn snorts. Her voice is thick when she says, "I would have helped him, you know."

"As would I," says Alizeh as she lands beside Wyn.

Torin continues to laugh. He looks from me to Vander, then to Wyn. He opens his mouth for one last jibe, a taunt about all the times he put Wyn on her back in training. The words never come. The light fades from his eyes as his soul abandons his broken body, but the smile... Oh, that winning smile. It remains.

We gave him all we could in his last moments. We sent him into the afterlife with a laugh. But now he's gone, limp and heavy in my arms. Now the tears come. They stream from my face with fierce determination as I bow my head, resting my brow against Torin's. My entire body shakes as I embrace him. I struggle to breathe through the pain.

I'm distantly aware of Alizeh's howling wind as she sends blasts of it over the battlefield. Her pain cuts through me with more savagery than the sharpest of blades. She and Torin had just found love with one another, and now it has been ripped away.

I am not aware of how much time has passed when Vander pulls Torin from my arms. "Come, Princess. Leave him to rest in peace." His voice is thick, strained. He helps me to my feet and wraps me in his embrace. "He wouldn't want this pain for you."

I nod against his chest and take a deep breath to calm myself. War demands sacrifice. It's an assurance I wish I did not have to endure. But Torin is not the only life lost. There are others who we must burn before the Mother Star, if she rises again, and send them into the afterlife with a prayer.

My swollen eyes protest when I wipe away the tears. My body aches, and my hands yearn to hold Torin longer. But I turn from his lifeless body and watch as the last fae falls by Ruith's sword.

This time, we are certain the war is over. There are no cheers or smiles or laughter. The air grows heavy. Melancholy settles over the field. We have won, it is true.

But nothing can bring back the dead. Defeating our enemy should not be celebrated, but mourned. Every life lost on this cruel night — a night where not even the moon shines bright — is worth remembering.

Chapter 31

I DO NOT KNOW what to do. The last of our enemies has fallen, Maude is gone, and the war is over. Yet, I am at a loss. Celebrating is not an option. We learned that in the hardest way imaginable. Do we just leave? Walk off this blood-stained field never to return? I would give anything to just rest, to lie down and refuse to surface until this unending pain subsides.

No one else seems to know what to do, either. Wherever I look, confusion pulls at eyes and frowns curl lips. A Winter male bends to heave a Spring soldier over his shoulder but thinks better of it. He straightens, scratches his forehead, then shrugs at his female companion. Beyond them, a pink-haired healer beckons a Dusk female over, who helps the healer to fold to the closest infirmary. That the healer is asking for help is telling.

Most fae here are feeling the strain of continuous magic use.

In fact, now I have a moment to breathe, aches and pains are making themselves known. My cheek throbs where my gauntlet somehow pierced through the metal of my helmet and sliced my skin. My legs are unsteady as I take a step towards Vander, and I know they will give way if I don't rest soon. I cannot feel the Autumn magic I control, and the Winter powers swirling inside me are running low.

"What do we do now?" I ask.

Several of those nearby turn to Vander, awaiting instruction. But it is Ruith, who refuses to relinquish his hold on Uma, who says, "Now we heal our injured and pay our final respects to the deceased."

"Jonik," says Vander. "Can you ask your healers to join us here? Those who are not busy in the infirmaries, of course."

"I'll put a team together of anyone willing to help with the deceased," says Wyn.

No one answers her, though we all watch her work. The thought of moving all those bodies is overwhelming at best and downright horrific at worst. The lack of response doesn't bother her, though, and she walks away to recruit helpers. It doesn't take long before there's an army of fae moving bodies into the centre of the field, right where Maude fell.

Jonik shakes his head, a few strands of long dark hair slipping free of their leather bindings. "Leilani, could you issue the order to the healers? Tasar and Larrad, set up a triage station." His eyes flick to the growing pile of bodies. "Away from the pyre, if you will."

Whoever had no use of the antidote for the blue mock hands the Dawn princes their vials. The injured need it more than we do now.

Vander asks Ruith, "Can we inform those hiding in the Bol-bala Ranges that they're free to leave whenever they wish?"

I tune out the rest of the conversation, my eyes locked on a forlorn male off to the side. His head is bowed, and his shoulders shake. He has lost his mother. His father suffers an unknown madness. The war ruined his mating ceremony. His grief must be unbearable.

I cross the field and stand beside him, avoiding the body at his feet. There is no strength left inside me to endure looking at Zentha's lifeless form. "Are you okay, Elmon? Can I get you anything?"

"Can you turn back time?" His voice is as hollow as his eyes.

"I... No, I cannot."

"Then there is nothing you can do for me."

I grip his shaking hand. "It does not seem like it right now, but it will get easier. I promise." I offer him one last glance before leaving him to his sorrow.

A Day fae crosses my path, and I stop them with a gentle hand on their elbow. Speaking low, I say, "Lady Zentha did not survive the war. High Lord Elmon needs his mate. Do you understand?"

Tears shine from her eyes. "Shall I fetch Lady Kyra?"

"Please," I croak. I do not know how much more of this I can take. The broken hearts. The injuries. The fallout of this unnecessary war. It is all too much.

She blesses me with a rare kindness and folds from the battlefield. Tears prick my eyes; acts of kindness have been few and far between since the Dusk island surfaced, and I am so thankful to witness such a moment. It will take time for Radelea to return to the realm it once was. But this, something so small and insignificant, is the perfect first step. A humble fae agreeing to bring solace to another.

"Are you okay?"

I'm so wrapped up in my thoughts that I startle at Wyn's words. My hand flies to my chest and presses against the cool armour. "You gave me a fright."

"Sorry." Standing beside me, she does not look my way. Her often warm skin is pale, betraying her wish to veil her exhaustion. She sighs. "It'll take time for everyone to feel safe again."

We watch the quiet movements of fae from every court — yes, even the rare few Night fae remained behind; those who disagreed with Maude's actions hope to make amends, with this as their starting point — as they continue adding bodies to the pyre. There are logs and branches surrounding it now, thanks to the Spring fae and their ability to manipulate plant life.

It takes me a while to see it, but eventually I see the system they have put in place. The Dawn fae are healing the injured and casting light over the dark scene. The Spring fae ready the pyre for the Summer fae to burn. Day fae work to clean injuries and weapons with their water, some of them offering blessings to spirits only they can see. Night, Autumn, and Winter fae move bodies to either the pyre or triage tent. Dusk fae use their power over the wind to lift bodies to the top of the pyre, where none other can reach.

Everyone is working together. Every court, playing a part.

More healers fold to the field, and a familiar head of silvery-blue hair catches my attention. I watch as Penna desperately searches around the field. Her entire body seems to sag with relief before she dashes across the grass to a waiting Xaria. They embrace for a lone heartbeat before her hands rove over Xaria's body, searching for injuries. I drag my eyes away when they kiss, offering them the only slice of privacy I can.

Watching the courts work together fills me with a sense of pride. I have to look away when Vander and Alizeh work together to place Torin's body at the top. It's too much. It's all too much.

"Breathe, Princess."

Vander's reminder comes just as my throat tightens. I have never been more thankful that he's inside my head. I offer him a tight smile, then turn to Wyn.

She does not look at me, not yet, not as she says, "Say what you need to."

"It's not that I need to. It's just... Why the guns? What purpose did killing Erthana and the Spring fae serve?" I don't want to remind her of the horrors Maude forced her to inflict on others, but I have been wondering this for a while now. Two fae were shot dead. We have never known why.

She looks at me at last, with tears lining her eyes. "You know I stole tasers from Earth. But did I tell you why?" I shake my head, and she says, "Maude wanted to equip every member of her army with guns."

"It would have been a bloodbath." Moreso than it was.

"Killing Erthana was Maude's way of testing the efficacy of human weapons. After... After I killed her, something inside me snapped. I just couldn't do it. A kind of shield formed in my mind that prevented Maude from issuing the order to use the gun. She broke through eventually."

"And that's when you killed the Spring fae?"

She nods. "If Maude was forcing me to kill, I was damn well going to make it benefit us in some way. That was all I could think of, short of using the gun on myself. Some days, I think I should have. At least then I wouldn't have to endure this pain."

I know the demon on her shoulder all too well. To live in such darkness... Sometimes it feels as if death is the only way out.

For myself and for Wyn, I say, "There's always a rainbow of light at the end of the tunnel. Sometimes, the darkness is so dense we cannot see it. Sometimes, the shadows trick you into thinking there's nothing but black. I couldn't see anything other than black and crimson for a long time, but after a while, the other colours revealed themselves. And let me tell you: the other colours are so very worth it. They're worth struggling through the darkness."

"Colours," she scoffs.

I am quiet for a moment while I watch thousands of fae fold onto the field from the safety of the Bolbala Ranges, where they were hiding until the battle ended. Fear still stains their faces, soon replaced by an equal mixture of heartache and relief when they realise the war is indeed over.

"Yes." I face her now, determined to make her see the rainbow. "Like the green grass that ripples with the wind, wafting the scent of nature towards you and calming the demonic thoughts. Or the golden yellow of the Mother Star and the way she warms your face and promises tomorrow will be better. The orange sunset that reminds you that you made it through another day. I could go on."

"There's beauty in colour." She sounds surprised by the revelation.

I echo the words and turn back to the pyre, where Summer fae stand waiting with flames in their palms. "Like the red of a flame. At first, it's lonely. But it soon finds other flames just like it, and they meld together, forming something so beautiful and deadly that the demons have no chance of winning. Find your flames, Wyn."

She wraps an arm around my shoulder. "You're one of them, Bria. The best kind, the kind that doesn't burn, but warms. Thank you."

"You are most welcome."

The fire wielders send crackling flames over the pyre. They catch on kindling and clothes, and within heartbeats the entire mound is blazing. It pops and sizzles, and the sound roars in my ears. There's something cathartic in watching the dancing red, orange, and amber.

It is the first time since fleeing Ad'Starrag the red doesn't haunt, but soothes.

I send prayers to the Mother Star for the lives lost. I pray for Argi, Nyana's consort and defender. For Dey and the rest of my students, who should not have died so young, at only one and twenty. For Zentha, who saved me from drowning and taught me to trust myself. For Tohminic, whose sacrifice I will never forget. For Torin, who I could count on to brighten the darkest of days. And for everyone else who died defending our realm. Father, Ulakas, Fayeth, Erthana, Nikolai, Blodwen. The list is endless.

Glowing embers flash within the churning smoke. They twist in rapid spirals as they race for the sky, where they fade beyond the stars. It's kind of fitting that tonight is a new moon. It is a symbol of new beginnings, of growth, transformation, and renewed energy. The absence of both the moon and Mother

Star allows us to focus on the light of the fire. It offers us a chance to say a proper farewell to those who burn.

As it should be.

A slight breeze tickles the hairs of my nape, sending tendrils of copper over my face. I brush them away, feeling the shorn hairs on the side of my head — longer now, and soft to touch — and remembering everything those hairs once stood for. In cutting them, I cut away the remnants of my old life. I shunned my family and my home court. Perhaps I was wrong to sever all ties. Perhaps Rennyn's mind would not have been controlled by Maude had I bothered to care about him.

Hindsight. It's a key to the door I have locked in my mind, the door that keeps the demons at bay. I cannot change the past. No one can. All I can do is move forward. That begins with forgiving my brother.

I twist from Wyn's grip and move through the enormous crowd, seeking Rennyn among the masses. I find him standing alone on the outskirts, head bowed and hands gripped together in prayer.

"Ren." My tone is tight, fighting to hold back the emotion clogging my throat.

He slowly lifts his head. "If you are here to say I told you so, I do not need nor want to hear it, sister."

"I have come to apologise." His golden-brown eyes brighten. I allow a lone tear to fall as I say, "I'm sorry I wasn't there to protect you. In my anger, I shunned the only family I had. It was immature and wrong, and I'm sorry. I should never have turned my back on Autumn."

"Your anger was understandable. I am sorry I kept your mother's identity from you. More than anything, I am sorry I broke your trust. Can you ever forgive me?"

I move to stand beside him, watching the dying flames as I fight the urge to say no. Instead, I offer a grim smile. "In time, perhaps. So much has happened, Ren. Just give me time. For now, can you come with me? I have an idea."

"Of course. Let it be known this is the first stepping stone to forgiveness."

"Don't push your luck," I say as we weave through the crowd.

Fae from every court fold away from the battlefield, their prayers having been sent to the Mother Star, and their sorrow having run its course for now. Two Dusk fae fold away, only to reappear moments later to declare the Dusk Court intact. It seems Maude ordered her armada's retreat when we fled. They sailed to Autumn's eastern border, according to Rennyn, and are yet to return to the Night Islands.

I gather those I need along the way, finding Ruith and Uma first, then Jonik, Leilani, and their sons. Elmon follows with Kyra tucked under his arm. Nyana, Darcel, and Imala join us, all sombre, with swollen and red eyes. Yaryn, too, agrees with my plan. By the time I find Wyn and Vander in the crowd, we are a large party of six and ten.

"Princess?" Vander turns towards me, his face cast in hues of amber and red from the fire. "What's going on?"

"Here. You may use this. It is a relic from ancient times." Ruith hands me a large chalice made of copper.

Rennyn beckons an Autumn female over and whispers something in her ear. She disappears for two heartbeats, folding back to us with a small barrel of plum wine.

Ren fills the chalice to the brim.

I say, "Before they signed the ancient treaty, the High fae all shared a chalice of wine. Drinking from the same cup reflected their love of the same land. I offer this wine as a sign of peace within Radelea." I hand the chalice to Vander first.

"Wait," says Wyn. "We need a Night fae." She hooks a thread of dense air around the waist of a passing male and drags him to the group. "You. You're the new High Lord of Night."

"B-but I am a lowly vendor. I... I sell apples."

"Do you have any intention of waging war on our land?" asks Yaryn.

"N-no."

Larrad pats him on the shoulder. "Then you are the perfect candidate, friend."

Vander raises the chalice. "The Dusk Court hid from you for centuries in order to protect the human realm. It was a foolish endeavour. The humans do not want nor need our protection. Instead, I vow to protect Radelea." He drinks.

Rennyn says, "Autumn agrees to this treaty. May Radelea remain peaceful forevermore."

"Summer agrees." Yaryn drinks.

"As does Spring," says Nyana before drinking.

Elmon's hands shake as he takes the chalice. "The Day Court mourns the loss of their High Lady, as we mourn the loss of every fae on this fateful night. We agree to no more war."

"Our healers will return to each court," says Jonik. "We agree."

The Night fae says, "My name is Folen, and I agree."

Ruith, the last High fae to take the chalice, raises it above his head. "May the realm thrive under our leadership. May the Mother Star grace us with her warmth once more. I agree." He drinks.

The stars flicker. One by one, they fade into the darkness.

For a moment, I fear we have made the wrong choice, that we have angered the lights of the night sky. A small heartbeat of uncertainty... then a golden glow lines the eastern horizon. Slither by slither, the Mother Star shines her light upon the realm. It starts as gold, like the ancient net of magic we used to bring down Maude, before shades of pink, orange, and lilac streak across the sky. Colours pierce the darkness.

Tears fall freely from my eyes at the sight.

Tears fall from the eyes of every fae still on this horrid field.

The return of the sun is the most beautiful thing I have ever seen. With the pyre still burning behind us, the weight of loss heavy on our shoulders, and the memory of war fresh in our minds, the sun brings a soothing calm. She kisses my cheeks with warmth, assuring me that everything will be okay. She casts light upon the field, revealing the true extent of damage done to her land, and I know we are forgiven.

I thread my fingers through Vander's and lean against him. *"I will never grow tired of watching her rise. For as long as I live, I will be thankful for this moment."*

He presses a kiss on my temple. *"You shunned the jaded crown you once wore. You fought the crimson haunting your soul. The land is no longer ruled by shadow. The time is ours, Princess. This is an era of peace."*

Not tentative as it once was, but true. True peace. The two words bring a smile to my face, and I take in the group of fae around me. Friends. Lovers. Comrades. Radelea's story is one of many.

I never knew how I wanted to spend my life. Now I do. The knowledge of my destiny thrums through me like a raging wind.

"I'm going to write about this," I tell Vander as I watch the sky fade from indigo to lapis lazuli. *"I want this war to be etched in the history books, accessible by all, so we may remember to stand together. The Chronicles of Radelea, as told by Bria of Dusk."*

THE END

Author's
Acknowledgements

I'm going to start by saying I hate these things. I never know who to thank or acknowledge, and I feel like a fool trying to word things so my readers don't think I'm a raving, over-caffeinated idiot.

But here goes...

Mum. Thank you for being the first to read every draft. Thank you for enduring those spicy scenes. Thank you for being excited every time new chapters hit your inbox. Your support and encouragement mean everything.

Dad. Thank you for your unconditional love and support. You're still not allowed to read my books. At least, not until I write one with no spice.

Daniel, your fairy corn jokes never fail to make me smile. Thanks for pretending to like what I like, and for not complaining every time I tell you I need new covers.

Thank you to my kiddies for taking an interest and never complaining when Mum spends too long at her laptop. I hope one day you'll each follow your dreams, just as I have.

Ash... I'm not sure whether I *should* thank you. It feels a little contradictory to our back-and-forth battle of wits. Seriously, though? If I didn't have you to bounce ideas off, bitch and moan to, and read the nonsense I send you, I doubt I'd publish anything. You're my book bestie, my sounding board, and my accountability partner. And sometimes, you tell me to shut the fuck up and get over it. You know what? Nope. You don't get a thanks. I take it back. Game on ;)

Kate at FireLily Australia and Megan at Enchanted Pages PR, you both took a chance on an indie author. To say thank you doesn't seem good enough. You're both genuinely kind and amazing people, and I hope one day I can meet you in real life to thank you in person. Your support means so much, your encouragement means more, but it's your belief in my books that I'm most appreciative of. Thank you, a million times over.

To every doctor, friend, loved one, and stranger who has ever been there for someone struggling with their mental health... THANK YOU. You are the flames, and you burn brighter than you know.

To anyone else who played a part in getting the Chronicles of Radelea published, whether you're a beta reader, ARC reader, editor, proofreader, cover designer, or some random stranger on the internet... This couldn't have happened without you. Thank you.

About the
Author

Samara is a fantasy author from Melbourne, Australia, where she lives with her partner, three kids, and an English Staffy named Boots. Though she loves Melbourne, she grew up surrounded by a large family in north-west Tasmania and misses the quiet life.

Some of her hobbies include reading, a good ol' Netflix binge, camping, and playing Monopoly with her kids.

You can follow her on social media for sneak peeks into up and coming works under the handle @samarasaward.author

Also by
Samara Saward

<u>The Opal Wolf</u>

<u>Helios Mage</u>
Heir of the Solstice
Prince of Persuasion
King of Deception

<u>Dragon's Oath</u>
Legacy
Enigma
Anarchy